THE

DOGS

of

BABEL

THE
DOGS
of
BABEL

CAROLYN PARKHURST

DOUBLEDAY LARGE PRINT HOME LIBRARY EDITION

LITTLE, BROWN AND COMPANY
Boston   New York   London

This Large Print Edition, prepared especially for Doubleday Large Print Home Library, contains the complete, unabridged text of the original Publisher's Edition.

ISBN 0-7394-3657-0

Printed in the United States of America

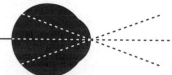

This Large Print Book carries the
Seal of Approval of N.A.V.H.

For Evan, with all my love

THE
DOGS
of
BABEL

O N E

Here is what we know, those of us who can speak to tell a story: On the afternoon of October 24, my wife, Lexy Ransome, climbed to the top of the apple tree in our backyard and fell to her death. There were no witnesses, save our dog, Lorelei; it was a weekday afternoon, and none of our neighbors were at home, sitting in their kitchens with their windows open, to hear whether, in that brief midair moment, my wife cried out or gasped or made no sound at all. None of them were working in their yards, enjoying the last of the warm weather, to see whether her body crumpled before she hit the ground, or whether she tried to right herself in the air, or whether she simply spread her arms open to the sky.

I was in the university library when it happened, doing research for a paper I was working on for an upcoming symposium. I had an evening seminar to teach that night, and if I hadn't called home to tell Lexy something interesting I'd read about a movie she'd been wanting to see, then I might have taught my class, gone out for my weekly beer with my graduate students, and spent a few last hours of normalcy, happily unaware that my yard was full of policemen kneeling in the dirt.

As it was, though, I dialed my home number and a man answered the phone. "Ransome residence," he said.

I paused for a moment, confused. I scanned my mental catalog of male voices, friends and relatives who might possibly be at the house for one reason or another, but I couldn't match any of them to the voice on the other end of the line. I was a bit thrown by the phrase "Ransome residence," as well; my last name is Iverson, and to hear a strange man refer to my house as if only Lexy lived there gave me the strange feeling that I'd somehow, in the course of a day, been written out of my own life's script.

"May I speak to Lexy?" I said finally.

"May I ask who's calling?" the man said.

"This is her husband, Paul. Iverson."

"Mr. Iverson, this is Detective Anthony Stack. I'm going to need you to come home now. There's been an accident."

Apparently Lorelei was the one responsible for summoning the police. As our neighbors returned home from work, one by one, they heard her endless, keening howl coming from our yard. They knew Lorelei, most of them, and were used to hearing her bark, barrel-chested and deep, when she chased birds and squirrels around the yard. But they'd never heard her make a sound like this. Our neighbor to the left, Jim Perasso, was the first to peer over the top of our fence and make the discovery. It was already dark out—the days were getting shorter, and dusk was coming earlier and earlier each day—but as Lorelei ran frantically between the apple tree and the back door of the house, her movements activated our backyard motion-sensor lights. With every circle Lorelei made, she'd pause to nudge Lexy's body with her nose, stopping long enough to allow the lights to go out; then, as she resumed her wild race to each corner of the yard, the lights would go on again. It was through this surreal, strobe-like flickering that Jim saw Lexy lying beneath the tree and called 911.

When I arrived, there was police tape marking off the backyard gate, and the man I had spoken to on the phone met me as I walked across the lawn. He introduced himself again and took me to sit in the living room. I followed him dumbly, all my half-questions stalled by the dread that seemed to have stopped the passage of air through my lungs. I guess I knew what was coming. Already, the house felt still and bare, as if it had been emptied of all the living complexity that had been there when I left. Even Lorelei was gone, having been sedated and taken away by animal control for the night.

Detective Stack told me what had happened as I sat there, numb.

"Do you have any idea what your wife might have been doing in the tree?" he asked.

"I don't know," I said. She had never, in the time I had known her, shown any interest in climbing trees, and this one couldn't have been an easy one to start with. The apple tree in our yard is unusually tall, a monster compared to the dwarf varieties you see in orchards and autumn pick your-own farms. We had neglected it, not pruning it even once in the time we'd lived there, and it had grown to an unruly height of twenty-five or thirty feet. I couldn't begin to guess what she might have been doing up there. Detective Stack was watching me closely. "Maybe she wanted to pick some apples," I said weakly.

"Well, that seems to be the logical answer." He looked at me and at the floor. "It seems pretty clear to us that your wife's death was an accident, but in cases like this when there are no witnesses, we need to do a brief investigation to rule out suicide. I have to ask—did your wife seem at all depressed lately? Did she ever mention suicide, even in a casual way?"

I shook my head.

"I didn't think so," he said. "I just had to ask."

When the men in the yard finished taking their pictures and collecting their evidence, Detective Stack talked to them and reported back to me that everyone was satisfied. It had been an accident, no question. Apparently there are two ways of falling, and each one tells a story. A person who jumps from a great height, even as high as seven or eight floors up, can control the way she falls; if she lands on her feet, she may sustain great injuries to her legs and spine, but she may survive. And if she does not survive, then the particular way her bones break, the way her ankles and knees shatter from the stress of the impact, lets us know that her jump was intentional. But a person who reaches the top branches of an apple tree, twenty-five feet off the ground, and simply loses her footing has no control over how she falls. She may tumble in the air and land on her stomach or her back or her head. She may land with her skin intact and still break every bone and crush every organ inside her. This is how we decide what is an accident and what is not. When they found Lexy, she was lying faceup, and her neck was broken. This is how we know that Lexy didn't jump.

Later, after the police had left and Lexy's body had been taken away, I went out into the yard. Underneath the tree, there was a scattering of apples that had fallen to the ground. Had Lexy climbed the tree to pick the last of the apples before they grew rotten on the branches? Perhaps she was going to bake something; perhaps she was going to put them in a pretty bowl and set them someplace sunny for us to snack on. I gathered them up carefully and brought them inside. I kept them on the kitchen table until the smell of their sweet rot began to draw flies.

It wasn't until a few days after the funeral that I began to find certain clues—well, I hesitate to use the word "clues," which excludes the possibility of sheer coincidence or overanalyzing on my part. To say I found clues would suggest that someone had laid out a careful trail of bits of information with the aim of leading me to a conclusion so well hidden and yet so obvious that its accuracy could not be disputed. I don't expect I'll be that lucky. I'll say instead that I began to discover certain anomalies, certain incongruities, that suggested that the day of Lexy's death had not been a usual day.

The first of these anomalies had to do with our bookshelves. Lexy and I were both big readers, and our bookshelves, like anyone's, I imagine, were halfheartedly organized according to a number of different systems. On some shelves, books were grouped by size, big coffee-table books all together on the bottommost shelf, and mass-market paperbacks crammed in where nothing else would fit. There were enclaves of books grouped by subject—our cookbooks were all on the same shelf, for example—but this type of classification was too painstaking to carry very far. Finally, there were her books and my books—books whose subject matter reflected our own individual interests, and books each of us had owned before we were married that just ended up in their own sections. Beyond that, it was a hodgepodge. Even so, I came to have a sense of which books belonged where. A mental impression that I had seen the novel I had loved when I was twenty sitting snugly between a book of poems we'd received as a wedding gift and a sci-fi thriller I had read on the beach one summer. If you asked me where you might find a particular textbook I coauthored, I could point you right to its place between a Beatles biography and a book about how to brew your own beer. This is how I know that Lexy rearranged the books before she died.

The second anomaly has to do with

Lorelei. As far as I can piece together, it seems that Lexy took a steak from the refrigerator, one we'd been planning to barbecue that night on the grill, cooked it, and gave it to the dog. At first I thought she must have eaten it herself and merely given Lorelei the bone to chew on—I found the bone several days later, hidden in a corner of the bedroom—but the thing is, there were no dirty plates or cutlery, only the frying pan sitting on the stove where she left it. The dishwasher was locked, having been run that morning after breakfast, and when I opened it up, I could still recognize my own handiwork in the way the dishes had been negotiated into place. The dishwasher hadn't been touched, the dish rack next to the sink was empty, and the dish towels weren't even moist. I have to conclude that one of two things happened: either Lexy surprised Lorelei with an unprecedented wealth of meat or she stood in our kitchen on the last day of her life and ate an entire twenty-ounce steak with her fingers. As I think about it now, it occurs to me that there might be a third scenario, and it might be the best one of all: perhaps the two of them shared it.

Maybe these events mean nothing. After all, I am a grieving man, and I am trying very hard to find some sense in my wife's death. But the evidence I have discovered is sufficiently strange to make me wonder what really happened that day, whether it was really a desire for apples that led my sweet wife to climb to the top of that tree. Lorelei is my witness, not just to Lexy's death itself but to all the events leading up to it. She watched Lexy move through her days and her nights. She was there for the unfolding of our marriage from its first day to its last. Simply put, she knows things I don't. I feel I must do whatever I can to unlock that knowledge.

TWO

Perhaps you're familiar with some of the more celebrated cases of language acquisition in dogs, but allow me to provide a brief history to refresh your memory. First off, of course, is the case of the sixteenth-century child-dog of Lyons. This dog, by most accounts a keeshond brought into the area by Dutch traders, was adopted at birth by a grieving mother whose baby had died soon after childbirth. The woman suckled the dog like a child and dressed him in little nighties and bonnets. As the pup grew, his "mother" took great pains to teach him to speak and succeeded to some degree by sheer perseverance, though listeners often had to ask the woman to translate. The dog became a celebrated member of the community but never learned to frolic and play like other dogs. The dog and his mother lived happily together for thirteen years, until the woman grew ill, and when she lay on her deathbed, the dog never left her side. On the night the woman closed her eyes for the last time, the dog spoke his last words: "Without your ear, I have no tongue." (I need hardly point out the double meaning of both the English "tongue" and the French *langue,* which refer both to the physical tongue and to language.) Though the dog lived another year after his mother's death, he never made another noise, either canine or human. After his death, the people of Lyons erected a statue in his honor, with his final words engraved on the base.

I think this story, so full of fairy-tale magic and sadness yet so well documented by the greatest scientific minds of their age, will be the perfect opener for my book, my earnest and scholarly work in which I try to explain to my baffled colleagues why, after twenty years of devoting my time to the study of linguistics, I have decided to turn my energies to teaching a dog to talk.

I'll need to begin with case histories to prove that I at least cracked a book before going completely off the deep end. They'll want me to remind them of the strange case of Vasil, the eighteenth-century Hungarian who, influenced by a philosopher named Geoffrey Longwell, who believed that dogs were the lost tribe of Israel, performed a series of experiments on a litter of vizsla puppies. Vasil took as his inspiration the biblical story of the Garden of Eden; though the Bible is unclear as to whether there were dogs in Eden, Vasil concluded that God would certainly not have omitted such a fine species of animal. Taking as evidence the serpent's speech to Eve, Vasil postulated that all animals must have been blessed with the power of speech in the earthly paradise, a power they lost when Adam and Eve left Eden. He felt that if he could restore that power, which had been unfairly wrested from the animals, he would uncover the first language ever spoken.

To recapture this language, Vasil placed each puppy in a walled-off garden, each one separate from its brothers and sisters, and attempted to re-create the conditions of Eden. He provided them with plentiful food and water, and he massaged their throats daily to encourage speech. He met with varied success. One puppy never spoke at all, one made sounds that resembled a mumbled French (although later researchers found it to be an Alsatian creole), and one learned only the Hungarian word for roast beef. The remaining five puppies merely barked, although they all seemed to understand one another.

Vasil's theories drew condemnation from the Church, especially his premise that God had acted unfairly in revoking dogs' powers of speech, and he spent the last twenty years of his life in prison. The vizslas were instrumental in his arrest; the dogs escaped and ran through the streets, with the French-speaking one barking out naughty and insulting limericks and the Hungarian-speaking one calling for roast beef, until the amazed crowd followed them to Vasil's house.

The real clincher, I think, will be the tragic case of Wendell Hollis, which, my colleagues will certainly recall, is the most prominent example of this kind of inquiry in the modern era. Over a period of several years, Hollis performed surgery on more than a hundred dogs, changing the shape of their palates to make them more conducive to the forming of words. Several of the dogs died as a result of the surgery, which Hollis performed in his New York apartment, and many of the others ran away. Hollis was arrested after the police received a complaint about the noise; after years of putting up with the mangled barking, a neighbor called the police when one of the dogs learned to cry for help. This one dog, with a scarred throat and misshapen mouth, testified at the trial. Though he didn't speak in complete sentences, he was able to say "hate" and "fire pain" and "brothers gone away." The jury took only one hour to reach a verdict, and Hollis was sentenced to five years in prison.

None of these cases can be considered completely successful, of course. But it's the very form these failures took, the "almost" quality of each half success, that makes me think there's more in this area to be explored.

In fact, I find lately that I can think of nothing else.

But if I am to keep my good name in the academic community, something I'm no longer sure I care about doing, I can't allow such subjectivity. I have to begin by telling my colleagues that there's a whole body of work out there already, nearly as old as the study of language itself. I have to tell them that I'm not doing anything new at all.

If I could, though, I would begin the way poets used to do when they told their stories of love and war and troubles rained down from the heavens. I would begin like this:

I sing of a woman with ink on her hands and pictures hidden beneath her hair. I sing of a dog with a skin like velvet pushed the wrong way. I sing of the shape a fallen body makes in the dirt beneath a tree, and I sing of an ordinary man who wanted to know things no human being could tell him. This is the true beginning.

Let me return for a moment to my preliminary comments regarding the project I am about to undertake. As I have mentioned, I have a dog named Lorelei, a Rhodesian Ridgeback. She was my wife's dog before she was mine. It is my proposal to work with Lorelei on a series of exercises and experiments designed to help her acquire language in whatever ways are possible, given her physiological and mental capacities. It is my proposal to teach Lorelei to talk.

I realize how this must sound. A year ago I would have been as skeptical as the rest of you. But you have to understand how the events of the past few months have changed my way of thinking. Let me remind you that we, as scientists, have witnessed in the past century the strange spectacle of apes speaking entire sentences with their hands. We've seen parrots who have learned to provide the punch lines of dirty jokes, much to the delight of their owners' friends. We've seen guide dogs trained to turn on light switches and to listen for the crying of babies born to deaf parents. I myself have seen, on an amateur video show, a dog who has learned to make the sound "I love you."

I'm not suggesting that any of the above examples offer conclusive proof I'll succeed. I'm aware, for a start, that dogs have considerably less cranial capacity than gorillas and other higher primates, and I'm not kidding myself that dogs who say "I love you" and parrots who curse like sailors are doing anything other than performing tricks they know will result in praise and bits of food.

But in the evenings when I sit with Lorelei

and she gazes up at me with her wide, inscrutable eyes, I wonder what she would tell me if she could. Sometimes I get down on the carpet with her to speak to her softly and ask her my questions while I rest my hand upon her great furrowed head. More than once I have awakened to find that I have fallen asleep with my head on the wide, rough expanse of her side.

The conclusion I have reached is that, above all, dogs are witnesses. They are allowed access to our most private moments. They are there when we think we are alone. Think of what they could tell us. They sit on the laps of presidents. They see acts of love and violence, quarrels and feuds, and the secret play of children. If they could tell us everything they have seen, all of the gaps of our lives would stitch themselves together. I feel I have no choice but to give it a try.

THREE

There's a talking-dog joke that goes like this: A man walks into a bar with a dog. The bartender says, "Sorry, buddy, no dogs allowed." The man says, "Oh, but you don't understand—this is a very special dog. He can talk." The bartender looks skeptical but says, "Okay, let's hear it." The man puts the dog on a bar stool and looks deeply into his eyes. "What do you call that thing on top of a house?" he asks. "Roof, roof!" barks the dog. "And how does sandpaper feel?" the man continues. "Ruff, ruff!" answers the dog. "And who was the greatest baseball player of all time?" the man asks. "Rooth, Rooth!" the dog says. "All right, buddy," the bartender says, "that's enough. Out of here, both of you." The man takes the dog off the bar stool, and together they leave the bar.

As they're walking out, the dog turns to the man and shrugs. "DiMaggio?" he says.

This is what I'm thinking of as I sit on the floor with Lorelei, looking into her deep brown eyes. I've been working with her for two hours now, running a few preliminary intelligence tests, and I have to fight the urge to give up my teacher persona and start talking silly puppy-dog talk to her. "Where have you gone, Joe DiMaggio?" I want to murmur in baby talk, taking her front paws and lifting them up high until she flops onto her back, a little roughhousing game we have. "Huh, girl?" I want to say, rubbing her belly. "Where's Joe DiMaggio?" But we've got a little more work to do, so I just give her a brief pat on the head and say "Good girl" in an authoritative tone of voice.

Rhodesian Ridgebacks are big dogs; Lorelei's head comes to well above my knee when we're both standing up. They were originally bred to hunt lions, and they are extremely strong and agile when in pursuit of rabbits or other small game (lions being rather rare in our small college town), but in domestic situations they are exceptionally earnest and gentle. They get their name from a distinctive ridge of hair running down the middle of their backs, hair that seems to grow the wrong way, standing up like a long cowlick against their sleek brown coats. When you run your hand across it, it feels bristly, like the buzz cuts boys used to get when I was small. More than anything, it reminds me of a very stiff velvet chair my grandmother had in her house; the fabric felt prickly against the skin whichever way you rubbed it—it was impossible to sit in if your arms or legs were bare—but when you flattened a bit of the nap with your finger, you could feel the softness that lay between the individual threads.

We began the morning by going through a list I've compiled of all the words I know Lorelei understands. She knows her name, of course; I did a brief experiment by calling out other words—broccoli, water bed, Santa Claus—in the same tone I normally use to call her name. She sat up and stared at me when she heard my voice and appeared to listen in a sort of rapture, but she didn't get up and come running over until I called out "Lorelei." Good girl, I told her. Good girl.

Next, we moved on to commands. Come, sit, and stay. Down. Paw and other paw.

Come on up (spoken while patting the couch cushion in invitation). Do you want to go out?

In the early days of our marriage, Lexy taught her the command "Where's Paul? Go get Paul," and on Saturday mornings when I slept late and Lexy got tired of waiting for me to wake up, I would wake to find Lorelei hovering over me, her front paws up on the bed and her face looking down into mine. Strangely, I was never able to retaliate; I was never able to make Lorelei understand "Go get Lexy." She responds splendidly to "Go get your ball" and "Go get your giraffe"—this last refers to a stuffed toy she likes because its long neck lends itself perfectly to games of tug-of-war—but never "Go get Lexy." Did she simply not know Lexy's name? Or did she understand me perfectly but refuse to obey, not wanting to violate the private joke she shared with Lexy, her first owner and love?

All in all, Lorelei knows the meaning of about fifty different words. Dinner and treat. Car and ride. Good and bad. This corresponds roughly to the number of words a human child understands by the age of thirteen months. This is perhaps not a very useful parallel, since by sixteen months or so, a baby will have doubled or tripled that number and will have begun to form rudimentary sentences like "Mama juice" or "Big truck vroom," whereas for a dog, the list of known words, once learned, will remain more or less static throughout his life. And, of course, at least to an outside observer, the capacity to link words and concepts into sentences as we know them remains outside the dog's ability.

What interests me, however, is that in children, language comprehension begins long before language production—between the ages of one and three, children understand about five times as many words as they can speak. By what mechanism does that thirteen-month-old make the leap from comprehension to speech? I believe this is the question that lies at the heart of my project.

The one advantage Lorelei has over human infants is that the sharpness of her senses allows her to pick up on nonverbal cues that we, as humans, are barely aware of. She can hear the tying of shoelaces two rooms away, and she stands and stretches, knowing it means that someone is going to leave the house, and that perhaps she'll be going with them. She understands the clatter of silverware in a drawer and the sound of someone settling down on the couch to read the newspaper. She knew what it meant for Lexy to stand before the bathroom mirror putting on her makeup, and when she smelled the particular combination of odors that comprised this event—perhaps the hair scent of the bristles on Lexy's cosmetic brushes, combined with the perfumed clay of her foundation and the thick, painty smell of her mascara—she would appear, out of nowhere, in front of the bathroom, and finding the door slightly ajar, she would poke her nose through the crack, waiting to see if she was going to be invited along on whatever adventure Lexy was preparing herself for.

Continuing my preliminary tests of Lorelei's intelligence, I get a dog treat, show it to her, then hide it underneath a cup. She noses the cup, overturns it, and retrieves the treat in six seconds, by my stopwatch. This is very good; it demonstrates impressive problem-solving ability. Next, I test her memory by making a show of hiding a treat in a corner while she watches, then taking her into another room for five minutes. When we return to the living room, she goes right for it. I'm very pleased.

Something odd happens during the third test. The test consists of covering the dog's head with a towel and timing how long it takes her to shake it off. It's another problem-solving task, and I'm expecting Lorelei to pass with flying colors. But when I put the towel over her head, she merely stands there, her head slightly bowed under the weight. I wait a full minute, then a minute and fifteen seconds. She makes no move to get out from underneath, and the hunched shape of her body, the thick green cloth covering her face as thoroughly as a widow's veil, seems to me suddenly very sad. I'm about to remove the towel myself when the phone rings. I turn to pick it up, and by the time I've turned back—it's a wrong number, and the call lasts no more than five or ten seconds—Lorelei has shaken off the towel and is sitting up, watching me. It occurs to me that maybe the reason she didn't try to free herself while I was watching is that she wasn't sure what it was I expected from her. Perhaps she thought I *wanted* her to stand quietly with a towel over her head. This was the strangest of all the strange games I'd spent the day playing with her, and for once, she couldn't figure out the rules.

Suddenly I feel tired; I think we've both had enough. I kneel down and put my arms around the dog. "Come on, girl," I say. "Let's go for a walk."

F O U R

A friend of mine from college used to live on the nineteenth floor of a high-rise in New York City. His next-door neighbors when he moved in were a youngish couple with a dog. I remember sitting on his balcony, drinking with him into the night, and seeing the woman of this couple come out onto her balcony, right next door, with the dog, a little pug. They had covered the sides of the balcony with chicken wire so that the dog could sit out there safely, without danger of slipping through the bars.

After my friend had lived there for a year or so, the man next door climbed onto the railing of the balcony and jumped. My friend was in bed when it happened—it was about one A.M.—and he heard a short piercing scream and then nothing more. It wasn't until the next day, when he was playing loud music and one of the family members who had gathered next door to grieve came by to ask him to turn it down, that he learned what sound he had heard.

I was in town a month or so later, and I stayed on his couch—this was during the young part of my life when I was happy to have someone else's couch to sleep on. As we sat drinking on the balcony, we couldn't stop talking about it. It haunted us, and every conversation seemed to lead back to it. Toward the end of the night, when we'd drunk quite a lot and had moved very quickly through the stages of grief for this man we hadn't known, we began to joke about it. We looked down from the balcony and tried to imagine the trajectory the man's body would have taken as it fell. We speculated about where exactly he might have landed—there was a building whose roof lay directly below us, ten stories or so down, but we thought that perhaps the wind might have blown his falling body out over the sidewalk—and it was only as dawn began to break that we realized we were talking quite loudly and that the young widow was sleeping next door. I never found out whether she heard us that night—I suspect not, because when she moved out a month later, she made a special point of thanking my friend for his kindness during that terrible time—but the very possibility of it still fills me with horror. If I were to meet this woman again (and I don't even know that I'd recognize her all these years later), I would fall to my knees and beg her forgiveness; I would tell her that I only now understand that what I did to her, whether she knew I did it or not, is the unkindest thing I have ever done in my life.

I was thirty-nine when I met Lexy. Before that, I was married for many years to a woman whose voice filled our house like a thick mortar, sealing every crack and corner. Maura, this first wife of mine, spoke so much while saying so little that I sometimes felt as if I were drowning in the heavy paste of her words. The most ordinary details of our lives had to be broken down and processed; in every conversation, I had to choose my words carefully, because I knew that any of them, innocuous though they seemed to me, might mire me in a nightlong conversation about my motives in uttering them. It seemed to me that Maura was anxious all the time, nervous she might not be doing it all right, and the only way she could keep control of the pieces of her life was to analyze them until there was no life left in them at all. Sometimes, in the car, we'd be driving in silence, and I'd glance over at her when her face was, for a rare moment, unguarded. "What are you worrying about right this second?" I'd ask. And she always had an answer.

Toward the end, after I'd begun to refuse to participate with her in these dialogues, she began leaving me notes. Just normal things at first—"Please pick up some milk" or "Don't forget dinner at Mike and Jane's tonight"—but as time went on, they became more and more complex and increasingly hostile.

Our marriage ended late one night when I came home to find a note that said, "I've asked you several times to do me the favor of putting your breakfast dishes in the dishwasher before you leave for work in the morning, and yet I've come home once again to find your coffee mug sitting on the table. I guess I've been wrong in assuming that I can expect you, as my husband, to listen to me when I voice my needs, and to honor my wishes with sensitivity and respect. We need to talk about this AS SOON AS POSSIBLE." The last four words were underlined twice.

I picked up a pen—this was not my finest moment, I'll admit—and wrote "Fuck you. I'm sick of your fucking notes" across the bottom of the paper. I stuck it on the refrigerator for her to find in the morning. We left each other the next day, but not until she'd tried to engage me in one last conversation. I walked out without saying a word.

I met Lexy less than a year later, and I knew from our first conversation that when she talked it was an easy thing, plain and open, with none of the byzantine turns and traps I found myself caught in when I talked to Maura.

We met because she was having a yard sale, and I happened to follow her handmade signs from the main road. Going to yard sales was something I had taken to doing after my divorce. I liked the treasure hunt of driving through neighborhoods I'd never visited before, and I liked investigating the small mysteries of the lives of the people I met—how had they come to acquire this particular combination of things (shower radios and ornate liquor decanters, hand-crocheted baby sweaters and limited edition Super Bowl Coke cans long since emptied of their contents), and what had happened along the way to make them decide these items no longer had a place in their home? I found a strange, childlike excitement in the promise that I might discover something I had been looking for for years without even knowing it, and it reassured me, humbled me somehow, to see that other people's lives, too, could be broken down into pieces and spread out on the lawn for anyone to examine.

On this particular Saturday, I pulled up in front of a small green house, set back from the street by a tree-shaded lawn. Lexy was sitting on the front steps, reading a paperback. She had dark blond hair, dipping just below her chin, and she was wearing a loose cotton dress printed with a pattern of vines and flowers. She was very pretty—I won't say I didn't notice—but I did little more than register the fact and let it go. She was easily eight or nine years younger than I was, and I immediately added her to the "wouldn't be interested" list that grew longer in my mind with each passing day.

She looked up and smiled as I got out of my car. "Hi," she called. "Let me know if you have any questions."

An enormous brown dog lay on the grass nearby. The dog looked up at me with wide-eyed interest for a moment, then laid her head once more on her thick paws.

I browsed the tables that had been set out. There was the usual collection of books and CDs, a worn-looking toaster oven, souvenir glasses with cartoon characters painted on them. I didn't find much that interested me, but I didn't want to leave just yet. At the back of the yard, toward the house, I noticed a rack of formal dresses of the shiny, oddly cut bridesmaid variety. A sign attached to the rack read, "Free to anyone who likes to play dress-up. One per customer. Free dyed-to-match shoes with every dress."

"Any takers?" I asked, pointing to the dresses.

"A couple of little girls who took the choice very seriously, and a guy who fell in love with this awful off-the-shoulder floral thing. It actually looked great on him. Sometimes I think bridesmaids' dresses are actually designed for drag queens."

I smiled. "My ex-wife has friends who still won't talk to her." I was surprised to find I had said this. Was I flirting? Letting her know I was available? This was certainly more information than I usually gave out to perfect strangers.

I was afraid I might have put her off— *Warning: pathetic, lonely man on the prowl*—but she laughed. "What color?" she asked.

"Lavender. With puffy sleeves and a big bow across the back."

"Ah, the butt bow. Why do they always insist on the butt bow?"

"I just don't know," I said. I turned away, unsure of what to say next, and began to examine a collection of objects spread on a blanket. A small cardboard box, labeled Square Egg Press, caught my eye. The picture on the front showed a plate of hard-boiled white cubes on a bed of parsley. One of the cubes was cut into careful slices, displaying the square shock of yellow yolk inside. I opened the box and found a hard plastic cylinder with a squat square base. According to the instructions, you were supposed to place a hard-boiled egg, warm and quivering and rid of its shell, into the square chamber, then drop a sort of plastic hat on top of it. There was a screw-on lid, which, I gathered, pushed down on this egg hat, applying the pressure necessary to negotiate the egg into its new, unnatural shape.

"What *is* this?" I asked, turning back to her.

"Well," she said, reading from the copy on the box, "apparently, it turns ordinary hard-boiled eggs into a unique square taste treat."

"Does it work?" I asked.

"You know, I never tried it," she said. "It belonged to an old roommate of mine, and when she moved out, she left it behind. I think she actually got it at a yard sale, too. She was an art history major in college, and she wrote a paper about it for a class on surrealism."

"Surreal is one word for it," I said. "How much are you asking?"

"Fifty cents," she said, turning the box over in her hands. She looked thoughtful, and a little troubled. "I can't believe I've had it all this time, and I never made a square egg."

"Well, I was going to buy it, but you don't have to sell it if you don't want to."

She shook off her troubled look and smiled. "No, no," she said. "It's the kind of thing that should be passed around to as many people as possible. Maybe someday when you're finished with it, you can sell it to someone else."

"Absolutely," I said. I gave her the money and stood there for a moment. "Well, thanks," I said. "Good luck with your sale." I started back toward my car.

"Thanks," she said. "Good luck with your square eggs."

I drove away with a feeling like laughter caught in my chest. I felt happier than I had felt in a long time. So I went home and made some square eggs.

It was late in the afternoon by the time I returned to her house, and she was beginning to take her unsold items inside. She was facing away from me as I drove up, the late sun in her hair, and I sat and watched her for a moment before I got out of the car. The plate of eggs sat beside me on the passenger seat. I had arranged them on a bed of parsley, just like the picture on the box, and cut one into careful squares. I hesitated for a moment—what odd courtship ritual was this?—but just then, she turned and saw me, and I figured I'd have to go through with it.

I walked toward her, holding out my strange offering. "I thought you might like these," I called out.

"Square eggs," she said. Her voice was almost reverent, and as she took the plate from me, her face was filled with a kind of wonder. "I can't believe you made me square eggs."

She looked up from the plate and studied my face. She smiled a slow smile that grew until her whole face was lit with it. "I'm going to ask you out on a date," she said.

"Well," I said. "Well. I'm going to say yes."

And we stood there smiling, with the plate between us, the egg cubes glowing palely in the growing dark.

FIVE

Here's another talking-dog joke. My colleagues have been sending them to me by e-mail. A man walks into a bar with a dog. He says to the bartender, "I'll sell you this dog for five bucks. He can talk." "Yeah, right," says the bartender. The man nudges the dog. "Go on, show him," he says. The dog looks up at the bartender and says, "Oh, please, kind sir, please buy me. This man mistreats me. He keeps me locked in a cage, he never takes me for walks, and he only feeds me once a week. He's a terrible, terrible man." The bartender is amazed. "This dog could make you rich," he says. "Why do you want to sell him for five bucks?" The man replies, "Because I'm sick of all his damn lies."

It's just a joke, but it brings up an interesting point: Who's to say that your average talking dog would be any more honest than your average talking person? Who's to say that Lorelei, if I could loose her tongue, would speak the truth?

I had never owned a dog before I married Lexy; to be honest, I was rather afraid of them. When I was a child, I knew a great mammoth of a dog named Rufus who was angry all of his days. His owner was a bitter and reclusive man named Bucky Jones who used to terrify neighborhood children by gutting deer carcasses in his yard and throwing bits of bloody viscera in our paths as we walked by on our way to school. I'm quite sure he abused the dog on a regular basis, but even so, Rufus was devoted to him. The same dog who spent his days tied to a tree, leaping and snarling bloody murder, would whimper with sweet puppy joy whenever his owner came into the yard. On summer evenings, when Bucky used to climb up onto the roof to sit and drink beer and say wild things to no one, he'd hoist Rufus up there with him, and the strange silhouette they made against the night sky is something I see in my dreams to this day.

The first time I met Lorelei, apart from the

wary once-over we gave each other the day of the yard sale, was when I arrived to pick up Lexy for our first date, a date that, as it turned out, would last a full week. As soon as I rang the bell, I could hear the enormous noise of Lorelei's bark beginning at some distant corner of the house and moving with alarming speed toward the other side of the door. I took an involuntary step backward and cowered against one of the porch posts as Lexy opened the door. Lorelei bounded out and leaped toward me, landing with her paws just below my shoulders. I stood rigid as she peered up into my face for a long moment, no longer barking, and I felt an unexpected calm run through me as I met her eyes. For one strange moment, my anxieties about the evening ahead of me faded, and without even thinking about it, I reached out and rested my hand gently on her head. This is the beginning of *our* story, mine and Lorelei's, a story separate in many ways from the one Lexy and I would begin to create that night. For the first time, I looked into those earnest eyes and touched that rough-soft fur. For the first time, I felt a hint of tenderness for this dog who has, through time and the earthly miracle of canine trust, come to be my own. All that we are together now, the sum of our grief and our play, the daily movement of man and dog through an empty house, following the passage of sun from room to room until it's gone, all of it began that moment on the porch, with Lexy standing in the background.

When she stepped forward then, my Lexy, and I turned finally to look at her for the first time that day—she was pulling the dog off me and apologizing, chiding Lorelei in low tones as she maneuvered her into the house and shut her inside—I felt nothing of the rapt nervousness, the deep-bone stage fright, I had felt on all the other first dates of my life. Lexy had kept our plans for the evening deliberately vague, which had left me with some uneasiness, an unfamiliar tilting feeling of not knowing where I might end up, but now as I watched her negotiate all of the everyday hubbub of calming the dog, putting on a jacket, locking the door, I knew that somehow, without even realizing it, I had made the decision to follow her wherever she wanted to take me.

"Hi," she said, turning to face me and relaxing into a smile. "I'm sorry about Lorelei.

She's really a sweetie, but sometimes it's hard to tell."

"Oh, I could tell," I said.

She looked lovely. She was wearing a kind of silky black T-shirt and a long slim skirt, and she had pulled her hair back from her face. In the week since we had met, it seemed as if I had spent my time doing nothing else but conjuring her image in my mind, but I saw now that I had remembered everything wrong. I saw now that the brown of her eyes was lightened with flecks of amber and that the heart-shape of her face was more round than angular. I saw the complex layering of pale gold and dark honey in her hair and the rose-flush of her skin. I saw now that she was beautiful.

"So," I said as we walked toward my car, "where are we going?"

"Well," she said, sounding rather apologetic, "I'm afraid the first thing we have to do is go to a wedding."

"A wedding." I did my best to quell rising panic. Socializing with strangers is not something I do well, as anyone I know will tell you.

She went on in a rush. "I know that's a really weird first-date activity, but they're clients of mine and I promised I'd put in an appearance. We don't have to stay long— don't worry, I'm not going to know anyone there either, and I *promise* we can do some- thing fun afterward."

"Great," I said resolutely. "That sounds like fun."

She laughed. "No, it doesn't," she said. "And if you want to back out, I won't mind. But I guarantee you, it won't be like any other wedding you've ever been to."

I opened the car door for her. "Well, then," I said. "What are we waiting for?"

We drove, following a small hand-drawn map that I imagine had been included in the wedding invitation.

"So," I said. "You said these people are clients of yours. I don't even know what you do."

She smiled. "Oh, that will become appar- ent," she said. "I think I'll keep it a secret for a while longer."

"Am I going to be dressed all right for this thing?" I asked. "It's not formal, is it?"

"No, not at all. I think it's going to be kind of New-Agey, actually. They made a big deal on the invitation about this being the day of the vernal equinox—you know, when day and night are equal. They called it 'the day the sun marries the moon.' " She laughed. "I guess they were looking for something more dramatic than just 'the day Brittany marries Todd.' "

We were in the country now. It was late afternoon, nearing sunset. Eventually, we turned down a long dirt road that dead-ended at a patch of tall grass and wildflowers. A path had been cut into the growth and marked with garlands of roses on either side.

A woman was standing at the entrance to the path, holding a large basket twined with ribbons. She smiled as we approached her, and she held the basket out toward us.

"Please choose your masks," she said.

I glanced at Lexy, who was watching me and smiling. "You go first," she said.

I leaned forward warily and looked into the basket. I think I was expecting something like the Halloween masks I wore as a child, flimsy plastic monster faces and shiny superheroes with no backs to their heads, elastic bands stapled to the sides of the masks to keep them from slipping off your face. Instead, the basket was filled with wonders the likes of which I had never seen. A dozen papier-mâché faces looked up at me with cutout eyes. I saw a frog first, then a zebra. A sunflower with vibrant yellow petals framing its face. A tall golden feather with ghostly features pressed into its wavy barbs. There were three-quarter-length masks with wrinkled brows and outrageously curved noses, and wild-looking jesters decked out in playing cards. A snaky-haired Medusa and a Bacchus crowned with grapes. I felt giddy with the choice.

"Go on," Lexy said. "What do you want to be today?"

I reached in and pulled out the first one I touched. It was a book, a thick, old-fashioned kind of book with its pages spread open. Eyes, nose, and mouth protruded from the gilded text.

"That's perfect," Lexy said. As she bent to rummage in the basket, I examined my mask. Across the two pages, a single phrase was written in a long, sloping hand: *You have taken the finest knight in all my company.* I fixed the mask to my face.

"Oh, good," I heard Lexy say. "I was hoping this one would still be here."

I turned toward her. She had covered her own lovely face with the smiling face of a dog. An earnest, familiar face.

"That's Lorelei," I said.

"Yes," she said. "It is. So have you figured out what I do for a living?"

"You made all these?" I asked.

"Mm-hmm," she said. She took my hand. "Let's go to the wedding."

We walked down the path until we reached a clearing. There were chairs set up around a center aisle, and each of them was filled with a person wearing a mask. I saw a sea nymph with starfish caught in her hair talking to a man with the head of a bull. I saw an angel with a halo talking on a cell phone. We took our seats, in between a splendid butterfly-woman and a man with an enormous iceberg perched on his head, the *Titanic* broken in two across the top.

Up at the front, a string quartet dressed in formal wear, with silver stars spread across their faces, began to play. We rose and turned to see the sun and the moon walking toward us through the crowd. The bride wore a dress of palest yellow silk with layer upon layer of iridescent gauze catching the light. Her face was a dazzling circle of gold, framed with fiery rays. The groom wore a tuxedo, his face masked with a tall crescent of silver. They were beautiful.

Lexy leaned toward me. "I'm curious to see how they're going to do the kiss," she whispered. I reached out for her hand and held it as we watched the sacred joining of sun and moon, silhouetted by the falling dusk.

S I X

Ah, but I've already let it slip, haven't I, that our first date lasted a week. It didn't end there in that perfect sunset moment of the masquerade wedding. There's more, there's always more to tell, and I'm already getting caught up in the accumulation of moments that led from the day of that wedding to the day of Lexy's fall.

But the more I think about Lexy, the more I try to sort it all out, the more I neglect my research. The truth is, now that I've arranged for a sabbatical and given myself all the time and space I could possibly need, I'm not sure how to proceed. My desk is piled with books on canine physiology and psychology, papers on language acquisition in apes and in children, studies of "the talking dog as motif" in folklore and literature. I have folders full of notes that I have compiled on famous dogs, ranging from Cerberus to Snoopy. Just yesterday, I spent several hours in the microfilm room of the university library, collecting clippings about the trial of Wendell Hollis and its star witness for the prosecution. The dog who sent Wendell Hollis to jail had been named Dog J by his captor, simply because he was the tenth in a series of alphabetically named dogs that Hollis had purchased from pet stores, picked up at pounds, or snatched off the streets, but after his rescue, the *New York Post* held a contest to rename him. Suggestions ranged from the cheerily naive Lucky to the wrongly gendered and grandiosely silly Harriet Pupman, but the name that stuck was Hero, and even the *Post*'s blaring headline of HERE, HERO! emblazoned above the famous photo of the dog being escorted out of the courthouse by a group of smiling police officers failed to detract from the dignity and the rightness of the name. This story fascinates me more than I can say, for reasons that should be obvious: This is a dog I would like to talk to.

So you can see I have been working; my desk is littered with the reading I have done, the tangents I have been willing to follow. But as I sit here, sifting through the paper, with Lorelei lying at my feet as inscrutable as ever, I realize that I have no idea where to begin.

I suppose the first step in teaching a dog to speak might be to teach her to "speak." That is, to teach her to bark on command in the parlor trick usually referred to as "speaking." I get a biscuit and call Lorelei over to me.

"Sit," I say, and she does.

"Speak." She just looks at me. "Speak," I say again. Uncertainly, she lies down.

"Up, up," I say. She stands.

"Good girl. Now sit." We're back to the beginning. She stares at me intently, her nose twitching at the nearness of the biscuit I hold. She sneaks a glance at the treat; hasn't she already performed several tricks?

"Speak," I say firmly. Then I start to bark at her. "Rrr, ruff!" I say, staring into her eyes. "Ruff, ruff! Speak! Ruff, ruff!"

Lorelei cocks her head to the side. This is unprecedented behavior on my part. Never before have I gotten down on the floor and barked at her. She waits to see what I'll do next.

"Speak, girl!" I say, pulling my face closer to hers. Our noses are almost touching. "Grr," I say, staring into her eyes. "Ruff! Ruff!" I'm nearly shouting. Finally, it works. Lorelei lets out a noise, not quite a bark, not quite a whine. It sounds, more than anything, like an expression of frustration— *When the hell do I get the biscuit?*—but it's progress.

"Good girl!" I say effusively. I break the biscuit in two and give her half. She settles down to gnaw on it. I wait until she's finished, then urge her back into a sitting position. I show her the other half of the biscuit. "Speak!" I say. "Ruff, ruff!" This time she gives a full throated bark, and then another. "Good dog," I say, "good speak!" I hold out the other piece of biscuit, but she ignores it. She stares into my eyes, her brow furrowed, and continues barking.

"Okay, now, good girl, quiet," I say. I pull away slowly, sliding back on the carpet, still sitting. "Quiet now!"

Lorelei stands up, drawing herself to her full height. She has to lean down to continue barking in my face.

"Good girl," I say soothingly. She's making me nervous. I stand up; my books have told me that in situations like this I need to assert my position as alpha male. "Quiet," I say more firmly. She looks up at me searchingly and barks again. She's less aggressive now, but I can't get her to stop. I reach out and gingerly pat her head. "Do you want a cookie? Nice dog, nice cookie." Finally, she takes the biscuit. She retreats to a corner of the room, where she drops it on the floor and pretends to bury it, using her nose to draw the folds of the carpet over the biscuit.

"Good girl," I call from across the room. I sink down on the sofa and watch her concentration as she goes about her task. I pick up my notebook. "Taught Lorelei the command Speak," I write. "Results inconclusive." I lean back and close my eyes. Across the room, Lorelei picks up her biscuit and takes it into a different corner to start over again.

SEVEN

I became a linguist in part because words have failed me all my life. I was born tongue-tied in the most literal sense: the tissue connecting my tongue to the floor of my mouth was short and thick, limiting lingual movement. It's a common enough condition; the doctor simply snipped the membrane in the delivery room, and I grew to speak like any normal child, with no lingering impediments. But the image stays with me as a kind of metaphor for all my subsequent dealings with language: I was born with a tongue not meant for speaking, and despite all artificial attempts to loosen it, it has stayed stuck in place at every important moment of my life.

But that first day with Lexy, I found I had plenty to say. Waiting in line to congratulate the bride and groom, radiant now in their own faces, for they had taken off their masks to kiss after all, I chatted with the other guests, happily introducing Lexy as the one who had made all the day's magic possible.

By the time we got through the receiving line, it was as if we were already a couple. As word spread that Lexy was the creator of the masks, a crowd formed around us, encircling us with such admiration and excitement that anyone looking on might have thought that we, and not Brittany and Todd, were the newlyweds. With my hand resting on the small of Lexy's back, I took on the role of proud partner and promoter, bragging about her work and allowing her to play the humble artist, basking shyly in the praise. Flushed and smiling, she answered questions about technique and inspiration and gave her business card to those who asked for it, art collectors and fairy-tale enthusiasts and people who liked to throw elaborate Halloween parties.

As the crowd around us thinned, Lexy squeezed my arm. "Thanks," she said. "You're good at that."

"Thanks," I said. "But I should tell you,

I'm not usually so suave. It must be the mask."

"Oh, I don't know," she said. "You were pretty suave with the square eggs. Those square eggs swept me off my feet."

"I'll bet those words have never been spoken before, in all the centuries of human language."

"Here's another one: 'Why don't you help me get this dog off my face so you can kiss me?' "

"Oh, I'm sure *someone* must've used that line before," I said. "In fact, I believe it appeared in the first draft of the balcony scene from *Romeo and Juliet.*"

But she was already kissing me.

"Let's get out of here," I said when we pulled apart.

"Very suave," she said. Hand in hand, we walked through the grass, past the crowds of dragons and princesses holding champagne flutes, of bunny rabbits dancing with demons, back to the real world of the car and the tall grass and the long, dusty road.

"So where to?" I asked Lexy, once we were settled in the car. "Maybe something more first-datey? Dinner, a movie, awkward conversation at a coffeehouse?"

She leaned back against the headrest, seeming to examine the ceiling. "Hmm," she said. "Let's see. Have you ever been to Disney World?"

"Disney World," I repeated. I should mention here that we were somewhere in suburban Virginia. Still, I pretended to consider it. "No, I can't say that I have."

Of course I hadn't been to Disney World. Disney World, the one in Florida, didn't even exist when I was a kid—I think I was fifteen or sixteen when it opened—and in any case, my parents never had enough money to take us on extravagant vacations. And as an adult, it had never occurred to me. When Maura and I went away, it was to cities— London, Rome, Athens. We both had a taste for ruins. Maura liked vacations that could be meted out into days just full enough and meals just sophisticated enough to leave us tired and sated when we returned to our hotel at night. On our honeymoon, we went to a Caribbean resort, and the sandy, sunny emptiness of each day drove her nearly crazy. We'd settle on the beach with a book for me and a straw

bag full of novels, magazines, and crossword puzzles for her, and within twenty minutes, she'd get up to take a walk in the
sand, dip herself briefly in the ocean, and
retreat into the air-conditioning to have a
piña colada in the dark bar, ignoring the
man in the flowered shirt who hovered near
us on the beach for the very purpose of
bringing us frothy drinks. I knew without
asking that the idea of spinning around in a
giant teacup and shaking hands with a
grown-up dressed up as a mouse would
not have appealed to her. So, no, I had
never been to Disney World.

Lexy turned to me with real excitement in
her face. "Really?" she asked. "Well, we
have to go. Now, tonight."

"Tonight it is," I said, playing along. "But
maybe we should get something to eat
first."

"Well, we can stop," she said, "but we'll
have to leave after the appetizers."

"Why?"

"Because if we finish dinner, then the
date will be over."

"Why is that?"

"Well, come on. We've already gone to a
wedding. Once we've gone out to dinner,

how much more could we reasonably expect to do? It's only the first date, after all."

"Okay," I said. "And if the date were over, then we couldn't go to Disney World because . . . ?"

She rolled her eyes. "Because that'd just be crazy. We don't even know each other, and we're taking off on a trip together? That's nuts. But if we decide that Disney World is the perfect place to go on our first date—and I believe it is—then we'll have a story to tell for the rest of our lives."

"You're serious, aren't you?" I asked.

"Of course." Her face was flushed with excitement. "Look, it's spring break, right, so you don't have any classes to teach. What were you planning to do with yourself for the next week?"

"Well, I have some papers to grade. And I was thinking about defrosting my refrigerator."

"Oh, yeah, you *need* a trip to Disney World."

I couldn't believe I was considering this. "What about your dog?" I asked.

"I have a neighbor I can call."

"What about clothes?"

She looked me up and down, appraising my khakis and button-down shirt.

"That'll do until we get there," she said. "Then we can get you a Mickey Mouse shirt. Or, no, not Mickey—Eeyore. That's who you remind me of. We'll find you an Eeyore shirt."

"Eeyore?" I asked. I scanned my memory of children's literature. "The sad donkey? That's who I remind you of?"

"Yup. But in a good way."

We stopped at an Italian place we saw on our way back to the highway. I guess I still thought she was going to call it off, but when we walked in, she excused herself to use the pay phone. When she came back to the table, she announced that everything was all set with her neighbor; he had agreed to take care of Lorelei while she was gone. I examined the menu. I was starving, and the entrées looked great. "Just appetizers?" I asked.

She nodded. "Doesn't sound very satisfying, does it?" She looked discouraged. Suddenly, I wanted to make this work for her, this whole crazy plan.

"Well, no one said we can only get one

apiece," I said. I looked at the list of appetizers. "There's enough here to make a meal from. We can share some bruschetta and that mozzarella salad. And look—it says here that you can get a half order of pasta. I think sharing is the important part. No one ever shares entrées, but everyone shares appetizers."

She looked at me and smiled. "Now you're getting into it," she said. "But I think we're also going to need some of those mussels. Is that too much?"

I shook my head. "It's perfect," I said. "Perfect."

And an hour later, we were in the car, stuffed and happy, heading south.

"So do you take all your dates to Disney World?" I asked. We'd been in the car a half hour or so and had reached a lull in the conversation. I was feeling strangely calm, given my cautious character and the enormity of this adventure I had agreed to undertake.

"No," she said. "But I do like to take people where they need to go."

"And why exactly do I need to go to Disney World?"

"Oh, just a feeling I have. Something about your sad Eeyore eyes and the papers you have to grade. I don't know what your ex-wife was like—and I'm not asking, that's just not good date conversation—but I bet she never would have taken you to Disney World."

"Well, you're right there." I was silent for a moment. "But what about you? Why don't we go someplace you need to go?"

"Oh, I've been to most of those places already. Anyway, I never know where I need to be until I get there."

"Wow," I said. "That sounds very deep."

"Well, then," she said. "It's time to play a word game."

We played games, off and on, all through the night. By four A.M., we were somewhere in South Carolina. We'd been driving for seven hours. I was getting sleepy.

"I don't think I can go much farther," I said. "Do you feel awake enough to drive, or should we find someplace to stop?"

"I can drive for a while," she said. "I'm a night person. Plus, I dozed a little earlier. Let's just get me some coffee."

We pulled off at the next exit. We found a gas station with an all-night convenience store, and while Lexy went in for coffee, I climbed over to the passenger side and put the seat back as far as it would go. As I eased myself into the softness of the seat, I thought for a moment, This is exactly where I want to be. I was asleep before she got back to the car.

I awoke to find a small girl peering at me through the window. I stirred a little and found that it was daylight, and we were in a rest stop parking lot. Lexy wasn't in the seat beside me; I turned and saw that she had crawled into the backseat and curled into a ball.

I looked again at the girl standing by my window. "Mommy, there's a man *sleeping* in there," I heard her say.

Without sitting up, I raised my hand and waved.

"He just *waved* at me," she said, her voice filled with horrified delight.

"Get away from there, April," her mother said. "Come on, this is just a quick potty break."

"But shouldn't I wave back?" the girl asked.

"No. Don't wave at strangers. It's a bad thing to do."

I heard Lexy move in the backseat. "Don't wave at strangers," she said sleepily. "I love how parents make up the rules as they go along."

"Yeah," I said. "She's going to grow up with some sort of strange waving complex." I watched as the girl and her mother walked across the parking lot toward the concrete octagon containing the rest rooms. Without turning back toward me, the girl stretched her hand out behind her and gave a small, secret wave, then skipped on ahead toward the building.

I laughed. "I take it back," I said. "She knows what's going on."

I looked at the clock. It was nine A.M. "How long have we been here?" I asked.

She pulled herself into a sitting position and stretched her arms. "Since about seven," she said. "I needed a break."

"Any idea where we are?" I asked.

"Somewhere near Savannah, I think. Come on, let's stretch our legs and then go get some breakfast."

We went to freshen up in the rest stop bathrooms. I splashed some water on my face and looked at myself in the mirror. I was unshaven and my skin was creased from the fabric of the car seat, but I saw something in my face that I hadn't seen in a long time. I looked relaxed, and happy. At peace. There was a small, easy smile on my lips. I felt exuberant, I felt the day stretched before me, filled with promise. I couldn't wait to spend it with Lexy. I straightened my clothes and walked out into the sunshine to take my place among the husbands and boyfriends waiting for their women to come out of the bathroom.

Breakfast, which we ate at a roadside coffee shop, presented some problems. As we slid into the booth, Lexy said, "I think we're going to need to establish some ground rules here. About eating."

It took me a minute, but I finally got it. "Oh," I said. "You mean, so we don't accidentally end our date somewhere on I-95."

"Right," she said. "I'd hate to see it end here at the Waffle House."

I scanned the menu. "Well," I said, "there aren't exactly any appetizers, but there's a whole list of side dishes."

"That's good," she said. "It's kind of a

paradox, isn't it? What is a side dish if it's not served on the side of anything? Does it become something else?"

"It's a regular Zen koan," I said. "I think I need some coffee before I can tackle that one."

We had a crazy meal, grapefruit sections and sausages, bananas sliced in cream and pieces of rye toast. On our way out, we bought a map; we were about two hundred eighty miles from Orlando. I was amazed to see how far we had already come.

All through that day with Lexy, that sleepy, sunny day, I couldn't seem to stop talking. The miracle of it is still so fresh in my mind, the strangeness she brought into my life almost from the moment we met. I felt as if, after a lifetime of listening, of parsing sentences and analyzing word choices without ever opening my mouth, I was having a conversation for the first time. When the day grew hotter and Lexy closed her eyes and slept in the light of the sun coming through the windshield, my mind was quick with questions I wanted to ask and stories I wanted to tell, and when we switched places and I slept for a while, I awoke with new words on my lips. By the time we reached Orlando, she knew most of what I had to say. She knew that I had grown up in New Hampshire, where my father worked in a slaughterhouse and came home smelling of blood. She knew that I spent a summer working in a mattress factory, where I once saw a man jump down the elevator shaft looking for a lost pencil, catch an elevator on his back, and live. I told her the name of the first girl I ever kissed. I told her things I hadn't thought about in years.

Somehow, the subject of dreams came up. Lexy told me that she had kept a book of her dreams by her bed since she was a child and that she wrote each new one down as soon as she awoke. She sometimes thought, she said, that to read this book was to know everything about her, all of her fears and strange wishes, all of the places she could not go when she was awake. One night, when she was no more than four or five, she told me, she met a king who yelled at her for hiding behind his throne. Another night, when she was twelve, she found herself naked at one of her mother's dinner parties. She told me her dreams, the most vivid ones, the ones that still came back on occasion and made her catch her breath, in a list, offering me her life in small pieces. She crawled through a basement on her hands and knees. She saw a horse cut apart until it was no more than a pile of bloody pieces, but still it lived and breathed and looked at her with one wide eye. She gave birth to a baby, but there had been no father. She fell from a great height. Her name changed from day to day. She planted a garden in her bed and awoke to find lush roses and daisies and ivy tendrils wrapped snug around her body. She wandered through a mansion, and her mouth was filled with broken glass. She swam underwater all the way to England without having to take a breath. Her arms grew long and her legs grew short. She visited an ice cream shop and ordered a flavor called Fury. The ice cream was greenish-red, cold and strong and meaty; even now, she could remember its taste. She told me how, once, her teeth had fallen out one by one, and how, another time, she had had the strength to lift a man over her head. She got married in a cathedral whose walls collapsed before she could meet her groom. Wild dogs chased her through a field. A horrible rash covered her from head to toe. She walked barefoot through the streets and grass sprang up before her. She was being chased but could not move. A swarm of butterflies landed all over her body.

The day was warm, and we drove with the windows open. Breeze on my arms as I drove. Savor it now, the day, the breeze. Run the memory of it over your tongue. Speak it aloud; there's no one listening. Say "sun" and "hot" and "day." Close your eyes and remember the moment, the warm pink life of it. Lexy's body in the seat next to mine. Her voice filling the car. Let it wash over you. It ends soon enough.

E I G H T

I have heard that sometimes when a person has an operation to transplant someone else's heart or liver or kidney into his body, his tastes in foods change, or his favorite colors, as if the organ has brought with it some memory of its life before, as if it holds within it a whole past that must find a place within its new host. This is the way I carry Lexy inside me. Since the moment she took up residency within me, she has lent her own color to the way I see and hear and taste, so that by now I can barely distinguish between the world as it seemed before and the way it seems now. I cannot say what air tasted like before I knew her or how the city smelled as I walked its streets at night. I have only one tongue in my head and one pair of eyes, and I stopped being able to trust them a long time ago. There's nothing new I can say about Disney World, nothing you haven't already heard or seen for yourself. All I can tell you is that I was there with Lexy.

We pulled into the parking lot of the Magic Kingdom about four-thirty that afternoon. I had suggested we find a hotel before making our way to the park—this was a popular vacation week, and I was a little worried about finding a place that had vacancies—but Lexy insisted.

"This is the best time," she said. "All the kids who have been here all day are getting cranky and leaving to take naps and have dinner. The lines are much shorter, and it's starting to get cooler."

"You're the expert," I said.

The closer we got to the park, the more excited she got. She talked in a rush, filling me in on all the unwritten rules she'd learned from a lifetime of Disney entertainment. "But the big rides, like Space Mountain, the ones with the *really* long lines, we don't go on those until the Electric Light Parade starts."

"Don't we want to see the parade?" I asked.

"Not when there's no one in line at Space Mountain."

We parked in the Goofy lot, took the tram to the ticket gate and the monorail from the ticket gate to the park. I have to admit, I was getting excited, too.

"So where to?" I asked when we finally reached the park proper.

"It's a Small World," she said. "You'll love it. It's naive but well intentioned."

We walked down Main Street, U.S.A., and through Cinderella's castle to Fantasyland. Lexy took my hand and led me, half running, to the ride. The sign told us to expect a forty-five-minute wait, but Lexy told me to ignore it.

"They always tell you it's going to take longer than it actually will. That way, you're happy when you get there ahead of schedule."

She was right. About twenty minutes later, we were ushered into a row of our own to wait for the next boat.

"We're in the last row," Lexy said. "Very romantic. If you like singing dolls, anyway."

The boat pulled up. The people in the

back row climbed out, and we slid in the other side. But the people in the seat in front of us, a couple with two small girls, stayed put. The man stood and leaned toward the ride operator, a clean-cut teenager in a Venetian gondolier outfit.

"Excuse me," he said in a serious, man-to-man voice. "I wonder if you could let us go through again. The little girl in front of us was yelling so loud we couldn't even hear the music."

The gondolier shook his head and said something I couldn't hear. In front of us, the woman started to get up and gather her things, but her husband waved her back.

"Please," he said to the gondolier. It wasn't a question. "We weren't able to enjoy the ride. It would mean a lot."

The guy shrugged. "Yeah, go ahead," he said.

The man sat down, and the boat pulled slowly into the canal.

"What'd you say, Daddy?" one of the little girls asked delightedly.

"Daddy told a lie," the man said in a stage whisper. "Daddy was bad."

His wife was shaking her head and laughing. "Yeah, kids," she said. "Do as Daddy says, not as Daddy does."

I looked at Lexy and rolled my eyes. "Great role models," I whispered.

Lexy's whole body had turned rigid. "I can't *stand* people like that," she said in a low, furious voice. "What makes them think the rules don't apply to them?"

I took her hand. "Don't worry about it," I said. "Look, singing dolls. Naive but well intentioned."

But she just sat still and stared straight ahead. Our boat sailed smoothly through the wide canals. The cool air felt good after the Florida heat. I watched the doll-children go by.

"What country is that supposed to be?" I asked, pointing toward an icy-blue landscape peopled by singing penguins. "Antarctica?"

Lexy shrugged.

The man in front of us turned to his daughters. "Come on, Ashley, Madison," he said. "You know the words. 'There is just one moon and one golden sun.' " The girls joined him, singing in loud, high-pitched voices.

"Shall we join in?" I said to Lexy. "Come on, Lexy, you know the words."

But she didn't smile. She looked down at her lap.

" 'There's so much that we share,' " shrieked the girls in front of us, " 'that it's time we're aware . . .' "

Lexy was still seething when we reached the end of the ride.

"Come on," I said, standing up and climbing out of the boat. "Let's go get one of those ice creams shaped like Mickey's head." But she was looking the other way.

"Excuse me," she said loudly to the ride operator. The little family group turned to hear what she was going to say. "Can we go through again? The people in front of us were so morally reprehensible that we couldn't enjoy the ride." She got out of the boat and started to walk, her body stiff, her arms held tightly at her sides.

"What does that mean, Daddy?" one of the girls asked.

Lexy turned back. "It means your daddy's an asshole," she said. And she walked quickly on ahead of me.

She was near tears when I caught up to

her. I reached out to touch her arm, but she jerked away from me.

"We were having such a good day, and now I've ruined it," she said.

"You haven't ruined it," I said. I'll admit I had been a bit taken aback by Lexy's outburst. I was surprised by the intensity of her emotion, the strength of her reaction to people she didn't even know. But there had been so much that had surprised me in the last twenty-four hours, not least of all my own willingness to follow Lexy's lead, to turn myself upside down to be with her. In my entire life, I'd never called anyone an asshole—not to their face, anyway—but it occurred to me now that maybe I should have. Maybe if I'd opened my mouth more often, let my own words come to the surface, I wouldn't have lived my life so alone.

"You were right," I said. "Daddy *was* an asshole. Let's go find him and kick his ass."

"I don't know why I get this way," she said, still not meeting my eyes. "If you want to just leave, that's okay."

I took her face in my hands and turned it upward until she was looking at me. I smiled. "I don't want to leave," I said.

"You don't?" she said. Her eyes were bright with tears.

"No. I don't."

"You're not—I don't know, mad or freaked out or embarrassed to be seen with me? I mean, you hardly know me, and here I am causing scenes with complete strangers."

"Well, I won't be cutting in line in front of you, that's for sure," I said. Finally, she smiled. "But how could I be mad at you? Look where you've brought me." I spread out my arms to include everything around us, the colors and the music, the rides, the crowds, the Florida sun. "You've brought me where I needed to go. Now come show me the rest of it."

NINE

I've mentioned the books, haven't I? The books Lexy rearranged on the day she died? Today I'm going to sit down and begin to make a list. As far as I can tell, Lexy's work on that day was concentrated on one bookcase in particular; even though every bookshelf in the house has been changed to some degree, with a single book removed here and there and a new one put in its place, it's only the bookcase in my den where everything is different. Every book that was there when I left that morning has been taken out, although a few of them have been put back in a different spot than they originally occupied. The rest of the space has been filled with books from other places in the house. I begin to type the titles into my laptop, in the order she placed

them, making notes about the subject matter and their history in our lives, as well as
noting which books were hers and which
are mine. So far, I can find no discernible
pattern.

I get as far as the top shelf, which is arranged as follows:

Mary Had a Little Lamb: Language Acqui-
*   sition in Early Childhood* (Mine.)
I Was George Washington (Lexy's. A book
    about past-life regression. She always
    had a weakness for that kind of thing.)
Love in the Known World (Hers. A criti-
    cally acclaimed novel that was later
    made into a truly awful movie.)
But That's Not a Duck! (Mine. A book of
    jokes I bought for an academic paper I
    was writing about punch lines.)
That's Not Where I Left It Yesterday (Hers.
    A coming-of-age story about a girl in
    1950s Brooklyn.)
What You Need to Know to Be a Game
*   Show Contestant* (Mine. I never did get
    to be on a game show, but I always
    thought I'd be good at it.)
I Wish I May, I Wish I Might (Hers. A book

of childhood folklore and customs from around the world.)

Know Your Rhodesian Ridgeback (Hers, although I've consulted it quite a few times lately.)

Didn't You Used to Be Someone? Stars of Yesterday and Where They Are Today (Hers.)

I'd Rather Be Parsing: The Linguistics of Bumper Stickers, Buttons, and T-shirt Slogans (Mine.)

Have You Never Been Mellow? The World's Worst Music (Mine. A joke gift from Lexy, who always insisted that I had terrible taste in music.)

How to Buy a Used Car Without Getting Taken for a Ride (Hers.)

As I said, this is only the top shelf. As soon as I've written down the last title, I begin to question my actions. What exactly do I think I'm looking for, a message from beyond the grave, arranged neatly in my study? I have a sudden memory of the eerie excitement I felt as a kid when the Beatles' "Paul is dead" clues started to surface. I was thirteen the year that story broke, and I was thrilled by it, the goose-bumpy feeling

of hearing backwards messages, the un-
canny idea of secret clues hidden in plain
sight. My friend Paul Muzzey, with whom I
shared not only a first name but also the
small excitement of being a namesake to
the corpse in this conspiracy, kept a long
list of all the clues published in music magazines and broadcast over the radio. He
called me up one afternoon and said,
"You've got to play 'A Day in the Life' right
now. Go do it while I'm still on the phone."

"Backwards?" I asked.

"No, just listen to it the right way. I'll tell
you when to stop."

So I put the phone down and walked over
to the hi-fi in the living room. I pulled *Ser-
geant Pepper* out of its sleeve and put it on
the turntable. My parents weren't home, so
I turned it up as loud as it went, then picked
up the phone again.

"Okay," I said as the familiar chords began.

"Okay," he said. "Just close your eyes
and listen."

I sat with my eyes closed, the phone to
my ear, and listened to the song I'd heard a
hundred times before. I heard nothing new.
The first verse came to an end with "No-

body was really sure if he was from the House of Lords," and Paul said, "Did you hear it?"

"Hear what?"

"He said 'house of Paul.' "

"No way," I said. "It's 'House of Lords.' 'Lords' doesn't even sound like 'Paul.' "

"Play it again and listen for it. He says 'Paul.' "

So I picked up the needle and dropped it back at the beginning of the song. And I heard it clear as day, my own name. "Nobody was really sure if he was from the house of Paul." A chill went through me.

"Oh, man," I breathed. "He does say 'Paul.' "

Paul and I sat there on opposite ends of the line and listened to the rest of the song in silence. It was a holy moment, a moment weighted down by the truth we had found. The house of Paul. It was really true.

Of course, it came out soon afterward that the whole conspiracy thing was a hoax and that Paul McCartney was very much alive. But to this day, I can't hear that song without hearing "house of Paul." I believe that what I learned that afternoon was true.

I would swear it on any pile of books you gave me.

Thirty years later, I'm still searching for hidden meanings in the ordinary objects that fill my life. Only now, I don't have a nation of DJs and keen-eyed teenaged fans to help me. I'm all alone in this. All I have is forty-nine books arranged on a shelf. And what do I think they mean? Something. Or nothing at all.

T E N

Back in Disney World, back among the nightly fireworks and the children in mouse-eared hats, Lexy and I walk hand in hand forever. I sometimes think that if I could, I would round up all of the people who visited the park during the days we were there, and I would ask them to show me their photos and videotapes, just on the chance that one of them might have caught us on film. I feel certain, looking back, that we must have walked through someone's family grouping at the exact moment the shutter closed; surely, some father wielding a video camera must have captured us somewhere, climbing into a teacup or reading the gravestones outside the Haunted Mansion, while his children, fidgety and drunk with excitement, ran around people's legs in the foreground. What would I give for that, to see how we looked, the two of us together, when we had known each other barely a week? Me in my Eeyore shirt, and Lexy with the sun in her hair. Everything. I would give everything.

We stayed in Orlando for four days. We arrived on a Sunday afternoon and didn't turn back for home until Thursday morning. And all the time, we ate nothing but appetizers. Appetizers, snacks, and side dishes. We didn't eat a meal until Friday night, when, almost home, we stopped again at the same Italian restaurant we had gone to the day of the wedding. We ate a big dinner, with entrées and desserts, wine and coffee, and then I dropped Lexy at her house and went home to grade my papers in an exuberant, generous mood. That was the end of our first date.

I haven't mentioned sleeping arrangements yet; I haven't told you how we slept in the same tiny motel room for four humid Florida nights, and how it wasn't until our last night there that Lexy crossed the room and came into my bed. How she whispered to me, "I don't usually do this on the first date" as she ran her hands over my long-forsaken body. I mention these things, the warm air and cool sheets, the fresh joy of Lexy lying beside me, in the interest of not skipping over anything that might prove to be important. But in truth, they are not things I can speak of very easily. I touched her and it felt like coming home. What more is there to say?

On Sunday afternoon, two days after our return, I arrived at Lexy's house with flowers and a chew toy for Lorelei. The flowers, the first I ever gave her, were dahlias, so dark and red they were almost black.

"Wow," Lexy said as she took them from me. "These are gorgeous. I've never seen flowers this color. They kind of remind me of the devil."

"The devil?" I said. "Yes, that's exactly what I was going for. It's a test, to see if you're receptive to the black arts. Now I can introduce you to the other members of the coven."

She laughed. "No, don't you see what I mean? They're this deep bloodred color, and they've got these kind of seductive honeycomb petals that just draw you in further and further." She waited a moment and then added grandly, "I believe I shall carry these flowers at my wedding."

I only paused for a moment. "Well," I said, "you'd better get married quickly. These are only going to last a day or two."

She laughed and put her arms around me. "Oh, I don't think you're going to get off that easily," she said. "But see what I mean about these flowers? They seduced me into asking you to marry me on our second date. I think we'd better put them in the other room before I lose control completely."

"Oh, let's keep them here and see what happens," I said, and pulled her down with me onto the couch.

Later that afternoon, she took me to see her basement workshop, the place where she made her masks. There was a large table in the center of the room, covered with an untidy litter of newspapers and jars of paint. Unfinished faces, bare and ghostly, were stacked in piles on the floor. Everything was coated with a fine white dust. I remembered the mask I had worn at the wedding.

"I meant to ask you," I said. "What does

that mean, 'You have taken the finest knight in all my company'? Is it from something?"

"It's from 'Tam Lin,' " she said. "Do you know that story?"

"No," I said. "I don't think so."

"It's from an old Scottish poem, but I first heard it as a fairy tale. There was a version of it on this record I used to have when I was a kid—I've always had trouble falling asleep, and I'd listen to these records of people reading stories, kind of like books on tape. It was always these washed-up actors doing the reading, people I'd never heard of but later saw on TV in old movies and stuff. Anyway, I loved this one. It's the story of a woman named Janet who falls in love with a knight named Tam Lin, who's been abducted by the fairy queen or the elf queen or something, and Janet has to rescue him and steal him back to the mortal world. She goes and waits for him in the woods at midnight on Halloween, and all the fairies ride by on horses, and Janet has to pull Tam Lin down from his horse and hold on to him while the fairy queen turns him into all kinds of horrible things—she turns him into a snake, and a snarling beast, and a red-hot bar of iron, but Janet has to hold on as tight as she can, until finally he turns into a 'mother-naked man'—isn't that a nice phrase, 'a mother-naked man'?—and then he's hers forever."

"So she's standing in the woods at midnight with a naked man in her arms? And this was a children's story?"

Lexy laughed. "That's nothing," she said. "When I was in college, I went and found an early version of the poem, and it turns out that Janet was pregnant. That's something they left out of the kids' version."

"So what about the 'finest knight in all my company' stuff?"

"Oh, that's the best part. After Janet rescues him, and everything's okay, the fairy queen throws a fit. The way it went in my version was, *Out then spoke the fairy queen, and an angry queen was she: 'You have taken the finest knight in all my company.'* And then there's this scary part that I found absolutely thrilling, where the fairy queen says to Tam Lin, *'Had I known but yesterday what I know today, I'd have taken out your two grey eyes and put in eyes of clay. And had I known but yesterday you'd be no more my own, I'd have taken out your heart of flesh and put in one of stone.'* It still gives me goose bumps."

"Lighthearted little story," I said. "I can see why that would stick in your mind."

She sank down onto a long, beat-up couch that ran along one wall. I sat down next to her. There was a series of soft thuds from the staircase as Lorelei loped down to join us. She came over to the couch and jumped up, insinuating her large, dense body into the small space between us.

"Can I help you?" I said to the dog as she wedged herself against my knees. Lexy stroked Lorelei, looking thoughtful.

"The thing is," she said, "I always identified with the fairy queen."

"Why is that?" I asked.

"I don't know," she said. "Maybe Janet was too goody-goody for me.

"Except for the getting knocked up part."

She smiled. "Except for that." She was quiet for a moment. "No, I guess I kind of identified with her anger. You know, she gets so mad, and it's presented like she's behaving totally inappropriately, but I can understand her point of view."

I considered it. "Absolutely," I said. "She's just doing her thing, being the fairy queen, and Janet comes along and steals away her finest knight."

"Right."

I watched her scratch Lorelei gently behind the ears. I thought of the queen in the story, stamping her feet and yelling into the night wind, and I thought of Lexy in the Magic Kingdom, leaning against a fiberglass tree, close to tears, trembling with all of an elf queen's fury. I picked up her hand and kissed it.

ELEVEN

There is a kind of grieving that dogs do, a patient waiting for homecoming, a sniffing for a scent that is no longer there. Since Lexy died, I have often seen Lorelei sitting at the top of the basement stairs, listening for noises from the workshop below. This morning, I find her in the bedroom, sleeping stretched out on one of Lexy's sweaters. I must have left the closet door open, and I can only assume that Lorelei, drawn by the scent of Lexy's perfume, her hair, her skin, still lingering on her clothes, jumped up and tugged at the garment until she had freed it from its slippery, padded hanger. I don't take the sweater away from her. Instead, I walk quietly out of the room and leave her to breathe in her memories, whatever they might be.

Today I have to go to the university to pick up some papers I left in my office. It's the first time I've been back since the day two months ago when I announced my research plans to my colleagues. It wasn't a very good day, the day I presented my proposal to the department; when I got to the part about canine language acquisition, the whole room turned very quiet, and people began to examine inanimate objects—their pens, their wedding rings, the conference table—with alarming intensity.

I'm hoping I won't run into anyone today, and in fact I've planned my trip for a time when I thought no one would be around, but it seems that in my absence they've changed the day on which faculty meetings are held. I arrive to find every professor in the department standing in the hallway outside the conference room, drinking coffee and talking. They grow silent as, one by one, they see me approaching.

Julia Desmond is the first to speak. Julia is a tall woman, blessed with family money and prone to wearing extravagant jewelry. Today it's rubies.

"Paul," she says brightly, coming toward

me with her arms outstretched. "How are you?"

I accept her embrace and kiss her lightly on the cheek. "Fine," I say. "Just fine." I look around at the group of people staring at me, smiles fixed on their faces. "I just came by to pick up a few things," I say.

"Great, great," says Julia. "We've missed you around here." She smiles at me a moment longer, her hands still on my arms. She seems unsure what to say next. "Well, good to see you," she says finally. She retreats into the conference room.

I make my way to my office, the crowd parting for me as if I were a holy man. Matthew Rice, the head of the department and a good friend of mine, comes up and stands beside me as I unlock the door. He follows me inside.

"So how are you really doing, Paul?" he asks, shutting the door behind him.

"So-so," I say.

"We've all been worried about you," he says. "But you're looking good."

"Thank you," I say. I'm pretty sure he's lying. I haven't been paying much attention to my appearance of late. I know I've lost weight since Lexy's death, and my clothes hang on me quite loosely.

"Are you keeping busy?" he asks, and seems immediately to regret it.

"Yes," I say. "My research has been occupying most of my time."

He nods and looks away from me. "Are you still working on that . . . project?" he asks. "The one with the dog?"

"Yes," I say, perhaps too brightly. "It's going quite well."

He doesn't meet my eyes. "That's great," he says, after a pause. "You know, Eleanor and I have that little beach house in Rehoboth, and you're welcome to borrow it if you'd like. It might do you good to get away for a while."

I think about it. Early morning walks on the beach with Lorelei running ahead of me, evenings bathed in the scent of sea air. It's not an unwelcome idea.

Matthew goes on. "The only thing is," he says, "Eleanor's allergic to dogs, so you wouldn't be able to bring Lorelei. But you can always board her or something for a week or two. Julia has dogs; she might be able to give you the name of a good kennel."

Of course, I think. Of course. "Thanks anyway," I say. My voice sounds thin and brittle as glass. "But I don't think I can leave my research at this particular point."

Matthew nods, looking down at the floor. "All right, then," he says, turning toward the door. He looks stricken. I soften a bit.

"Really, I'm fine," I say. "I'm sure this whole thing sounds crazy to you, but I really think there's something there. I feel like I'm on the verge of something important. I just need some time to work it out."

He smiles doubtfully, but at least he's meeting my eyes. "Just imagine," he says, "what it will mean if you succeed." He pauses thoughtfully, considering it. "Well, I've got to get back to the meeting. Keep in touch, okay?"

"I will," I say. "Give my love to Eleanor."

I gather up the things I need and prepare to leave. On my way out, I notice a scrap of pink paper that has, apparently, been slid under the door. I pick it up. It's a While You Were Out slip. Scrawled across the top it says, "Your dog called." In the message space below, there are two words: "Woof, woof." I crumple up the note and throw it away.

Back at home, I pick up Lexy's sweater from the bedroom floor and hold it to my face. I wonder what she would think of the turns my life has taken. Lorelei wanders in to greet me, and I give her a little scratch behind the ears.

"Where's Lexy?" I say to her. She looks up at me sharply. "Go get Lexy," I say. And all of a sudden, she's off, running wildly from room to room. I watch, heart-struck, as she charges through the house, sniffing in corners and barking. "Lorelei," I call after her. "No! Stop it, girl! Quiet! Come!" I run through every command she knows. But it's no use. I can't stop her, not now that I've spoken those magic words. Around and around the house she runs, searching and yowling for what she has lost.

TWELVE

The first time I asked Lexy to marry me, she said no. It was early December, about nine months since we'd first met, and we'd gone away for the weekend. We were staying at a small inn on the beach, and the day had been rainy and blustery. We'd spent most of our time inside, with the fireplace lit, playing board games and drinking wine.

Now, as we lay in bed, Lexy reached over and picked up a felt-tip pen from the bedside table and took hold of both my hands. "This is what you give to me," she said, and she began to write. She started on the backs of my hands and then turned them over to write on the palms. She covered my hands with words. *Square eggs,* she wrote, and *beaches in winter. Your lips on my neck* and *a week of appetizers,* and *really bad music.* She wrote, *Coffee milk,* and *Scrabble* and *flowers that look like the devil.* By the time she had finished, there was no space left at all.

"Now it's your turn," she said. She gave me the pen and offered up her hands. I didn't know what to write. Hunger, I thought, and fullness. A feeling like wings inside me. The days and the seasons and a dog with a rough velvet hide. But instead I took her hand, and writing upside down so she could read it, I wrote letter by letter and finger by finger, *whole world.*

It was the truest, most romantic thing I had ever said, and I didn't even say it out loud. Caught up as I was in the wide generosity of my emotions, I turned her hands over and, almost without thinking about it, wrote across her palms, *Will you marry me?*

She drew back and pulled her hands away. "Are you serious?" she said. She wasn't smiling.

"I am completely serious," I said, surprised to find that I was.

"You're asking me to marry you."

"I'm asking you to marry me."

She searched my face. "Well . . . no," she said. She looked away. "I have to say no.

We don't know enough about each other yet."

I was perfectly calm. I was prepared to give her some time to get used to the idea. "You know everything there is to know about me," I said. "And I know enough about you to know that I love you."

She turned away from me. "What's the matter?" I asked.

She didn't speak for a moment. She had made her back stiff and hard, and when I reached out to touch her, she flinched away. "I know you love me," she said finally. Her voice was ragged. "But how do you *know* that you love me?"

"Well, I know it because I want to be with you all the time," I began.

"No. That's not what I mean. I mean, how does it occur to you? How often do you really *know* it?"

"Always. I always know it."

"Yes, you always know it, but it's . . . it's like in the back of your mind, right? It's like . . . it's like the way that you know that you're going to die."

I reached for her shoulder and rolled her over so that she was looking at me again.

"Lexy, I don't understand what you're saying."

"Well, I mean, everyone knows that they're going to die, right, but most of the time you let it slip from your mind. I mean, it's always there in your head, and if anyone asked, you'd know the answer. But then there are some moments when all of a sudden you just *know* it, you know? It suddenly hits you that you're going to die someday, and you say, 'Oh, my God, this is the biggest fact of my life, and I'd almost forgotten.' "

"Well, so what?" I said. "What does that have to do with anything? No, I don't think about my own death every moment of every day, but that's because I want to forget it. You can't go on with your life if you don't forget about it sometimes. But that's not the way I feel about you."

"But still. That's the way you experience it, right? It's in fits and starts." She turned away again.

I ran my hands over my face, rubbing hard at the skin, trying to feel the sturdiness underneath. We had not fought like this before, and I felt as if I were trying to swim through molasses. "Come on, Lexy, why are you doing this? I love you all the time. It's always with me. But what do you want me to say? You can't maintain that level of intensity every minute of your life."

She was very quiet. "Well, I can. I do. I can't take one breath, not one single breath, without knowing that I love you."

I just lay there for a moment, looking at the long line of her back. "Where is this coming from?" I asked.

She didn't say anything for a moment. Then she turned and looked at me. "I don't know," she said. "I'm sorry. I guess you just kind of freaked me out a little, proposing like that, out of the blue."

"Do you want me to take it back?"

She held her hands up in front of her face, looking at the words I'd written. "No," she said. "I don't want you to take it back." She sighed. "But I can't say yes yet. I don't think you know enough about me. What if you find out more and you change your mind?"

"Well, I don't think that's likely. But, okay, go ahead—tell me the things I don't know."

"Okay," she said. Her voice was very quiet and even. "I'll marry you if you can answer this question for me: Do I have any tattoos?"

I stared at her. I knew the whole of her skin by heart. Did she think there was anything I had missed? "No," I said. "You don't."

She lowered her head and parted her hair for me. I could see black ink on her scalp. "Sorry," she said.

I bent over her head, examining. I couldn't make it out. "What is it?" I asked.

"It's snake hair," she said. "Like Medusa."

"Wow," I said. I tried to follow the lines on her head, to make out the scales and the angry snake faces, but her hair was too thick. "When did you get it?"

"When I was seventeen." She pulled away from my hands, still resting in her hair, and raised her head to look at me. "I used to pull my hair out. It's kind of a nervous disorder."

I nodded. "I've heard of that," I said. "Let me think, what's it called?" I puzzled out the possible Latin and Greek roots. "Trichotillomania?"

Lexy stared at me and shook her head. "You know the damnedest things," she said. "Anyway, my parents took me to a couple of different doctors, and they put me on medication for it, but nothing worked. So one day, I just decided to shave my head and be done with it."

I thought about my Lexy as a young girl, standing bald and brazen before the world. It was a strangely moving thought. "And did it work?" I asked.

"Well, yeah. There was nothing left to pull on."

"Right."

"So I kept it shaved for a year or so, until I felt like things were better in my life and it'd be safe to grow it back. I got the tattoo as kind of a talisman. It's my secret strength. It protects me from falling back into that place where I used to be."

I reached out tentatively. She took my hand. "I'm sorry," she said.

"For what?"

"For ruining your nice proposal." She held her hands out before her and looked at the words again. "It was very sweet."

"That's okay."

"I just need some time," she said. "To trust that this is all real."

"Don't worry," I said. "I'm not going any-where."

* * *

So I waited. I waited for five more months. And one morning, I awoke to find a single word printed across my palm. *Yes,* it said.

THIRTEEN

Here's the thing: I wasn't entirely honest with Detective Anthony Stack when he asked me if Lexy had ever mentioned suicide. In fact, I wasn't honest at all. Which is not to say that I had any reason to believe Lexy was suicidal in the months and weeks leading up to her death; at least, I had no such reasons at the time. But it would be dishonest of me not to reveal at this point that she did, during the sweet, breath-holding time of our engagement, tell me that there had been moments in her life when she had thought about killing herself.

The only time she came close, she told me, occurred during that hair-tearing year of her adolescence, the year the snakes took up residence on her scalp. Her parents were going through a divorce, and she was having a hard time in school—but I say that as if those are reasons. As if the fabric of human misery can be spooled apart into threads just like that. How many young girls that year had trouble in school, had trouble with their parents, and still never thought to pick up a knife and press its cold point against their wrist? No. There's more to it than that, and more scientific minds than mine have yet to piece it all together.

But whatever that fatal elixir is, that mixture of circumstance and temperament that leads a person to the edge of death and sometimes back again, it flowed through Lexy's body like blood. She fell into a deep depression, and the effort of wading through each day, the weight she carried like a stone in her gut, left her exhausted. She would come home from school and crawl into her bed and stay there until it was almost time for her mother to come home from work, and she knew she had to rouse herself and create some semblance of normalcy. During those afternoons, lying in bed until the light faded, she wrote things on her arms and legs, places that she knew could be hidden with clothing, digging deep into her flesh with the pen. *Sometimes,* she wrote, *I feel like I could start crying and not stop for a day and a night, and maybe that would be enough. And maybe it wouldn't.* She wrote, *Sometimes I feel like I have a ragged hole inside me, and it gets bigger every day.* She wrote, *Once upon a time, there was a girl who just disappeared.* She laughed when she told me these things, making fun of the drama of her teen angst, but I could see that it hurt her to remember. It was during those afternoons in bed that she began to pull out her hair. She wanted, she said, to make her pain tangible, to feel something on the outside. As she lined up the strands of hair on the sheet next to her, she told me, she felt a sense of accomplishment.

It was on the night of her senior prom that all those months of unhappiness crystallized into a single moment of action, and she actually thought she would kill herself.

Lexy had two close friends at the time, Brian and Sara. Brian was gay, and Sara had a boyfriend named Jon who was a year older and in college. Since Sara was going to the prom with Jon, it just made sense for Lexy and Brian to go together. Neither of them wanted to miss out. So Sara and Lexy

went dress shopping. Sara wanted something black and sexy, as unpromlike as possible. Lexy wanted to be pretty, in spite of
herself. She wanted a prom dress. She
found something perfect at a vintage clothing store, a pale blue 1950s strapless gown
with a spray of pink roses embroidered di-
agonally across the dress from bodice to
hem. She loved the dress, but she was embarrassed about her hair, about the bald
spots that showed in between the few
wispy tendrils that were left, so the day of
the prom, she took a razor and shaved her
head. She was pleased with the way it
looked; she liked the way her smooth scalp
felt when she ran her hands over it. The effect of the bald girl in the satin evening
gown was unusual, to say the least, but it
made her feel glamorous.

The prom was not what she thought it
would be. People stared at her newly
shaven head with open disdain, and she felt
lonely dancing with Brian, good friend
though he was. She wanted to be one of
the girls with boyfriends, handsome in their
tuxes, boyfriends who stroked their bare
shoulders and whispered in their ears what
they would do to them later on. She didn't

even like these boys, there wasn't a single one she could point to and honestly say she could imagine being with, but she wanted someone who wanted her back. She thought about dancing with a boy who'd become aroused at the press of her body, who'd close his eyes and touch his lips to the top of her head. She wanted the fantasy of romance and feeling grown-up, not her awkward friend Brian whose hands were light and unsure on her arms and whose eyes kept drifting to look at Michael Patterson, the boy he'd had a crush on all spring. She envied Sara, sophisticated in her sheer black dress and heavy eye make-up, who knew she'd be kissing someone and more when the night came to an end. Afterward, they went to a Holiday Inn where they'd arranged a couple of rooms for the night— Lexy's mom had even agreed to pay her share, knowing nothing was going to happen between her and Brian—and got drunk, the four of them, until Sara and Jon started making out and decided to slip off to their own room, leaving Lexy and Brian alone together.

"So that was the prom," Lexy said to Brian, reaching over for the bottle of vodka they'd gotten hold of. She poured some into her glass of orange juice.

"Yeah," said Brian. "Kind of a letdown."

"Michael looked good," Lexy said. Brian ducked his head and looked down into his drink. He was still shy about talking about it, even though Lexy had done everything she could to be supportive.

"Yeah," he said. "Do you think he and Bethany are having sex right now?"

"Probably," Lexy said. "Probably everyone's having sex with somebody except us."

"Yup." He lay back on the bed and closed his eyes. "Everyone except the bald girl and the homo."

"What would you do if Michael were here right now?" Lexy asked.

"Probably nothing. I'd probably clam up and be afraid to talk to him, as usual."

"How drunk are you?" she asked.

"Pretty drunk."

"Let's pretend I'm Michael."

He kept his eyes closed. "I don't think it's possible to get that drunk."

She swallowed the rest of her drink. "Sure it is," she said. "Come on. I'll turn out the light."

She lay down next to him on the bed and nuzzled his neck.

"Lexy," he said.

"Quiet," she said. She bit his earlobe lightly. "Think about Michael."

As she touched him, she whispered to him all the things that Michael might do. "He's wanted to do this to you all year," she murmured. "He's finally here with you. Just think about Michael doing this to you. Shhh," she said as she felt Brian's body respond to her touch. "Just pretend I'm Michael."

Afterward, Brian reached out in the dark and squeezed her shoulder.

"Thanks, Lexy," he said. "That was cool."

She waited a few minutes until she was sure he was asleep. Then she went into the bathroom and closed the door and put her head in her hands and cried. She paced back and forth in the tiny bathroom, her sobs growing louder and more convulsive until finally she sat down on the edge of the tub and buried her face in a towel so Brian wouldn't hear her. And it was as she was perched there on the narrow ledge of porcelain with her face pressed to the rough fabric that the thought came to her that she could kill herself, and she was filled with a sudden calm. I could just do it, she thought, and the idea had a kind of beautiful simplicity to it.

She stood up and began pacing the room again, but she wasn't crying anymore. She was filled with a clarity of purpose that exhilarated her. I'm just going to do it, she thought, and then it will all be done. But how? She looked around the bathroom for inspiration. Brian had left a small bag of toiletries by the sink, and she considered breaking apart his safety razor, but the blade looked too small and dull to do the job. There was little else in the room that seemed promising—this was a hotel room, after all, and there were no bottles of prescription pills in the medicine chest, no kitchen nearby with a butcher block full of knives to choose from, none of the deadly everyday objects people fill their homes with.

Then she saw the water glasses sitting on the counter, each one topped with a white paper cap attesting to its cleanliness. She picked up one of the glasses and threw it onto the hard tile floor. It shattered with a loud crash, and she was afraid for a moment that Brian would wake up, but when a minute passed without any sound from the other room, she bent down and picked up a large pointed shard. She stood over the sink and looked into the mirror for a moment, seeing herself in the strange, harsh bathroom light, a bald girl with swollen eyes and mascara smeared on her cheeks. And she didn't hesitate. She pushed the jagged point into her wrist.

She didn't get very far; as soon as the first drops of blood hit the basin of the sink, she grew terrified and pulled the piece of glass away. She ran her wrist under water and pressed a wash-cloth to the wound until the bleeding stopped. Then she cleaned up the broken glass from the floor as well as she could and opened the door to the bedroom. Brian was snoring lightly on top of the bedclothes, his pants still unzipped. Lexy climbed into bed next to him, cradling her hurt arm beneath her, and cried to think what she had done.

No one ever knew. The cut on her wrist turned out to be fairly inconspicuous in the light of day; she was surprised to see how little damage there was. Two days after the prom, she went out by herself into the city and found a tattoo parlor. She presented her scalp to the man who owned the place—he was a big man, and his name was Goldie—and she asked him to cover her head with snakes. She wore long sleeves until the wound on her wrist had healed completely, and her parents thought that a snaky-haired daughter was the worst they had to fear. Within a few months, Lexy went off to college, and by and by, the heaviness that had inhabited her body for so long began to lift. But that night in the bathroom became part of her. Every breath she drew was colored by what she had learned that night.

Suicide is just a moment, Lexy told me. This is how she described it to me. For just a moment, it doesn't matter that you've got people who love you and the sun is shining and there's a movie coming out this weekend that you've been dying to see. It hits you all of a sudden that nothing is ever going to be okay, ever, and you kind of dare yourself: Is this it? You start thinking that you've known this was coming all along, but you don't know if today's going to be the day. And if you think about it too much, it's probably not. But you dare yourself. You pick up a knife and press it gently to your skin, you look out a nineteenth-story window and you think, I could just do it. I could just do it. And most of the time, you look at the height and you get scared, or you think about the poor people on the sidewalk below—what if there are kids coming home from school and they have to spend the rest of their lives trying to forget this terrible thing you're going to make them see? And the moment's over. You think about how sad it would've been if you never got to see that movie, and you look at your dog and wonder who would've taken care of her if you had gone. And you go back to normal. But you keep it there in your mind. Even if you never take yourself up on it, it gives you a kind of comfort to know that the day is yours to choose. You tuck it away in your brain like sour candy tucked in your cheek, and the puckering memory it leaves behind, the rough pleasure of running your tongue over its strange terrain, is exactly the same.

This is what we know, those of us who can speak to tell a story: Lexy didn't jump. The wounds she suffered in her fall, the break of her bones and the wreck of her organs, the haphazard spill of her blood in the dirt, have told us this much. But perhaps, and this is where my breath catches in my throat, perhaps she let herself fall. The day was hers to choose, and perhaps in that treetop moment when she looked down and saw the yard, the world, her life, spread out below her, perhaps she chose to plunge toward it headlong. Perhaps she saw before her a lifetime of walking on the ruined earth and chose instead a single moment in the air.

FOURTEEN

I think it was fairly early in our courtship that Lexy told me the story of how Lorelei came to be her dog. Lorelei was maybe five months old when she first entered Lexy's life. She showed up on Lexy's doorstep one day during a sudden summer storm, a big bleeding puppy under a dark and shrunken sky. Lexy was walking around the house, closing windows, when she heard a low whine from outside, followed by a short, insistent bark. She opened the door to find a puppy with big ears and a ridge down her back and a gash in her throat that matted her fur with blood. "Hi," Lexy said. "Who are you?" She bent down to check for a collar and tags, but there were none. "Wait here," she said, and she ran to get a towel. She brought the dog inside and washed the cut with a warm soapy cloth. Lorelei flinched as Lexy touched the cloth to the wound, but she didn't make a sound and she didn't snap at Lexy. The gash wasn't big, but it looked deep. Lexy took the phone book down from the top of the refrigerator, and she looked up veterinarians. When she brought her back home from the vet, Lorelei had four stitches in her throat. The doctor wasn't sure what had caused the injury. There were no bite marks, so he didn't think it had resulted from a fight with another dog. He thought that perhaps Lorelei had gotten tangled in some low brambles or had somehow torn her flesh on a piece of rough metal, although the edges of the cut were fairly smooth. He allowed that the wound could have been inflicted by a human being, although he couldn't imagine what the purpose might have been.

Lexy had had every intention of trying to find the puppy's owner, but this last possibility made her hesitate. Besides, the more time she spent with Lorelei, the more reluctant she was to give her up. The Found Puppy ad she had composed to send to the paper sat on the kitchen table unmailed, and the signs she had photocopied to post around the neighborhood never went up. She kept an eye out to see if anyone reported a missing Ridgeback—the doctor had identified the breed for her—but when no one did, she was glad. By then, Lorelei was sleeping in Lexy's bed every night, her big puppy paws twitching in dreams, and following Lexy around during the day as she worked. And that's how Lorelei and Lexy came to belong to one another.

Lately, my work has involved studying Lorelei's vocalizations, the sounds she already knows how to make. So far, I've isolated and cataloged six distinct kinds of bark, four different yelps, three whines, and two growls. There is, for example, a certain sharp, staccato burst of noise she makes only when she has been trying to get my attention when it's past her feeding time, say, or time to go for a walk, and she utters it only when a sustained period of sitting at my feet and staring pointedly up at me has failed to elicit a response. There is a soft, low growl, almost leisurely in its cadences, that rises from deep in her throat when she hears the slam of a car door outside the house, which is entirely different from the angry warning growl that precedes a bout of barking in the event that the owner of said car has the nerve to walk up the front steps and knock on the door. When I arrive home after an absence, she greets me in short, joyful syllables, and when I make a wrong step and inadvertently land on her tail, the sweet, shocked outrage of her yelp can nearly bring me to tears. I have come to recognize the differences in these sounds and the wide spectrum of canine emotion contained within them in the same way that a new mother learns to understand the different pitches and tremors of her child's wail. I have reached the point where, when Lorelei makes a sound, I know exactly what she means.

I've been paying special attention to the sounds she makes that might be translated into human language, the English phonemes buried within every bark and every whimper. The rolling *r* of her growl, for example, and the wide *o* of her howl. It's an alphabet rich in vowels and softly voiced consonants. She can make a *w* sound as well as a kind of *h,* which evolves into a hard, guttural *ch* when she coughs. When she lies on her back and offers me her belly, the lolling of her tongue sometimes results in something close to an *l*. The sounds that elude her are the harder consonants, the ones that require movement of the lips: she has no *b*, no *p*, no *v* in her repertoire. She will never speak my name, that much seems clear, but I still dare to hope she may one day speak her own.

I read yesterday that the prison which houses Wendell Hollis has just instituted a program that allows inmates in good standing to train guide dogs for the blind as part of their rehabilitation. It seems unlikely—at least, I hope it is—that the infamous Dog Butcher of Brooklyn will be eligible for participation. But how must it be for Hollis, after three years condemned to the company of humans, when he looks out of the narrow window of his cell and sees dogs at play?

I cannot say exactly what it is that fascinates me about Hollis. I suppose I feel a sort of kinship with him. Whatever the differences in our methodologies, we are both driven by the same desire. We both want, more than anything, to coax words from the canine throat. The only difference is that I would not use a knife to do it.

I am curious about him. The turns my life

has taken to bring me to the jumping-off point for this strange inquiry I have undertaken are so complex that I can hardly imagine them replicated in a single other life. And yet here we are, the two of us; we have wound up in the same place.

I think I may write him a letter.

FIFTEEN

Lexy and I had a small and lovely wedding. Lexy wore a sheath of white silk and carried red dahlias. She let her bridesmaids pick their own dresses. We wore no masks at all, save those of our own shining faces.

The morning after we were married, Lexy woke up and said, "I had the strangest dream. I have to remember to write it down in my book."

"What was it about?" I asked.

"Well, I was a writer, and I was really famous, but I had only ever written one sentence."

"What was the sentence?"

" 'I remember my wife in white.' It just made people weep to hear it. In the dream,

I couldn't even say it all the way through without choking up."

She was beautiful in the morning sun, and I gathered her to me. We were naked except for our wedding rings, and I had never been so happy.

" 'I remember my wife in white'?" I said into her hair.

"Yeah. Everybody just thought it was the saddest sentence that was ever written. And it didn't matter if I never wrote another word. This one sentence had put an end to the need for any future sentences. I had said it all."

I could see her wedding dress hanging in the wardrobe next to my tux from the night before. I liked the tableau it created, the two of us dancing together without our bodies.

"I don't think it's a sad sentence," I said. "My whole life I'll remember the way you looked last night, and there's no way it could ever make me anything but happy."

She smiled. "Know what it's time for?" she said.

"Room service?"

"No. I think it's time to reconsummate the marriage. I'm not sure it took the first time."

*   *   *

On our honeymoon, we went on a cruise, and Lexy was sick for two days. For two days, I wandered the ship on my own, playing cards with the old men and looking out at the great sea, returning from time to time to check on my bride, who lay weak in the bed and retched emptily into the commode in the tiny lavatory.

On the third morning, Lexy sat up and asked me to bring her some breakfast. I ordered a feast for her—eggs and sausages and fresh fruit, bacon and coffee and tiny pancakes arranged prettily on a plate. I persuaded the waiter to give up his white jacket for a few moments so that I could deliver the food to my wife myself. When I returned to Lexy, I found her sitting up against the pillows, her hair lovely and wild around her face. Now, I thought, our life begins.

I fed her with my fingers until she protested that she had better not overdo it. Then I helped her dress and took her out to see what she had been missing. Here is the sea and the bright hot day. Here are the men playing cards. Here I am with the woman I love, walking under the sun.

SIXTEEN

I've had a dream that Lorelei speaks to me. In the dream, I'm sitting at the kitchen table, eating a plate of spaghetti and meatballs, when Lorelei walks in on her two hind legs. She speaks, and her voice is surprisingly high-pitched. She sounds like a character in a cartoon.

"Give me a meatball," she says, "and I'll tell you everything you need to know."

I spear a meatball with my fork and hold it out to her. She gives it a tentative lick, then grabs it with her teeth and charges out of the room. I jump up and run after her. When I catch up with her, she's in my office, lying in front of a door I've never seen before.

"She's in there," says Lorelei, her mouth full of meat.

I open the door. Inside is a small closet.

Lexy sits huddled on the floor. She's dressed in a blue nightgown. She is very thin. "What took you so long?" she says.

I wake up then with a start, my chest filled with a wild joy. It's a moment before I can situate myself, before I come to myself again and remember that I am alone in my bed and my wife is gone. Disappointment runs through me with a terrible heat.

I sit up and turn on the light. It's almost dawn. Lorelei is sleeping on the floor next to the bed. "Lorelei," I call. She raises her head. "Come on up, girl. Up, up." I pat the bed.

This is an unusual request on my part, and I have to repeat it a second time before she obeys. She yawns, then stands and stretches, and finally jumps up on the bed and settles herself next to me. I stroke her fur. "I had a dream about you, girl," I say. "Do you want to hear my dream?" She sighs deeply—one of her most human sounds—and closes her eyes.

I lie next to her for a minute, my hand on her stomach, feeling the sleepy rise and fall of her breath. I want nothing more than to close my eyes and to find my way back to Lexy's hiding place, to gather her in my arms and lift her thin body out into the light, but as the moments pass, it becomes clear to me that I'm not going to get back to sleep, and I know that even if I do, I would probably find myself in a different dream entirely. The sad truth of dreams is that they rarely let you travel to the same place twice.

I decide to go for a walk. I get out of bed and put on my shoes, without changing out of the sweats and T-shirt I slept in. I grab my keys and my wallet and walk out into the misty dawn.

I'm not headed anywhere in particular, but after a few blocks I see the all-night supermarket looming ahead of me, an oasis of light in the dark landscape. It seems as good a destination as any.

The supermarket is a strange place at five A.M. You find a surprisingly wide cross-section of people—guys who have worked the night shift stopping by to pick up beer and cigarettes on their way home, mothers who have come out after a sleepless night to buy diapers, baby aspirin, Popsicles to soothe sore throats. I see a woman in a black cocktail dress buying a pint of ice cream. I see a homeless man with a basketful of groceries, holding up a jar of marinated artichoke hearts, examining it closely. He reads the ingredients on the back with great interest and then gently places the jar in his cart. I see that his cart is full of all kinds of luxury food—cans of smoked oysters, a cake from the bakery, a family-size frozen lasagne. I want to offer him some money—actually, I want to pay for his entire basket of food—but I have the sense that it would ruin the fantasy for him, the illusion that he's just another customer wandering the bright aisles. I leave him in the condiment section, where he's comparing two different brands of barbecue sauce.

I walk through the aisles like a ghost, my basket empty. What do I want? It's all laid out before me, anything I could possibly need. I have only to choose. I remember a time early in our relationship when Lexy and I stayed up all night, talking and making love, and ventured out at dawn to walk to this very supermarket to buy bagels and juice. "Don't think about it," I say out loud. "Don't think about it." I think about my dream, Lexy hidden in the closet all those months, waiting for me to find her. And then I know what I want. I want spaghetti and meatballs.

I gather ground beef and parsley, tomatoes and bread crumbs and Parmesan cheese. I pay for my purchases and walk home under the pale morning sun.

I put on some music while I chop the onions and garlic, break the eggs, measure the bread crumbs. Lorelei comes into the kitchen as soon as I pull the cellophane from the package of meat, and she sits on the floor, watching me with interest. I focus on each small task completely, letting it occupy all of my mind. Now you heat the oil in the pan. Now you plunge your hands into the cold meat and squeeze it between your fingers.

By seven A.M., the house is filled with the warm scent of it. For the first time in months, it smells like someone lives here. I eat a big plateful, and when I'm done, I feed Lorelei three meatballs, one after another, from my fork. The way she takes them in her teeth is surprisingly delicate. I crawl back into bed and fall into a welcome, dreamless sleep.

SEVENTEEN

After our honeymoon, Lexy and I returned home to her little house, the house with the apple tree in the backyard, and settled in with a fresh sense of adventure. It was September, one of Lexy's busiest times, work-wise—something about the changing colors, the new chill in the air, the glimpse of Halloween looming on the horizon, makes people think about magic and masquerade in a way they rarely do in the warmer months.

I loved to watch her work. She made her masks through a lamination process of layering torn bits of paper into a clay mold and brushing them with glue. She had experimented with other methods—there's a commercially produced paper pulp mixture you can buy, and she had also tried a method of pureeing paper and wallpaper paste in a blender—but this was her favorite. Sometimes she left the masks to dry outside in the sun or the wind; more often she used an electric fan. After they were dry, she painted them with acrylic paints and finished them with a coat of varnish.

She sold her masks at craft fairs and Renaissance fairs and over the Internet, and she also did occasional work for local theater companies; I remember in particular a wonderful donkey head she made for a production of *A Midsummer Night's Dream.* She had about a hundred designs, and she was always coming up with new ones. She got a lot of special orders. We're not far from Washington, so there were always requests for political figures, especially in election years, but she also filled a few more unusual requests: a giant pepperoni pizza for a restaurant trade show, a bashed and bloody cow's head for an animal rights protest. I never knew what strange new creature I might find in my home when I returned at the end of the day.

One day, maybe a month into our marriage, Lexy greeted me at the door wearing a mask of my own face. The likeness was quite good; she had a particular talent for the details that make up a human face. "Hi," she said in a gruff voice. "I'm Paul."

I laughed. "Wow," I said. "That's amazing. And I see you were kind enough to leave off the lines around my eyes."

She swatted me with something she held in her hand, a second mask. "Don't be silly," she said, in the same deep Paul voice. "I have an extremely youthful face."

"What's that one?" I asked, pointing to the mask in her hand.

She held it up. It was her own beautiful face. "Here," she said, handing me the Lexy mask. "I'll be you and you be me."

I covered my face with hers. "My name is Lexy," I said. "My husband is a wonderful, wonderful man."

"Hi, Lexy," she said. "You are one hot mama."

"I don't talk like that," I said.

"Well, maybe you should." She took me by the hand and led me into the living room. We sat down on the couch. "So," she said. "Tell me about yourself."

"Well," I said in my best Lexy voice,

which wasn't very convincing. "As you've already noticed, I am one hot mama."

She laughed. "See?" she said. "It just rolls off the tongue."

"I'm also a very talented artist, and I'm smart, and I'm funny, and . . ." I looked around the living room for inspiration. "And it looks like I even cleaned the house today, which was super-nice of me and above the call of duty. I hope I'm not turning into a housewife."

"You know, it's funny you should say that. That's exactly the thought you had while you were doing it, but you decided that since you'd already gotten your work done and you had some free time, it was probably okay. But enough about you. Let's talk about me."

"Okay," I said. "What are you like?"

"Well, let's see. I am a brilliant man, a wonderful professor, and I'm sweet and caring, and I can be very sexy in a befuddled sort of way."

"Stop," I said. "You're making yourself blush."

"Now, you, Lexy, are going to get up and open a bottle of wine and make your husband a wonderful dinner."

"No," I said. "You'll make dinner. You insist."

The next day, I nailed two hooks into the wall over the couch and hung our masks there. They are there still, the faces of Paul and Lexy, smiling and newly wed, presiding over everything I do. Now, when I lift the Lexy mask off its hook, I can run my fingers over all the curves of her face. Here is her nose, and here is her chin. Here are the holes where her eyes should be. Here are her own lips, though rendered forever stiff and hard, which I once kissed in every room of this house.

And another day—I sink into the memory as if it were a warm bath—another day, I came home to find that Lexy had painted the kitchen while I was at work. We had spoken once or twice about doing something to brighten the room, but months had passed, and we still hadn't gotten around to going to the paint store and picking out a color. That morning, I'd drunk my coffee in a room with the same dingy beige walls that had been there since before I moved in, but when I came home, I found my wife sitting in a room with walls the color of pale sunshine.

"So what do you think?" she asked, smiling up at me as I walked into the kitchen. It was a cool night, but she had the back door open to let the evening air wash away the smell of fresh paint.

"I love it," I said, looking around. "It looks great. I can't believe you did all this."

"Yeah," she said. "It was more work than I expected. But I wanted to get it done before you got home."

"It's wonderful," I said. "What a nice surprise." I bent to kiss her. She had a smudge of yellow paint just above her top lip.

"There's another surprise, too," she said. "But you're going to have to find it yourself."

"Here in the kitchen?"

She nodded.

I looked around, but I couldn't see anything else that was different. I opened a cupboard and scanned its contents.

"Chickpeas," I said, pulling out a can. "What a nice surprise."

She laughed. "That's not it."

"Are these new sponges?" I asked, picking one up from the sink ledge.

"Relatively. But that's not it either."

I went through the kitchen slowly, going through the cabinets, picking up mugs, heads of garlic, decorative platters we never used. "I give up," I said finally.

"You'll find it," she said. "Eventually."

I found it the next morning. I was sitting at the table, having breakfast, when I looked up from my newspaper and saw, toward the top of the wall in front of me, the word "you" glinting in a square of sunlight. The word was almost transparent; it was only the slant of the morning sun that made it visible. Trailing my eyes farther along the wall, I saw the word "I" and the word "love," followed again by the word "you." Following the line of words across the top edge of the wall, I could see that Lexy had written "I love you" over and over again, a hidden border that could only be seen in the morning light.

Lexy came into the kitchen just then and saw me looking up. "Did you find it?" she asked.

I got up and put my arms around her. "I found it," I said.

"It's a translucent glaze," she said. "I think you'll be able to see it every morning."

And I do. In the beginning, right after Lexy died, I avoided the kitchen during those morning hours. If I had to go into the room, I kept my gaze focused on the floor. I couldn't bear to lift my eyes. But now I look forward to it. I like knowing it's there; it helps me greet each new day. Some mornings I sit in the kitchen and linger over my coffee for an hour or more, watching the sun shift across the wall, illuminating each repetition of the phrase until the afternoon shadows come and the words are gone.

Do you see, then, the way that my Lexy liked to make a game of the things of this life? That she carried within her a fine sense of play that colored everything she did? Is it any wonder that I look around at everything she left behind and wonder if she may be playing with me still?

EIGHTEEN

I think I may finally be making some progress with Lorelei. I believe I am on my way to teaching her her first word.

Here's the way it happens: Lorelei is lazing on the carpet in a patch of sun, lolling on her back, and I'm observing her from across the room. As she lies there, she lets out a yawn, and as she yawns, she makes a noise that sounds like *wa*. I jump up from where I've been sitting.

"Good girl!" I cry. I run to the kitchen and pick up her water bowl. It sloshes dangerously as I run back to the living room. Lorelei is sitting up now, roused by my sudden activity. "Good girl," I repeat, and set the bowl down in front of her. She looks up at me, then at the bowl. Lazily, she sniffs at the water, then gives it a single lap with her tongue.

"Wa," I say. *"Wa."* I remove the bowl and put it aside, up on the coffee table. I sit down on the floor next to Lorelei. I have to get her to repeat the sound.

"Roll over, girl," I say, pushing on her flank. She resists. "Come on, girl," I cajole. "Roll over." After a few tries, I'm able to roll her onto her back. But how to make her yawn again?

She's eyeing me warily. I remember a time, years earlier, when my nephew was an infant and I was watching my sister hold him in her arms. As I watched, my sister looked down into the baby's face and fluttered her eyelids slowly up and down. She looked as if she were having trouble staying awake.

"Are you tired?" I had asked. "Do you want me to take him?"

"No," she said. "I'm trying to get him to fall asleep. Sometimes this works."

To my surprise, after watching my sister do this for a moment or two, the baby let his eyes droop once or twice. In another minute, he was asleep.

Perhaps the same tactic would work on Lorelei. I stretch out on the floor next to her and look into her face. I let my eyes flutter shut, then open them again as if it's a very great effort. I close them as if they were made of lead. When I open them again, Lorelei is staring at me, her eyes open wide. I try a few more times, with no luck.

Trying another tack, I yawn grandiosely. *"Wa,"* I say, yawning. *"Wa."* I reach over and retrieve her bowl from the coffee table and set it down in front of me. *"Wa,"* I repeat, then lean over the bowl and pretend to drink. I sneak a glance at Lorelei. She looks, if this is possible for a dog, surprised. Just do it, I think. Don't think about Lorelei's tongue and the other places she puts it. You've got her attention; just go all the way. *"Wa,"* I say again, and plunge my tongue into the bowl. The water tastes stale. I lap it up and drink two big swallows.

"Wa," I say. *"Wa."*

Lorelei stands up, shakes herself, and walks out of the room, leaving me sitting on the floor in her patch of sun, the taste of dog water fresh on my tongue.

Sighing, I get up and pick up the dish to take it back to the kitchen. I empty it into the sink—if I've learned anything from this little exercise, it's that I owe it to Lorelei to change her water more often—and wash the bowl with soap, something I haven't done in quite a while. I refill the bowl from the tap, but as I'm about to put it back in its regular spot on the floor, I stop. What if I make Lorelei ask for her water? I flinch slightly at the idea. One of the cardinal rules of dog ownership is that you never withhold water. Every dog book I've read contains this rule, set apart from the text in bold letters: Always have fresh, clean water available for your dog to drink. But I'm not talking about long-term dehydration. I'll simply watch to see when Lorelei goes looking for a drink, and I'll take the opportunity to work with her on the *wa* command. If it doesn't work, I'll give it to her anyway. I'm not heartless. I place the full bowl on the counter and wait for Lorelei to get thirsty.

In the meantime, I go into my study. I take out my laptop to continue my task of listing the titles of the books Lexy rearranged. The books on the second shelf from the top are arranged as follows:

You're Out! A History of Baseball (Mine.)
And Your Little Dog Too: Hollywood Dogs from Rin Tin Tin to Beethoven (Hers. I came across it in a used bookstore and

thought she'd be interested. She seemed to like it.)

Cooking for Two (Ours. Wedding gift.)

Gray Girls (Mine. A collection of interviews with women who were in the audience of *The Ed Sullivan Show* for the Beatles' first appearance.)

Don't Close Your Eyes (Lexy's. She had a weakness for horror novels.)

First Aid for Dogs and Cats (Lexy's.)

Put Me in the Zoo (Lexy's. A picture book she'd had since childhood.)

Where to Stay in Northern California (Ours. We'd been invited to a wedding in San Francisco, and we talked about taking a side trip to the wine country. But the wedding was canceled at the last minute—we never quite got the whole story, but there was some kind of scandal involving the bride and the father of the groom—and we never made the trip.)

A Feast for the Eyes (Lexy's. It's a big, glossy cookbook with complicated recipes and beautiful pictures. Neither of us ever used it.)

Thrill Rides of North America (Lexy's. She loved roller coasters; she always said

she planned to ride every single one in this book before she . . . well, that's what she said. Before she died.)
Clay Masks from Around the World (Lexy's.)
I'm Taking My Hatchback to Hackensack and Other Travel Games (Ours. We bought it on that first trip to Florida before we set out for the long drive back.)

As I write down the last title, I hear Lorelei padding down the hallway on her way to the kitchen. I get up and follow her. I watch as she sniffs around the corner where I put her bowls. She licks her empty food dish, perhaps finding some microscopic particle left over from her breakfast. Then she sniffs the floor where her water bowl should be.

"*Wa,* Lorelei?" I say. "Do you want some *wa*?" She looks up at me and twitches her tail in a miniature wag.

"Say '*wa,*' Lorelei." I massage the folds of her throat. She lets out an impatient whine. The sound it makes is more *mmnnnn* than *wa,* but it's progress.

"Good girl," I say. "Now say '*wa.*' "

She turns away from me and goes back to sniffing around the empty bowl corner, as if a dish of water might have appeared there in a moment when she wasn't looking.

Maybe she's not thirsty enough for this to work. I decide to up the ante. I take a bag of potato chips from the kitchen cabinet and give her one, then another. The sound of her crunching fills the kitchen. When she's finished, I turn on the faucet. She looks expectantly toward the sound of running water.

"Wa, Lorelei," I say. *"Wa, wa."*

I stand and wait. Lorelei watches me for a moment, then turns and walks out of the kitchen. I start to follow her, but by the time I'm halfway down the hall, I can hear the unmistakable sound of lapping coming from the bathroom. With a heavy heart, I turn into the room. There's Lorelei, her head in the toilet, drinking long and deep from the bowl.

NINETEEN

During that first winter of our marriage, Lexy and I fought a battle between us.

I wanted us to have a child. A baby with my features and hers. I imagined Lexy pregnant, holding our child within her, cradling it with her blood and her bones wherever she went. I imagined walking the leafy streets, pushing my son or my daughter—or both! Twins are not an unheard-of occurrence in my family—in a carriage, narrating the life of the neighborhood as we walked. "Look," I would say. "The leaves are changing color. Look, there goes Mrs. Singh in her red car." My child lying on her back, taking in the sky. I could almost see the soft curl of her hair. I wanted it very much. I wanted to spread a blanket on the grass when the weather got warm and to set my baby down upon it so she could reach for handfuls of grass and wriggling worms. I wanted to rescue a worm from her pudgy fingers before she put it in her mouth. I wanted to lift her up to the sky and hear her laugh. I wanted to dance her around the room when she was fussy and wouldn't sleep.

We were at a restaurant the first time I brought it up. At the table next to us was a couple with a baby, a boy maybe eight months old. I was in love with the scene of it, the mother and father taking turns entertaining the baby with a parade of toys produced one by one from a voluminous diaper bag, feeding him a snack from a plastic bag full of dry Cheerios, offering him a bottle of juice. From time to time, the baby would let out a string of nonsense syllables, and the happy sound filled the restaurant.

At one point, the baby's mother scooped up a spoonful of couscous from her plate and offered it to the baby. "Look at that," she said to her husband as the baby swallowed it. "His first couscous."

Lexy smiled at me. "His first couscous," she said in a low voice. "If I ever had a kid, it'd probably be more like, 'Aw, look at that, his first Big Mac.' "

I laughed. "His first taco chip. Wasn't that a Norman Rockwell painting?"

"Or one of those Precious Moments figurines. His first Hostess snack cake."

"His first onion ring."

"His first Mountain Dew."

"I had a friend in college who told me his mother used to put Coke in his baby bottle."

"Wow. Nothing like an infant hopped up on caffeine."

I paused to take a bite of my salad. "So," I said. "Do you ever think about that?"

"What," she said, "babies hopped up on caffeine?"

"No," I said. "Babies, period."

"Sure, I think about it," she said. "But mostly I think no." She looked at me to see my reaction.

"Why not?" I asked. "Don't you like kids?"

"I love them. I'm just not sure I should have one."

"That's a strange choice of words," I said. "You didn't say, 'I'm not sure I *want* to have one' or 'I'm not sure I'd *like* to have one,' you said, 'I'm not sure I *should* have one.' What does that mean?"

"Oh, here we go," Lexy said, rolling her eyes. "The perils of dining with a linguist."

"No, really," I said. "I'm curious. Why don't you think you should have a baby?"

She searched my face for a long minute before she spoke. "I'm just not sure it's fair to give a child me for a mother. And that's the last I'll say about it."

I stared at her, astonished. "Are you seri ous? My God, Lexy, I think you'd make a wonderful mother. You're caring and gener-ous—"

She put up her hand to stop me. "No," she said. "Don't. I don't want to talk about it anymore, okay?"

"But, Lexy, I can't believe you'd think such a thing."

She stood up. "I'm going to the bath-room," she said, "and when I come back, we're going to talk about something else."

She started to get up, then stopped. "You know I'd never actually feed that kind of stuff to a baby, right?" she said.

"See?" I said, smiling. "There's that ma-ternal instinct kicking in."

We didn't discuss it again that night. But the conversation wasn't over. I found myself thinking about the subject almost constantly in the weeks that followed. At the time, I had a graduate student in one of my seminars, a woman named Angelica Raza, who was pregnant with her first child. One day, she and I both arrived early to class, and after we exchanged a few pleasantries, I decided to ask her some questions that might help me figure things out.

"So," I asked. "Did you always want kids?"

She thought about it. "Yeah, pretty much always," she said. "My husband was a little harder to sell on the idea. But he came around eventually. Obviously," she added, placing her hands on her rounded belly.

"How'd you bring him around?"

"Well, basically, I tried not to pressure him. He's just a cautious guy, and he likes to make decisions in his own time. It took him seven years to decide to marry me. And we'd been living together for five."

"Wow," I said.

"Tell me about it," she laughed. "I knew he'd eventually decide he was ready for kids, but I was afraid I'd be eighty by that time."

"But you didn't pressure him?"

"No. One thing I've learned about John is

that he doesn't respond well to pressure. So I kept it light. I'd drop little comments about people we knew who were having babies, and I'd make jokes. For a while, we had this game where we'd try to come up with the most inappropriate baby names we could think of. I think the winner was Tabula, for a girl. Get it? Tabula Raza?"

I laughed.

"And then one day," she went on, "he just turned to me out of the blue, I think we were watching a cop show or something, and said, 'Let's have a baby.' "

"That's great," I said.

"Yeah, and now he can't wait. He's read more baby books than I have."

Just then, a couple of other students arrived, and the conversation shifted to something else. But later that night, when I got home, I decided to give Angelica's method a try.

I started by telling Lexy Angelica's story about naming a girl Tabula. She smiled and said, "Oh, you linguistics scholars. Never a dull moment."

"So then," I said, "I was wondering if there were any names that wouldn't go with our last names, but I couldn't think of any for Iverson. I guess Ivan Iverson would be pretty bad."

"Well, not as bad as Stinky Iverson," Lexy said. "It doesn't matter what your last name is, I think if you name a child Stinky, you're setting him up for a life of hardship."

This seemed to be going pretty well, I thought. "What about Ransome?" I said. "Is there anything that doesn't go with Ransome? Kings, I guess. You wouldn't want to name a kid Kings Ransome. But that's not a real name, anyway."

"My dad used to have some complicated joke that took forever to tell, and I was too young to really get it anyway, about how he should have two sons and name them both William. God, I wish I could remember the whole thing, it'd tell you a lot about what my father was like. Anyway, the punch line was something about paying a Ransome in small Bills."

I laughed, maybe a little too hard.

Lexy looked at me. She had a serious expression on her face, suddenly. "Sweetie, I know what you're doing," she said. "And I don't think it's going to work."

"No?" I took her hand. "Look, Lexy, I don't want to put any pressure on you, but don't you think it's possible you might change your mind?"

"Well, anything's possible, but I don't think so." She looked away. "I guess this is something we should have talked about before we got married," she said, and it was like a question. "I guess it might have changed things." Her voice sounded fragile suddenly, like a little girl's.

"No, of course not," I said. "Nothing could have stopped me from marrying you." She smiled at me tentatively. "I can't say I'm not disappointed, and I can't say I don't hope you'll reconsider, but I'm in this with you for good. No matter what."

And so I agreed to it. I agreed to a life without children. I agreed it would be just the two of us, here in the tilting world. What would our days be like, I wondered, with that space in them, the space where a child might be, the space where a child might walk between us, holding each of our hands? But no, I resolved. Our days could be filled with the two of us. We would walk through our days together, and the shadow we would cast on the ground would be tall, the shadow of two adults walking together, not the familiar H of adult-child-adult walking hand in hand. We would live a good, quiet life, uninterrupted by the shouts of children at play, the daily chaos of cuts and scrapes and quarrels over the sharing of toys. There would still be the two of us, and the bright sky of our love. I could do this for her. This was not so bad. There would be hard times, but what did I care if we had hard times? The branches of my love were wide, and they caught the rain and the snow. We would be okay, the two of us together. We would be okay.

TWENTY

When I was a little boy, my mother, who was given to hyperbole, used to tell me that if the world were to come to an end, her last thought would be of me, and she would fling my name out to the heavens as the mortar of the earth burst apart and the ground fell from beneath her feet. It is only now, when I am surprised to find that I am growing older every day, it's only now that I am beginning to believe that my mother was not just speaking extravagantly. I think every one of us carries with us a name like this, a name whose importance may not be clear to us until we find it on our lips in those final moments. I don't think it is ever, perhaps not even for my mother, who we expect it to be.

All this to say: I am forty-three years old. I

may yet live another forty. What do I do with those years? How do I fill them without Lexy? When I come to tell the story of my life, there will be a line, creased and blurred and soft with age, where she stops. If I win the lottery, if I father a child, if I lose the use of my legs, it will be after she has finished knowing me. "When I get to Heaven," my grandmother used to say, widowed at thirty-nine, "your grandfather won't even recognize me."

Lately, I've been having trouble sleeping. It's the getting to sleep that causes me problems. During the day, I go from one task to the next, not thinking much about the shadow areas of my life, Lexy's death, my grief and the strange way I have chosen to respond to it, the laughingstock I have become in my field. I can go the whole day without thinking of any of it. And then I get into bed. All those hours spread before me, and nothing to do but think. I would get up and work on my research, but Lorelei has made it clear she will not work between the hours of eight P.M. and six A.M. Dogs sleep a lot—one lesson I've learned in my two months of research is that dogs sleep a hell of a lot more than they do anything else.

And so it is that on this night, my wife four months dead, I find myself sitting in the dark watching an infomercial for a telephone psychic.

I've never been much of a believer in the mystical arts, although as a child I indulged all the natural curiosities for ghost stories, Ouija boards, and the like. In fact, the powers of the Ouija board have become legendary in my family: once when my sister and I were children, a Ouija board told her that she would marry a man with the initials PJM, and as it turned out, she did. My sister's first husband, to whom she was married for a scant eight months right after college, was named Peter James Marsh. Now, happily married for almost fifteen years to a man with the initials LRS, the only thing she will say about her first marriage is that she should have known better than to marry a man based on his initials.

But in my adult years I've always been something of a skeptic. I don't believe in ESP or UFOs, past lives or parallel worlds or spirits of the dead that haunt the living. I don't believe in anything I can't put my hands on. Still, something about this woman on the screen intrigues me, and I find myself not wanting to change the channel. I suppose everyone is a skeptic until they have a reason to believe.

Lady Arabelle is her name. She could not be more of a cliché—colorful scarves knotted about her head, a jangle of gold necklaces at her throat—but there's something so sincere about her you forget all that. Something about her manner, the warmth she displays, draws you in right away. I can see why you'd want to believe what she has to say. The people who phone in with their problems, she calls them honey and baby, and she makes it sound like she means it. There's something distinctly motherly about her. If she called me baby, I think I'd want to cry.

"Check him out, honey," she's telling the woman on the phone. "Make sure his divorce is final, because I don't think he's being honest with you. He's hiding something. Did he ask you not to call him at home?"

"Well, he told me he has this roommate he doesn't like, so he's not home much. He told me I should call his pager."

"That's no roommate, honey. That's his wife."

They flash a phone number. "Lady Arabelle knows all your secrets," the voice-over tells me. "She answers your questions about the future, your questions about the past." Well, that's something. Your questions about the past. Idly, I imagine the conversation that would follow if I called the number on the screen. "I see a large dog. The dog has something to tell you."

Another caller, a man this time. "I'm sorry, hon," Lady Arabelle tells him. "But that's not your baby."

"It's not?"

"No, honey, it's not. Tell me this, did she go out of town a few months ago, maybe for her job? Did she go to an Eastern city?"

"Yeah," he says, his voice gone flat. "She went to Boston in June."

"Well, that's when it happened. Ask her about it. Ask her if she ran into an old boyfriend in Boston, and see what she has to say for herself."

I give some thought to this man whose marriage may now be over as the result of a phone call to a stranger. I wonder if it's true, this scenario she's put in his mind. I picture the confrontations that will follow this phone call.

Another voice-over, some fine print about rates per minute. I find myself tempted to write the phone number down. Then Lady Arabelle is back, talking to another woman.

"There's something you're not telling me about," she says. "You're all excited about something. Something you found in his coat?"

"Yes," the woman says. "I found a ring. I think he's going to propose!"

"Well, I'm gonna tell you something, baby. That ring's for someone else. That ring is not for you."

It's the specificity that seals the deal. The Eastern city, the hidden ring. She's very convincing. But something about the desperation of these callers, the faith they put in this woman who, sincere though she seems, knows nothing about their lives, bothers me. I stand up, ready to turn off the TV—I have the remote in my hand—but what I hear next makes my heart stop.

Because the next voice I hear is Lexy's.

TWENTY-ONE

It's her. It's her. I know it the way I know the pound of my blood in my chest. Lexy's voice, like a homecoming for me. Lexy's voice, filling the room once more.

"I'm lost," she says, and I lose my legs beneath me. "I don't know what to do," she says, and I make a sound like an animal struck.

My hands are shaking, and I feel dizzy. My heart is beating so hard I think it will break. I pick up the remote from where I've dropped it, and I turn the volume up as high as it will go. Lady Arabelle, her voice like a lullaby, gives her reply.

"Listen to me, honey," she says, so loud I can feel it in my teeth. "You have more strength than you know."

I wait for more, I wait for Lexy to come

back and say something else, but that's all there is. They're back to the voice-over about rates and phone numbers.

Lexy's voice gone once more. I cover my face with my hands and give myself over to the wave of sound racking my body. A tightness in my chest gives voice to a bottomless noise like a howl. I kneel on the floor in the half-light of the television and wail loud enough to wake the dead.

I feel a wet pressure on the back of my hand, and I look up to see Lorelei staring me in the face. "Lorelei," I say, my voice wrecked and uneven. "Did you hear it, girl?" She licks my face. I gather her in my arms and lift her, all of her dense, heavy weight, onto my lap. I press my face into the rough warmth of her neck, the thick leather band of her collar. I'm sobbing now, and her fur grows damp beneath my face. "Did you hear it, Lorelei?" I say. "It was her, it was her, it was her."

Later, later, when I've calmed down enough that my body has stopped shaking and I've quieted my breath, I get a piece of paper and I write down the number on the screen. I stare at the number. My head is pounding. What does it mean? For a wild minute, I imagine Lexy alive, sitting in a room someplace, with a phone pressed to her ear. But no. Just as quickly, I see it all again, Lexy lying in her coffin, her body strange and still. Who knows how long ago she made this call? It could have been months before her death, it could have been years. For the first time, I think about Lexy's words. "I'm lost," she said. "I don't know what to do." What kind of trouble was she in? And where was I? It occurs to me that there must have been more to this phone call. I have to talk to this woman. I have to hear the rest of the story. But will she even remember Lexy? She talks to a hundred people a day. And all their problems are the same. All the world's troubles and secrets, none of them new. She gives them all the same advice, *Follow your heart* and *You know what you have to do.* There's no mystery there. The people who call know the answers already. They just need someone to say them out loud.

I get up and walk to my study. For once I'm glad I never throw anything away. In my desk drawer, I find a thick folder filled with old bills, and I begin to go through it. Nothing's in any order; I always just cram papers in here at random after paying the bills. Here's a water bill from three years ago; here's the credit card bill I paid last week. I go through, separating out the phone bills and throwing the rest on the floor.

It takes me an hour to find it. That phone number, the one I've just written down, 11:23 P.M. Forty-six minutes in length. What desperate night was this? While I slept, she sat in this very room and made a phone call to a television psychic. "I'm lost," she said, and I was asleep. And then she came in and lay beside me. She was lost, and I had no idea. She lay beside me, lost and scared.

The charge is $229.54. How could I have missed this? I tend to be a bit absent-minded when it comes to such things—it once took me six months to notice I was being charged a monthly membership fee for a health club I didn't belong to—but a two-hundred-dollar phone call? And then I see the date. October 23 of last year. The day before Lexy's death. Of course I paid my bills that month in a fog.

Lorelei comes into the room and whines to be let out. It's late; she had her nightly walk hours ago, and there are hours still until morning. This is a strange night for us both. I follow her to the back door and let her out into the yard. She sniffs around the base of the apple tree. I wonder if Lexy's scent is still there, embedded in the damp earth. Strange that Lorelei didn't respond to Lexy's voice on the TV. She slept through the whole thing, awakening only when she heard me cry out. How could she have missed it, with all her strong canine powers of hearing? Has she forgotten Lexy's voice in this short time? Or is there something about the filtering effect of the tape recording, the tinny TV speakers, that reduces even the most beloved voice to mere background noise? I've noticed before that Lorelei doesn't respond to familiar voices on the telephone answering machine either. The doorbell, though. Whenever she hears a doorbell on TV, she jumps up and runs to the door, barking. And our doorbell hasn't worked as long as I've lived here.

After we come back inside, I go into the living room and pick up the phone. I dial the number I've written down. It rings once and picks up. There's some tinny, mysterious-sounding music, then a recorded voice. "You have reached the Psychic Helpline, your gateway to psychic adventure. You must be over eighteen to enjoy our services. Our rates are four dollars ninety-nine cents per minute. The Psychic Helpline is for entertainment purposes only. Please hold for your personal psychic adviser."

The extension rings, and a woman answers. She sounds young, Midwestern.

"Thank you for calling our Psychic Helpline. This is Caitlin, extension 79642. I'm going to do a tarot card reading for you today. Let me begin by getting your name, birth date, and address."

"Um, actually, I'm not looking for a reading. I'd like to speak with Lady Arabelle."

"Lady Arabelle's not available right now. Why don't you let me help you?"

"Well, maybe you could put me on hold. It's very important that I speak to Lady Arabelle directly. I'm willing to wait until she's free."

"No, I'm afraid Lady Arabelle's not here right now. Tell me, are you a Pisces? I'm getting a strong vibe here—"

"Maybe I could leave a message for you to give to her. Or maybe you could tell me when she'll be there, and I can call back then?"

"I'm afraid that's not going to be possible. But I assure you, I'm a qualified professional psychic, and I'll be more than happy to help you. I'm sensing you've had some trouble in your life lately—"

"Listen," I interrupt. "This is very important. It's a matter of life and death." Well, it is, in a manner of speaking. "You've got to tell me how to reach Lady Arabelle. I'm sure you're not allowed to give me her home number, but maybe if I explain why I need to speak to her—"

Caitlin sighs. "I'm sorry, but I don't have any idea how to reach her." She's dropped the ethereal quality she's been trying to inject into her voice.

"What do you mean? She does exist, doesn't she? I've seen her on TV."

"Well, I'm sure she exists, but the thing is, there are hundreds of psychics who work for this network, and when you call, they just connect you to whoever's available. You don't get to pick who you get to talk to."

"Well, even so, you all work together. There must be some way you can leave a note or something."

"No, it doesn't work that way. See, right

now, I'm sitting here in my apartment in Dayton, Ohio, and for all I know, this Lady Arabelle, who I'm sorry but I've never heard of, could be in California or Texas or anywhere. It's not like we're all sitting around in some big psychic room or something, looking into crystal balls. We don't all even work for the same company. There are, like, a hundred little companies, and they all sign up with this other company that runs a big central computer in Florida or someplace, and when someone calls, the computer checks to see who's logged on, and then the phone rings right here in my living room, and I pick it up. You could call a hundred times and never get the same person twice."

"I see," I say. I feel deflated. "But there must be some phone number I can call to talk to someone who's in charge. Whoever runs the big computer in Florida, I guess."

"Well, if there is, I don't know it." Her voice softens a little. "But, listen, if you tell me a little more about this life-or-death situation, maybe I can help you find some answers. Come on, honey, tell me your birthday."

It's the "honey" that does it. Even in that

thin, young voice of hers, the word makes my chest ache. Do I crave kindness and tenderness that much?

"September twentieth," I say. I press the phone to my ear, ready to hear whatever she has to tell me.

TWENTY-TWO

When I was a child, one of my favorite games on long car trips and rainy afternoons was to write a word, any word, at the top of a piece of paper and list beneath all the words that could be made from its letters. The point wasn't so much to count the number of words that I found, it was more to see what those words revealed about the word they came from. It was like magic to me, like a secret code to crack. Break apart *family,* and you find both *yam,* homey as Thanksgiving, and *lam,* the inevitable flight from the nest. Is it any accident that *loser* contains the letters to form *sore?*

I liked the surprise of the images this game conjured up and the way that the pictures it painted were often so right. I broke down *father,* and I saw the way my own father was like a *raft,* bobbing along, holding us all up. I broke down *mother,* and I saw the way my mother hovered around us like a *moth.*

I find myself playing the same game now, writing down names and seeing what they can tell me. Look inside *Lorelei* and you find *roll* and *lie,* two very doggy verbs, two things she does very well. But look further and you'll see she carries within her a story to tell (see, there it is—*lore*) and a *role* she herself plays in that story.

Break open *Lexy Ransome* and you find *omen* and *sexy* and *soar. Lost* and *rose. Yearn* and *near* and *anymore.* See how it works? It doesn't bear thinking about. It couldn't be clearer. Only one letter away from *remorse,* and one letter away from *answer.*

My own name, Paul Iverson, holds a wealth of words within it. Many of them, disconcertingly, have to do with the life of the body. Look and you'll see that I am made up of *veins* and *liver* and *pores, nape* and *penis, loins* and *pulse.* Try as I might, I cannot escape this body of mine that breathes and beats and lives, that still sweats in the sun and craves water to drink.

That passes urine like any living thing. I am tangible as the earth. I am *soil*; I am *vapor.* But look again: I am more than my body, I am more than my living self. Look again and you'll find *soul* and *reason, prose* and *salve* and *lover.* I am *nervous* and *son* and *naive.* I'm as human as you can get. I *snore* and I *pine.* (One letter away from *passion.* One letter away from *reveal.*)

These are the notes I made during my talk with Caitlin, and they tell me more than anything she said. She told me I had faced great sadness in my life. (And who, I wanted to ask her, who hasn't? Who, at least among those willing to pay three hundred dollars an hour for advice, hasn't faced some misery they don't know how to bear?) She told me things would get better. She told me she saw a woman in my future, and when I balked, when I told her I couldn't imagine such a thing ever again, she told me she saw a man. Granted, I didn't give her much to work with. I told her my real birthday and my real name, but when she asked if I was married, I said only, "Not any-more," and I left her to draw her own con-clusions. I resisted her attempts to draw my story out of me; if she's being paid to be a psychic, I thought, then let her figure it out. Part of me, I admit, wanted her to tell me something true; part of me wanted her powers to be real. It's a strange role they play, these "psychics," part priest-confessor, part therapist, and I was half hoping she would tell me something that would make everything make sense. I was half hoping that somehow she would save me. But in the end, she was just some woman from Ohio sitting in her living room, talking to a stranger in the middle of the night. And me, I was just some schmuck paying for a phone call he couldn't afford.

Now, outside, the dawn is breaking. It's been a very long night. I feel empty now, too tired to think anymore about Lexy and her call to Lady Arabelle and what it all means. When I go into the bedroom, I find Lorelei sleeping across the foot of the bed, and I decide not to shoo her off. I crawl between the sheets, curling myself into a ball so as not to kick her, and almost immediately, I am asleep.

TWENTY-THREE

I run into Maura today. The ex-wife. Or, well, when I say I run into her, I mean I run into her on my front porch. I open the door to get the newspaper and there she is. It's quite a surprise. She hasn't knocked. She has a note in her hand, and I guess she's trying to decide whether to leave it. She jumps when I open the door.

"Hi," I say. I'm a little taken aback to see her there.

"Oh, Paul," she says. "I didn't know you were home."

"Well, here I am."

She smiles and goes into a kind of artificial sympathy mode. "I just heard about Lexy," she says. "Paul, I'm so sorry."

I nod and smile sadly and look at my feet and mumble my thanks. I'm still not very good at accepting condolences from people, especially people who didn't know Lexy.

"Well, would you like to come in for a cup of coffee?" I ask finally. It's strange to see Maura standing on my porch smiling at me. We didn't part on very good terms, as I think I've mentioned. But it's kind of nice to see her. I realize I haven't spoken to an actual human being in two days.

"That would be nice," she says.

Don't worry. This isn't headed where you might think.

As she comes in, I look around the house and see it as she must see it. It's a mess. There are dishes everywhere, and stacks of books piled precariously high. I'm sure I look rumpled as well. I am certainly unshaven.

It's not until Maura is already inside the house that Lorelei comes barreling in, barking. She must be losing her watchdog touch, I think. There was a time when she would've known Maura was standing on the porch before I even opened the door. It occurs to me for the first time that Lorelei is getting older—she must be eight years old by now—and that I may not have unlimited time to conduct my research. Or to enjoy the quiet pleasure of her company. I will lose her someday, that much is certain, and it makes me ache to think of it. But, as all dog owners must, I put the thought quickly out of my mind.

Maura backs away and shrinks against the wall when Lorelei comes into view. She never was a dog person.

"Down, girl," I say in my most command-ing voice. "It's okay." To Maura I say, "Let her sniff your hand. Don't worry, she won't bite."

Maura holds her hand out uncertainly. Lorelei sniffs it avidly and thoroughly and gives it a tentative lick. Satisfied, I guess, that the situation is under control, she turns and walks away.

"So," Maura says. "I guess that's Lorelei."

"How do you know her name?"

"I'll be honest with you, Paul. Matthew Rice called me." She brightens for a mo-ment. "He told me he's head of the depart-ment now. That's great. Good for him." Then she puts her concerned face back on. "He's worried about you, Paul. He thought maybe I should talk to you."

I feel a flash of annoyance at Matthew

Rice. He knows how I feel about Maura. And I have work to do. This unexpected visit is quite a disruption.

"Well, come and sit down then and talk to me," I say. I'm sure the irritation is clear in my voice.

I lead her into the living room. She stops to look at a picture on a side table, a photograph of Lexy and me taken on our wedding day.

"So this is Lexy," she says. There's a brittleness to her voice that she doesn't quite manage to hide. "She was pretty." She sounds as if she's accusing me of something.

"Yes," I say. "She was."

I clear the couch of newspapers and notepads and gesture for Maura to sit down.

"God, Paul," she says. "Look how you're living."

"Well, I wasn't expecting company," I say shortly. "Did you want some coffee?"

She eyes a pile of dishes on the table with a kind of horror. "No," she says. "That's all right."

I sit down in a chair facing her. "So," I say. "How have you been?"

"Fine. Thank you."

"How's work?"

"Fine."

"Are you . . . seeing anyone?" The question sounds absurd.

"No. Not at the moment."

"Okay," I say. "Well, let's get down to business. What'd you come here to say?"

"Paul, Matthew thinks you've lost your mind. He says you've stopped interacting with people, and you didn't show up for dinner at his house . . ."

That's true. It was on a day when I felt I was very close to making some headway with Lorelei—it was the day of the *wa* breakthrough, as a matter of fact—and I simply forgot I had made plans with Matthew and Eleanor. I called the next day and apologized, and I thought I had explained the situation perfectly well. Matthew himself is extremely single-minded when it comes to research. I thought he, of all people, would understand.

Maura's still listing my shortcomings. "And he says you actually think you're going to teach that dog to talk. I mean, really, Paul, you don't believe that, do you?"

"I believe that interspecies communica-

tion is an area that has not been fully explored," I begin. "And I think that we have
much to learn—"

"Jesus Christ," Maura breaks in. "Paul,
do you hear yourself? You need help. Look,
I'm sorry Lexy died, that's a tragedy, but
you have to get over it. You're ruining your
life and you're ruining your career."

I stand up. Haven't I spent enough of my
life already listening to this woman? So she
thinks I'm crazy. Fine. I'll give her something
to take back to Matthew.

"Lorelei," I roar. I'm surprised at the fe-
rocity in my voice.

Maura looks nervous. "Paul, what are you
doing?" she asks.

"Lorelei," I yell again. Lorelei appears in
the doorway. "Sic!" I say, and point at
Maura. Lorelei just looks at me.

Maura jumps up. "Oh, my God," she
says.

"Get her, girl!" I shout. Lorelei looks from
me to Maura and back again. She lets out a
single bark, responding, I suppose, to the
loudness of my voice.

"Are you nuts?" Maura says to me.

"Apparently," I say. "Go on, Lorelei! Get
her!"

"I'm leaving," Maura says. "You've really lost it, Paul. Let me out of here." She grabs her purse and walks quickly to the door, giving Lorelei a wide berth.

I follow her and stand in the doorway as she retreats down the front path.

"And stay out!" I yell after her. It's strangely satisfying. I start to laugh. I watch Maura drive away, and then, laughing, I walk back into my cluttered living room to continue my research.

TWENTY-FOUR

Lexy and I had been married six or seven months, I think, when she got the call to make the mask of the dead girl. She called me at work.

"Hi," she said. "Do you know where Van Buren's Funeral Home is?"

"Um, I'm not sure," I said. "Why, did somebody die?"

"No. Well, somebody did, but it's not anyone I know."

"What?"

"I just got this call, out of the blue," she said. "It was from a woman whose daughter just died, and she wants me to make a mask from the girl's face."

"Oh, my God," I said. "And you're going to do it?"

"Well, I was a little put off when she first

started telling me what she wanted, but the more she explained it, the more sense it made. I guess this girl—she was nineteen, she was in college—it sounds like she had some kind of cancer. Her mother sounded very calm and rational; I think they knew this was coming for a long time. Anyway, this girl was a theater major, and she was kind of quirky, and she wasn't afraid of death, her mother said. Her parents think she would've approved of this. They think it would be a nice way to remember her."

"Uck," I said. "I think it sounds creepy. Don't you think? It doesn't sound like a very healthy way to grieve, to keep a mold of your daughter's dead face around. What are they going to do with it, display it on the coffee table?"

"Yeah, I know," she said. "It's kind of weird. But there's something about this that appeals to me. It's important work, you know? More important than most of the things I take on. I mean, this is the last chance they have to capture their daughter's face the way it really looks."

"The way it looks *in death.* Don't they have any pictures of her, pictures of the way she looked when she was *alive*?"

Lexy sighed. "Maybe I'm not going to be able to explain it to you," she said. "But I think I understand. You know, death masks have been around for thousands of years. And I read once that back when photography was new, people used to have pictures taken of their loved ones in their coffins. Or mothers would take their dead babies to be photographed. It would be the only thing they'd have to remember them by."

"That's very sad. But I still think it's a strange request."

"I don't know. I think there's something sacred about capturing the human face in the moment of death. Think about this—if no one ever wanted to remember the way their loved ones looked after they died, then why would we have open caskets at funerals?"

"Well, I'm not too crazy about that either," I said.

"I think there's something comforting about it," she said. "You know, death is this big mystery, and it's something we're all afraid of, but when you see someone who's actually dead, they look peaceful. It doesn't look so bad. Especially if it's someone who's been through a lot of pain and is finally at rest. Maybe that's what this girl's parents want to capture."

"I suppose," I said. "But are you sure you want to be a part of this?"

"Yes," she said. "I'm sure."

At the time, I found the whole business unsavory. It seemed to me an act of desperation on the part of the girl's parents, an unwillingness to let go. Even without knowing this dead girl, I doubted she would have chosen this as the way she wanted her parents to grieve. To keep her dead face in their home, always in sight? To keep them rooted forever to the moment of her death? If the goal of grief is to learn to move on, I thought, to learn how to inhabit the same space as absence and to keep living anyhow, then surely these sad people were doing a disservice not only to themselves but to the memory of their poor lost daughter.

But now, having come to know grief as intimately as I have, having lived in its bare rooms for so long and walked its empty halls, I'm not so sure they were wrong.

When Lexy died, I admit I took some cloistered comfort in seeing that her face had not been bruised in the fall. And in spite of what I may have said, when the time

came I did have an open casket at her funeral, and every time someone said to me,
"Oh, she looks so beautiful," it was like a
balm to me. When I knelt by her coffin, my
mind wiped suddenly blank of all my childhood prayers, and I reached out to touch
her cheek, I stared as hard as I could bear
to and I fixed in my mind every detail of the
way she looked, because I knew it would be
the last time I would ever lay my eyes on
her. Would I want a mask of Lexy as she
looked in death, to hang on the wall, perhaps, next to the mask of Lexy as she
looked in life? No. But I would not presume
to tell any other grief-sick wanderer that
what he needs is wrong. I would not dare.

I was afraid that embarking on such a
morbid project would throw Lexy into a fit of
melancholy, but when she came home she
was glowing.

"She was beautiful," she said. "Very
gaunt, from the illness, but you could see
she had really beautiful features."

I tried to picture the dead girl, waiflike on
the slab. I could not quite imagine beauty
there.

"They hadn't put the makeup on her yet,

you know, for the funeral, so her skin was very pale. I had to work quickly—they needed me to be done by this afternoon. But it didn't take me very long to make the mold. Not to be morbid, but it's easier when you don't have to keep telling the person to stay still."

"Was she cold?" I asked. I hadn't spent much time around dead bodies. Even when my father died, I had kind of kept my distance at the funeral.

"Not ice-cold. But cool. Cooler than a living person."

"Did you talk to the parents?"

"Yeah, of course. I sat down with them to discuss what they wanted the end product to be like."

"And what were they like?" At this point, I still couldn't imagine a healthy-minded person doing such a thing.

"They seemed very normal. Sad, of course. The father started crying at one point. But they were very grateful that I was willing to do this for them. They were afraid they wouldn't find anyone."

With good reason, I wanted to say. But I kept quiet.

"Listen," I said instead. "What do you say

we go out and get some dinner? After a day like that, you need to be among the living."

"Actually," she said, "do you mind if we just order something in? I'm kind of anxious to go downstairs and get to work on this while it's all fresh in my mind."

"Okay," I said. I was disappointed. It was a Friday night, and I'd been looking forward to spending it with Lexy, doing something nice together, getting a start on the weekend. We were still newlyweds, after all. But it had been a while since I'd seen her so excited about a project, and as distasteful as I found it myself, I didn't want to ruin her good mood. I went into the kitchen and ordered a pizza.

Lexy worked all weekend on the mask, coming upstairs only to get food from the kitchen or to pace around the living room, deep in thought. Lorelei spent most of the time down in the basement with Lexy, as she always did when Lexy was working, so it was a rather solitary couple of days for me. On Sunday night, I was sitting in the living room reading when I looked up to see Lorelei standing in front of me.

"Hi, girl," I said. I reached out to pat her head, and as I did, I noticed there was a piece of paper sticking out of her collar. I removed it. It said, "Ms. Alexandra Ransome requests the honour of your presence in the basement for an unveiling of her latest work." I laughed, and all was forgiven. I walked to the basement door, with Lorelei trailing behind me.

Lexy was stretched out on the battered couch when I got downstairs. The mask was on the worktable, covered with a cloth.

"Did you just get the note?" she asked, standing up. "I sent Lorelei up a half hour ago."

"I guess the Ridgeback Express isn't as quick as it could be. You never know when she'll have to make an unscheduled stop to eat a bug or something."

"So are you ready to see it?" I could feel her excitement from across the room.

"Absolutely," I said. I steeled myself and got ready to lie when she asked me what I thought.

She sat me down and made me close my eyes. She put the mask in my hands. I opened my eyes with some trepidation.

It was beautiful, what she had made. I was surprised at how beautiful it was. In my narrow imagination, I had supposed she would paint the mask from life (or from death, as it were), the color of pale flesh, the lips blanched and barely pink, fine lash-lines highlighting the bumps of the closed eyes. I had imagined, I guess, that the mask would look dead. But that was not the way she did it at all. She had painted the face white, a stark white background, with a field of bright flowers that stretched from cheek to cheek. The colors were vibrant—no soft pastels, no pinks and baby blues. There were stems and leaves in bright, vivid greens, topped with blossoms of red and purple and yellow and teal, their petals touched with gold like a glint of sunglow. These were not the kinds of flowers that would have been sent to the girl's funeral, formal and somber, carefully arranged. These were wildflowers, windblown and growing every which way.

The girl's features were barely visible. Lexy hadn't emphasized them at all; in fact, you could look at the piece and not realize right away that it was a face. The soft hollows of the eyes, the bump of the nose, the curve of the lips, were written beneath the flowers like a palimpsest. But once I noticed them, I couldn't stop looking. I could see the youth in the face, the promise of a beauty she might have grown into. But the mask wasn't sad, that was the extraordinary thing. Even knowing that the girl whose face had served as the model had since been laid in the ground, it didn't make me sad to look at it. In a way, I think that a photograph of the girl, laughing and alive, might have been more upsetting—think of those yearbook photos that appear in the newspaper every spring alongside stories of tragic car crashes on graduation night. The lost potential of those newly dead kids, shown in their uncomfortable new suits and their formal smiles. It breaks your heart; it never fails. But this mask was different, somehow. It lacked that pathos. It portrayed what *was,* not what might have been. Looking at it, I saw that there can be grace in death, and beauty. I saw what I imagined the girl's parents must have seen when they took Lexy by the arm and asked her to look upon their daughter.

I sat silent for a moment, gazing at the mask. All of the quick words of false praise that I had prepared melted away.

"Well?" Lexy asked.

"It's beautiful," I said. "It's nothing like what I expected."

"You thought it would be terrible, didn't you?" she said, smiling.

"Honestly? Yes." I studied the mask a moment more. "But do you think it's what the parents had in mind? It's a little abstract. Maybe they're expecting something a little more realistic."

She regarded me warily. "What do you mean?" she said.

"Well, I just wonder if they were expecting more of a realistic likeness, painted the way she actually looked."

Lexy stiffened. "It's her face," she said. "That's what they wanted. They wanted her face."

"Well, yes, of course, but did you tell them you might be doing something like this?"

" 'Something like this'?" she said. "What do you mean, 'something like this'?" Her voice rose as she spoke.

I stood up and took a step toward her, reaching out to put my hand on her arm, but she shook it away.

"Don't get upset," I said. "I think this is wonderful—I think it's one of the best pieces you've done. I just wonder if the parents are in the right state of mind to appreciate it."

"You think they're going to hate it," she said. "You don't think it's good. Give it to me." She grabbed the mask from my hands.

"No, Lexy, that's not what I said at all. Calm down."

She looked down at the mask, which was trembling in her hands. "You hate it," she said, her voice ragged. She began to cry, painful, racking sobs. "You hate it. It's terrible."

"No," I said.

"Yes," she said. "You hate it." She threw the mask to the floor and stepped on it hard. The pâpier-maché was stiff and resisted the force of her bare foot.

"Stop it, Lexy," I said. "You're being ridiculous. Stop it."

She picked up the mask and flung it violently onto the worktable. She picked up a knife that she used to trim masks after they had hardened, and she pounded the blade into the mask again and again. The pâpier-maché splintered and sent up a cloud of fine white dust. She kept stabbing at it until the surface of the face was pocked with holes and the nose had dissolved into powder. Then she put the knife down and stared at what she had done. She dropped her face into her hands and sobbed until her body shook.

I stood back, horrified and a little angry. "What did you do that for?" I asked roughly.

"I don't know," she said. Her voice sounded strangled, as if she weren't getting enough air. "I don't know."

I stood and watched her, unable to move forward and comfort her. Finally, she took her hands away from her face and looked at me. Her skin was red, and there was a string of pale crescents across her forehead, where she had dug her fingernails into her flesh.

"Do you see?" she said. "Do you see why I can't have children?" She turned and walked up the stairs. I stood in the basement, staring at the ruined mask, and listened to her footsteps cross the floor above me. I heard the front door open and close, and I knew I was alone.

TWENTY-FIVE

I call the Psychic Helpline compulsively every day, hoping to hear Lady Arabelle's voice. Usually I hang up when I hear the psychic's name, when I know that it's not her, but sometimes, when I'm feeling lonely, I get pulled in by a certain voice, and I wait to find out what she has to tell me. (Or he. But it's almost always a woman.) Sometimes I tell her my whole story, and sometimes I let her try to figure it out for herself. "I'm sure it was an accident," they always say. "It sounds like she loved you very much." They tell me, "You are not alone, although you might feel like you are." They tell me that if I only wait a little longer, I'll have financial windfalls and love will come my way. They tell me not to lose hope. They tell me that the cards show bright skies ahead. The Death card means change, not death. They ask me if I have a specific question, and I don't know what to say. Did she kill herself? I can't bring myself to form the words. Will I teach my dog to talk? How can I ask such a question without inviting ridicule? I asked one of them, "Do you see anything about animals? Do you see anything about a dog?" and she assured me that my lost dog was alive and well and would return home soon. Some of them are sly and cruel and will resort to anything to keep you on the phone. One of them told me I was sick, and one of them told me she foresaw an accident, but that if I stayed on the line a little longer, we might be able to find a way to prevent it. "Have you been feeling run-down lately?" they ask, and who can honestly say they haven't when it's one A.M. and they're talking on the phone to a stranger? They say, "There's a woman you work with . . . I'm seeing an *S* name maybe? Or an *R* name?" The first time one of them asked me if I knew a woman with an *L* name, I felt my heart quicken. But when I didn't answer right away, not trusting my voice to be steady, she said, "No, maybe it's a *T* name. Terry? Theresa?" and I knew she had nothing. On the occasions when I tell them about Lexy, and I must say those are becoming more frequent, they ask me for her birthday. They tell me to picture her face as they deal the cards. And I do. I focus on her face with all my might. They tell me things about our marriage based on my astrological sign and hers. It's all kind of hit-or-miss. "She was very neat, wasn't she?" they'll say, and I'll say no. But then they'll say, "Sometimes you fought about money," and I'll remember a time when I forgot to record an ATM withdrawal, causing Lexy to bounce a check. "Yes," I say, wanting it all to be true. "Yes. Sometimes we fought about money." They know what I want to hear. Sometimes their questions are so right it makes my heart stop. "She died suddenly," they'll say, and it's not a question. But then I realize they can hear it in my voice, in the desperate note I didn't realize was there. They can tell it's not the voice of a man who nursed his wife through a long illness. They can tell it's the voice of a man who still wakes up every day surprised to find her gone.

*   *   *

But on the dog front, things couldn't be going better. I've had the most wonderful idea, an idea that I think may be the key to the success of my project with Lorelei. The idea comes to me quite accidentally. I'm sitting in my study, working on my laptop—I'm cataloging the contents of the third shelf of books, the ones Lexy arranged on the day of her death—and I've typed in the following titles:

I Had a Dream: The Civil Rights Movement and Real Life (Mine.)
796 Ways to Say "I Love You" (Mine. I always wanted to be as spontaneous and romantic as Lexy, to be able to surprise her the way she always surprised me. So I bought this book to help plan my spontaneity. I didn't know she knew about it.)
Things I Wish I'd Known (Hers. A book of poetry.)
Strange but True: Aliens in Our Midst (Hers. She bought this book for the illustrations after a customer of hers requested an alien mask for a play.)
Forget About Yesterday and Make the Most of Today (Hers.)

You'd Better Believe It! The World's Most Famous Hoaxes and Practical Jokes (Mine.)

How to Be a Success While Doing What You Love (Hers.)

And No Pets Step on DNA (Mine. A rather silly collection of palindromes. The cover shows a laboratory full of dogs in lab coats. A sign on the wall shows a cat standing on a double helix, with a line drawn through it.)

More 10-Minute Recipes (Hers, though I often used it. It contains some surprisingly good recipes, although they seldom live up to the ten-minute promise.)

My Ántonia (Mine from college. I never read it.)

A Room of One's Own (Hers from college. I don't know if she read it or not.)

Places I'd Never Dreamed Of (Mine. A collection of travel writing.)

As I type, I'm attempting at the same time to eat a ham and cheese sandwich. It's rather awkward, and at one point, as I take a bite out of the sandwich, a morsel of cheese and a drop of mustard fall onto the letters *K* and *L* on my keyboard. I set the computer down on the floor and go to the kitchen to get a sponge, and when I return, I find Lorelei standing in front of the computer, her head bent to the keys, lapping at the space where the cheese had been. I shoo her away—who knows what damage dog saliva might do to an expensive computer?—but when I bend to wipe off the keys, I see that something quite wonderful has happened. Beneath the title of the last book I listed, Lorelei has typed a string of letters with her tongue. KKKLKLLKIK-KLMLK, she has written. And that's when it hits me, this marvelous idea, that's when it breaks on me like day: I am going to teach Lorelei to type.

It seems to me a perfect solution. Several weeks have gone by since the *wa* incident, with no further breakthroughs. Perhaps, I think, Lorelei's vocal cords are not suited to speech per se, but that doesn't mean communication isn't possible.

I begin to devise a plan. I am not expecting her to type words, of course, but it occurs to me that if I can teach her to associate the words she already knows—"ball," "out," "treat," "Lexy"—with specific visual symbols, I can then devise a special keyboard with those same symbols, and Lorelei can type an entire word with a single touch of her nose. The keys would need to be a bit bigger than usual, to allow for the wideness of her nose as well as to provide room to display symbols large enough for Lorelei to be able to "read" them. I get to work with the flash cards. I show Lorelei a card with a single wavy line. "Water," I say. "Water." Then a card with a childlike lollipop drawing of a tree. "Tree," I say. And so on. I draw Lexy as a smiling face with a curl of hair coming down each side of her head. I draw "out" with an arrow. I draw "treat" with a bone.

But this isn't enough. I have to teach her "sad." I have to teach her "fall." And "jump." I have to make her understand the difference.

In the end, I just create symbols for every word I think I might need. I can always teach her the meanings later.

For the keyboard, I decide to go see an acquaintance of mine, a man named Mike Wolfe who works in the electrical engineering department at the university. Mike has an interest in linguistics, so I think he might be willing to help me out. A former student of mine once asked Mike to help him write a program that would put together random sounds to create nonsense words for a project the student was doing on language formation. It was a rather meaningless project—in fact, as I recall, the student left the department soon afterward without receiving his degree—but I was impressed with what Mike came up with.

So I go to see Mike, and I tell him what I'm looking for. I don't tell him it's for a dog; I tell him I'm working with severely disabled children. I emphasize that several of them will need to hit the buttons with their noses. He nods respectfully and seems to believe me, but when I return to pick up the machine two weeks later, I see a cartoon, clearly cut from the campus newspaper, posted to the office door of one of Mike's colleagues in the department. It shows a dog sitting in front of a computer, tongue hanging out, with a goofy look on its face. Its paws are resting on the keyboard, and a string of nonsense words are visible on the screen. Behind the dog stands a man, looking nothing like me, I must say, peering over the dog's shoulder. "Brilliant!" the man is saying. "Don't stop now!" The cartoon's caption reads, "Arguments Against Tenure."

But the machine is everything I could have hoped for. Mike has modified an old laptop—it will be a bit slow, he tells me, but it should meet my needs. The keys are large and marked clearly with the symbols I gave him. Since he was working with a standard keyboard, the keys when pressed each type a single letter. I'll simply need to make a note of which letters result from which symbols, and I can translate what Lorelei meant to type. BNL, for example, translates to "Lexy tree fall." And so on.

I spend two weeks working with Lorelei on memorizing the visual symbols before introducing the keyboard to her. First, I show her a flash card with a particular symbol on it—the symbol for tree, say—and I repeat the word several times. Next, I shuffle the card together with two other cards, making a big show out of it, like the magician I'm trying so hard to be, and I lay the three cards faceup on the floor.

"Water, Lorelei," I say. "Where's the water? Go find the water." At first, she doesn't seem to understand what I want from her. The first time I give this order, she goes uncertainly to the corner of the room and picks up her toy giraffe in her teeth. Great, I think—now I'm making her question the meanings of words she already knows. So I begin to demonstrate what I want her to do. I cast my eyes down toward the card I want her to pick. I point to it. I bend and touch my own nose to the symbol. Eventually, she seems to understand. When she lowers her head to sniff at the card I've indicated, I praise her well.

After two weeks, she's pointing to the right card about fifty percent of the time. Not bad, considering she's choosing from *three* cards; if she'd been simply picking cards at random, I'd expect only a thirty-three percent success rate. But still not great. It occurs to me that maybe the visual cues are a problem. Sight is not her best sense. Maybe I need to assign a different scent to each key. A scratch-and-sniff keyboard. But how do I sum up how Lexy smelled to Lorelei? Rub her sweater on the keys? Spray her perfume, dab her hair gel, smear her lipstick on a palette, and mix them together? What of Lexy's own un-adorned scent, the scent beneath all those other scents she added to her body? I can't re-create that. (Oh, but if I could! If I could lift up an atomizer and spray that scent into the air!) And the smell of water? And the smell of an apple tree on an October day? Is the scent of air rushing as a person falls different from the scent of the air if that person jumps? Is the scent of the flying dust as the body hits the ground any different?

So I suppose I must stick to the visual. But today, as I work with Lorelei on the flash cards, I realize something. I have neglected to make a card for myself. I have not created a symbol to represent the concept "Paul." I suppose there has to be one. Certainly, I am a part of the story she has to tell. Or am I deluding myself? What if the story she has to tell has nothing to do with me or with Lexy but with her own puppyhood, of which I know very little? The story she chooses to tell, the one it's most important for her to get out, may not be the one I want to hear. I think again about the story of how Lorelei came to belong to Lexy. Maybe this is what Lorelei will want to tell me about: salvation from the storm, the tearing pain in her throat. Or maybe something from even before that. Does she remember her mother, her brothers and sisters? The tragedy of puppies, taken from their families, all of them, never to see each other again. This is the sadness we inflict on the beasts we love. Am I anthropomorphizing? Of course I am. It can hardly be helped. But still. Who am I to know what heart beats beneath that fur? What leg-twitching dreams project themselves behind those wide, inscrutable eyes? Does she dream of walking on big, unsteady puppy paws, of struggling to find a place to suckle alongside her siblings? Does she remember all of that, or is it like our own infancy, lost in the prelanguage mist of babyhood?

Maybe she wants to tell me about a single moment of summer grass, looking for something to chase, the feel of damp earth on bare paws. That may be what she has to tell me. The joy of muscle and bone working together to run as she chases a car. The wind blowing her ears as she sticks her head out a car window. The loneliness of the door closing, leaving her alone in the house. The patient waiting beneath the table, the smell of dinners not meant for her, the thrill of being in the right place at the right time when human fingers slip and a piece of meat falls to the floor. The drool-inducing terror of pulling up in front of the vet's office. The sweet sadness of Lexy gone, the constant vigil for her return. Seeing things happen and not knowing why. The smells of other dogs. The softness of couch cushions. The satisfying give as a pillow rips apart in her teeth. The hunt. The sun. Rolling in the dirt.

"Where's the tree, Lorelei?" I say, nodding to the cards on the floor before me. "Where's the tree?"

She noses the card that means Lexy.

"All right, girl," I say. "That's enough for now."

I am tired. I am so very tired. I gather up my cards and put them away. Then I sit down at my desk to write a letter to Wendell Hollis.

TWENTY-SIX

The night of the death-mask incident, Lexy didn't come home at all. I sat up all night waiting for her. Finally, around eight in the morning, I heard her key in the door.

She walked in looking tired and disheveled. She didn't seem surprised to see me sitting in the living room.

"Hi," she said. She wouldn't meet my eyes.

"Hi."

She just stood there, looking at the floor, her keys in her hand.

"Where have you been?" I asked.

"I drove to Delaware and back."

"Why?"

"I don't know. I just started driving. I wasn't going to come back."

"Ever?"

"Ever. I was going to just disappear."

"That's crazy, Lexy."

She laughed without smiling. "Yeah."

"What made you change your mind?"

"I started thinking about you sitting here waiting up for me. I couldn't leave you sitting here."

"Well, I wish you'd called," I said. "I was afraid . . ." I didn't finish.

"I'm sorry," she said. There was a long silence. "You're scared of me now," she finally said.

"Well, yeah, a little." I could hear my voice rising. I was angrier than I realized. I stopped and regulated my tone. "You were out of control," I said as evenly as I could. "I didn't know what you might do."

"Well, I didn't know either."

"God, Lexy," I said, and this time I couldn't keep the anger out of my voice. "Do you know how much it terrifies me to hear you talk like that? Do you know what it's been like for me, sitting here all night, not knowing if you were alive or dead?"

Finally, she raised her eyes and looked at me. I could see her face crumpling. "I'm sorry," she said. She started to cry. "I'm sorry."

I watched her stand there crying, in the middle of the room. I couldn't get up and go to her. I couldn't.

"Lexy, I think you need to get some help," I said. "It scares me when you get like this. You need to talk to someone."

She began to cry harder. "You think I'm crazy," she said.

"No, I don't think you're crazy. I just think it might help you to talk to someone."

She turned from me, still sobbing. "I shouldn't be here," she said. "I should go away."

"No," I said. "That's not what I want. I just want to talk about this."

"I don't want to talk now," she said, trying to keep her voice steady. "I'm too tired. I just want to go take a shower."

She turned and walked away. She made her back look hard and sturdy as she walked, but as soon as the bathroom door closed, I could hear her sobbing grow louder. I heard her turn the shower on. I sat on the couch for a few moments more, then got up and walked to the bathroom. I knocked on the door.

"Lexy," I called. "Let me in."

"No," she cried. "Leave me alone."

"Lexy," I said. "It's going to be all right."

"Go away," she said. "I can't look at you right now."

"Lexy, we need to talk about this."

She didn't answer me. I could hear her ragged weeping through the door.

I tried the doorknob and found it was unlocked. "I'm coming in," I said.

Lexy wasn't in the shower. She was sitting naked on the tile floor, her knees gathered up to her chin. Her face was hidden in her hands. The room was beginning to fill with steam.

The sight of her sitting so forlorn broke something inside of me. I didn't feel angry anymore.

I knelt down beside her. "Shh, Lexy," I said. "It's going to be okay."

I reached out to touch her, but she jerked away.

"Go away," she said. "I don't want you to see me. Go away." She turned her blotchy face toward the wall.

"I'm not going to go away," I said.

"Well, then I will," she said. She was on her feet in a minute, but I was right behind her. I grabbed her and folded her reluctant body into my arms.

"Let me go," she said.

"No. I will not."

She cried and struggled, but still I held her fast. I stood as strong as a tree, rooted firm to the ground. The more she pulled, the tighter I held.

"I won't let go," I said. "I will not let you go."

Her skin was hot as iron. Her skin was hot to the touch.

She let out a guttural sound, an animal noise of frustration and resistance. And still I held her fast.

"Let me go," she hissed, wriggling in my grip. She was slippery as an eel. And still I held her fast.

We stood together in the bathroom steam, with Lexy twisting and crying out and me holding her tight, until her sobs quieted and I felt her body relax. Until at last I held her still and mother-naked in my arms.

"My poor little girl," I said into her hair. "You always thought you were the elf queen, didn't you? But you're not the elf queen. Don't you see? You're Tam Lin. You're Tam Lin. And I will not let you go."

*   *   *

Later, when Lexy had calmed down enough to talk and the water in the shower had run cold, I asked her what she was going to do about the mask.

"I'm going to make another one," she said, "and I'm going to paint it exactly the same way. In spite of everything, I think I made the right choice to do it that way. If the parents don't like it, I'll make them one that's more realistic. But I think they're going to like it. I just wish I'd trusted myself from the beginning."

"Yeah," I said. "So do I."

The parents did love the mask. The first mask, the ruined one, lay untouched on the basement table for several weeks; Lexy and I walked carefully around the wreckage, neither of us quite willing to throw it away. And if the colors on the second mask weren't quite as bright, if the flowers painted across the face didn't seem to dance quite as freely in the wind as they had before, the girl's parents never knew the difference.

TWENTY-SEVEN

The letter I write to Wendell Hollis is fairly straightforward. I know from everything I've read about Hollis that he considers himself to be a noble figure, a martyr to science. I know that if I hope to receive an answer from him, I'll have to play up to that image. Flatter him, I think. Show that you believe him to be a scholar, that you take his work seriously. Don't appear to be scared off by his methods. Don't give any hint of the revulsion you feel at the sound of his name.

Here's what I come up with.

Dear Mr. Hollis,

You don't know me, but I am very interested in the research you have done. As a fellow scholar in the area of canine language study, I feel I have much to

learn from you. I have a dog named
Lorelei, a Rhodesian Ridgeback, that
I've been working with for several
months with only minimal success.
Can you give me any tips? How did
you become interested in this topic?
Do you have any plans to continue af-
ter you get out? Any advice you might
have would be appreciated.
   Sincerely,
   Paul Iverson

To my surprise, barely two weeks pass
before I receive a response. When the letter
appears in my mailbox, with Hollis's correc-
tional facility listed as the return address, I
feel some sudden trepidation at what I've
done, a feeling that only increases as I read
what Hollis has written.

Dear Paul Iverson,
   I get a lot of letters, not many positive I can tell you, so yours stood out.
I'm glad to hear my legacy lives on
while I waste away in here and I'm glad
there are serious scholars such as
yourself still working on the Dog Problem. Tell me more about what you're

doing with Lorelei. Have you started the operations yet? I'm sure a learned man like you knows she'll have to be modified if you want to get results. I'm sending along some of the diagrams I used in my own surgeries. If you send me a picture of the dog you're using that will help too.

Here's how I got interested dogs were always looking at me. I wanted to know what they were thinking when they looked at me like that. There was this one little dog that lived next door to me, wouldn't stop barking. It was like he was yelling all the time without saying anything just noise. Day and night and when I'd see that little dog in the hallway with the old lady that owned him, that little ratdog would pull on his leash just for the pleasure of jumping at me and barking. And I thought What the hell's your problem? You got something to say to me you say it. Well, one day the old lady drops dead, and I see all these cops in the hall, and I say what's gonna happen to her poor little puppydog? Can't you just hear me, I put on a good show. So they say we're taking him down to the pound and I start laying it on about how me and the dog are such good buddies and please can't you let me take him I'll give him a good home. It's what she would have wanted, she always said If anything happens to me, take care of my sweet little dog. So I lay it on real thick and the cops say okay cause this little yappy mutt's driving them all nuts anyway. So I took that dog and the first thing I do is I build him a soundproof room. Well, actually, I just made some changes to this spare bedroom I had but it worked pretty well. And I put him down in the middle of the room and I say okay let's see what you've been trying to say to me all this time. Let's find out what you been trying to tell me all this time. And the rest is history, ha ha. He was a cute little guy, I got to admit it, but I didn't let that get in the way. I had some real serious work to do with him, and I wasn't going to let anything get in the way of my contribution to science.

So that's my story. Now you gotta tell me yours. I gave your name and address to a friend of mine, calls himself Remo, who lives in your area. He runs a group, kind of an underground club, for people who share our interests. He will be getting in touch with you.

Write back soon. We men of science have to stick together.

Yours,
Wendell Hollis

Attached to the letter are the diagrams Hollis has promised. Horrible sketches of dogs cut open, their bodies vivisected, their faces taken apart and put back together in entirely the wrong way. There's a drawing of a dog's brain, the different parts labeled with names like "speech node" and "hunger center" and "home of dog aggressiveness." There's a long handwritten explanation of how a human jaw might be attached to a dog's skull, "if you can lay your hands on one without getting caught."

I put down the papers, horrified. Break down the words *Wendell Hollis,* and he reveals himself to be made up of *lies* and *sin* and *Hell. Slew* and *woe.* He is *low.* He is *swine.* What am I doing corresponding with this maniac? And who is this Remo who will be "getting in touch with me"? I shudder at the thought.

And yet—how can I say "and yet," you're wondering, with all this carnage dia-grammed before me, with this madman's ravings fresh in my mind? But this is where my mind takes me—and yet, I think, it can-not be disputed that Wendell Hollis has succeeded where I have failed. A whole courtroom full of people heard Dog J speak his piece. I look at Lorelei dozing on the couch, her body whole and untouched. No, I think, I will never resort to his methods. I will never do anything to hurt my dog. But what harm can it do to see what this Remo person has to say?

TWENTY-EIGHT

I was glad when the death-mask business was over. Except that, as it turned out, it wasn't over at all. The dead girl's parents were so pleased with their mask that they put it on prominent display in their home and showed it off to all their friends, several of whom they'd met through a support group for families of cancer patients. As a result, Lexy started getting requests for death masks rather frequently. After the fourth or fifth one, she got a call from a reporter who'd seen one of her masks at a funeral; the dead man had been in a car accident, his body too mangled to allow for an open casket, so instead, his family displayed Lexy's mask on top of the coffin. The reporter was haunted by the mask, he told Lexy, so ghostly and tangible at the same time, and he wanted to do a story for the paper. The headline was ARTIST FINDS BEAUTY IN DEATH, and the story hailed Lexy as a pioneer in a new "trend" in memorializing the dead. The reporter called her work "eerily delicate" and said that with each mask she succeeded in capturing "the substance and texture of grief itself, while still managing to celebrate life as it was lived by her subjects." It was a glowing article, accompanied by several photographs of the masks (and one of Lexy herself—look how lovely she was!), and it started a flurry of interest in her work. She received so many requests for death masks that she was forced to put aside her other projects, her vibrant theatrical masks, her gaudy Mardi Gras faces, for how could she say no to a grief-sick mother or lover in order to work on something as trivial as a summer-stock play?

Eventually, she began to advertise herself as a maker of death masks. She liked doing them, she told me; it fulfilled her to see how moved people were by them, the solace it seemed to give. "It's important work," she said. "People need this. It helps them. It helps the living." It is often said that when a loved one passes away, it helps to see the body lying still and dead. It helps make it real. People whose loved ones have disappeared, never to turn up again, they suffer forever. Lexy believed that by fixing her gaze upon the moment of death, she was helping the world's survivors carry on with the business of living.

She began leaving her card with funeral directors, and she took out ads in the obituary section of the paper. She visited the dying in hospitals, the ones who knew they were going to die and had reached some acceptance of it. And she did not lack for work.

The masks she made were beautiful, I have to admit it. She took great care in designing each one. She met with families, listened to their stories, took notes. It did them good, the survivors, to talk. She never said "the deceased" the way the funeral home people did. She said, "Tell me about your mother. Tell me what you remember." She asked leave to surprise them, to come up with something unexpected. Always with a promise that she'd make a new one if they weren't pleased. But that only happened once.

Her goal was to figure out the one image that would forever call to mind the person who had been lost. Not just what that person's life was, but who he was, summed up in a drawing, an emblem, a single scene. A person's life written across his face, as personal as a tattoo. Nothing so obvious as golf clubs for a golfer or a caduceus for a physician. Her paintings had the quality of a dream. The dream-life of the dead. She painted shadowy figures, dark against the bright sky. She painted pastoral scenes, trees on hills, birds in nests. A cityscape, a skyline. Constellations and shooting stars. A name in graffiti. There was a joy in what she painted. A nudge to remember the good things. A young girl dancing and spinning across the face of an old woman. For a pilot, middle-aged—dead of a heart attack, not a plane crash—she painted not an airplane but a view of the world from above, with the words *Call it Heaven or call it flying* written among the stars. For another man, an AIDS activist who had succumbed to the disease, a picture of the virus itself, unfathomably pretty for something so deadly, surrounded by scenes from the man's life. For an old woman who had been a seamstress, a patchwork design covering the entire face, each square painted in the texture of a fabric from a loved article of clothing—here a wedding gown, there a baby blanket. And always, in every mask, the face hidden beneath the painting, adding its poignant topography.

Lexy took special care with the suicides. She had two of them. The first was a man in his fifties. He had been depressed for a long time, but his family thought he had recently shown signs of getting better. It was July when he died, but after his death, his family found a closetful of Christmas gifts, wrapped and waiting for them. For this man, Lexy painted a winter scene, peaceful but impenetrable: snowdrifts, bare trees, icicles like shards of glass. A tiny figure stood in the foreground, looking upward; if you followed his gaze, you would see that, off in the distance, just barely visible, there was a tiny cottage with a light in its window. The man had a long road ahead of him—the steep hill he would have to climb looked almost insurmountable—but he could see that light and warmth were not so far away.

The second suicide was a teenage girl. Her name was Jennifer. Lexy met with her parents, their faces blank with shock. They seemed hardly able to tell Lexy what their daughter was like; each detail, each thing they thought they knew about her, had been called into question, and they wondered now if they had really known her at all. They gave Lexy the girl's diary to read. Lexy read it in a single night and returned it to the parents in time for them to bury it with their daughter. They didn't read it themselves. They didn't want to know what it said.

I don't know what Lexy learned from the diary, if anything. She wouldn't talk to me about it. Usually when Lexy took a job, she would tell me about the person she was working on. She would tell me what she had learned of their lives, and she would discuss her ideas for the design of the mask. But not this one. She seemed to carry this girl's story inside her. Sometimes, months later, when she seemed sad and I would ask her what was wrong, she would say, "Oh, I was just thinking about Jennifer."

For Jennifer, Lexy painted a mask upon a mask. At first glance, it appeared as if she had simply painted Jennifer's own face, smiling. But when you looked closer, you could see that the smiling face was itself a mask; there was a faint outline, shield shaped, like those happy-and-sad faces used to symbolize the theater, drawn around the painted features, and painted ribbons extended from each side, as if to hold the mask in place. Underneath it all, Jennifer's own features stood in somber contrast to the bright, bright smile and the wide, happy eyes.

It was a masterwork. But it was not what Jennifer's parents were hoping for. As far as I can remember, this was the only time that Lexy's clients refused the mask she offered them. It made them angry to see it, she told me. Jennifer's mother cried, and Jennifer's father actually yelled at Lexy. "This is not my daughter," he told her.

She agreed to make a replacement mask. The new mask was very pretty but not particularly substantive. It showed a swarm of butterflies taking flight. There was a feeling of lightness about it, of being freed from the gravity of the earth. There were bright colors and fluffy clouds. It was just what the parents wanted.

Lexy kept the first mask. She hung it on the wall above her worktable, and sometimes when I went downstairs to see what she was doing or to say hello, I would find her sitting on the couch, staring at the mask of the smiling girl.

TWENTY-NINE

In a strange coincidence, the day after I receive Wendell Hollis's letter, Hollis's name is in the news again. It seems that Dog J has disappeared.

After the trial, after Wendell Hollis went to prison, Dog J was adopted by one of the policemen who rescued him in the raid on Hollis's apartment. The policeman received many offers to show off Dog J (or Hero, as he was now known) on talk shows and at state fairs, but he declined them all. "This dog has been exploited enough," he said. "I just want to give him a quiet life."

But now Hero has vanished from the man's Brooklyn apartment. The police officer had gone to work as usual, leaving Hero asleep on the couch, and when he returned home on his lunch hour to walk him, the front door was wide open and the dog was gone. The door showed signs of forced entry, and the policeman's TV and stereo were missing as well. As far as anyone can tell, the dog must have slipped out the door while the intruder was carrying out the stolen goods. An enormous search effort is in progress, but so far there has been no luck. All over the city, signs have been posted, asking people to be on the lookout for a four-year-old yellow Lab with the power of speech. "At least," the grief-struck police officer was quoted as saying, "at least he'll be able to ask for help."

It's on the day this news story breaks that Matthew Rice and his wife, Eleanor, come knocking at my door. I'm lying on the couch when I hear the knock, watching TV and hoping for more news on Dog J, and I almost don't answer the door. It's early afternoon, and I'm still in my pajamas and robe. But when I stand up to peek out through the closed blinds and see who it is, I stumble over a pile of books on the floor and let out an involuntary oath so loud that I figure I can't possibly pretend I'm not home.

I open the door to find Matthew and

Eleanor standing there, smiling brightly. Matthew is carrying a stack of Tupperware containers and baking pans covered in foil, and Eleanor is holding a large bucket filled with cleaning supplies. I wonder for a moment if I'm expecting them, if they called and said they were coming, and I've somehow forgotten.

"Hello," I say tentatively.

"Hi, Paul," says Eleanor warmly. "I hope you'll forgive our barging in on you like this, but we haven't had much luck reaching you by phone." It's true that I haven't been answering the phone lately. I've gotten a little bit sick of my mother and my sister calling, expressing their well-meaning concern. I've been letting the machine pick up, and it's been a while since I've listened to my messages.

"Oh," I say. "No problem." Just then, Lorelei comes trotting to the door to see what's going on. She pushes past me and begins to sniff first at Eleanor's legs, then at Matthew's, looking for the source of the food aromas that are emanating from the containers in Matthew's arms. I grab her collar and pull her back.

"Down, girl," I say. "Do you want me to

put her in the back? You're allergic, aren't you?" I ask Eleanor.

"Don't worry about it," she says, setting down her bucket and stooping to pet the dog. "I took a pill. I'll be fine."

"So what brings you by?" I ask. I'm aware that I should invite them in, but I'm embarrassed to let them see the state of the house.

"Well, we talked to Maura after she came by," Matthew says. "It sounded like you could use some help."

"Help?" I say, stiffening.

"Oh, just a little friendly help around the house," Eleanor says quickly. "I've brought you some food to stick in your freezer. There's a lasagne and some chili and a pot of navy bean soup."

"And macaroni and cheese," Matthew adds. "With ham in it, like Eleanor made for the Christmas potluck the year before last. I remember you said you liked it."

The list of food makes my stomach ache with hunger. It's been weeks since I've been to the grocery store. I've been eating mostly crackers and dry cereal. There have been days when I've thought about snacking on handfuls of dog food from the economy-size bag in the garage.

Eleanor continues talking. "And I'm going to roll up my sleeves and do a little cleaning while you and Matthew have a nice visit."

"Well, that's awfully kind of you," I say, "but I'm not sure this is the best time. . . ."

Eleanor smiles at me and reaches out to touch my cheek, my rough, stubble-ridden cheek. "Let us in, Paul," she says. "There's nothing to be embarrassed about." The gentleness of her touch nearly brings tears to my eyes. "I made you a pan of those peppermint brownies you like."

I look at the floor and nod. I feel humbled, I feel like a small child. "All right," I say, and I step aside for them to pass.

If they feel any revulsion on entering, they don't let on. "Good," Eleanor says. "Now why don't you go shower and get dressed, while I heat up some soup for you."

"I don't know if there are any clean pots," I say. "Or bowls."

"I'll take care of it," she says.

By the time I emerge from my bedroom, clean and dressed, the house already looks better. Eleanor has opened all the curtains, and the rooms are filled with light. She's cleared the dirty dishes off the kitchen table and set a place for me. I sit down and she sets before me a bowl of steaming soup and a plate of buttered toast. I eat ravenously.

Afterward, Matthew and I sit on the living room couch with mugs of fresh coffee and a plate of brownies in front of us. Eleanor has vacuumed the rug, and she's cleared away the piles of clutter from the table and the floor. She's opened a window, and the room feels fresh, airy.

"So how's your work going?" Matthew asks me. He even manages to meet my eyes as he says it.

"It's great," I begin, then stop. "Well, it's okay. Honestly, it's hard to say if I'm making any progress." I tell him about Lorelei's adventures in typing.

He nods thoughtfully. "That's an interesting approach," he says. "You know, I read once that Thomas Mann's daughter tried something similar. She had her dog composing poetry on a typewriter."

"Really?" I say. "Anything good?"

Matthew shrugs. "About what you'd expect, I think. Or what I'd expect, anyway." He smiles. "I think eventually the dog rebelled and wouldn't go anywhere near the typewriter."

"Yeah," I say. "They don't much like typing. It's hard on the nose."

We're quiet for a moment, both of us looking at Lorelei, snoring on the carpet in front of us. From the other room, I hear the washing machine click on.

"You know, Paul," Matthew says, "I'm not quite sure I've ever fully understood this project of yours. I guess I'm not exactly clear on what you're hoping to learn."

"Well, I suppose . . ." I falter for a moment, trying to remember the scholarly goals I outlined when I began. "I suppose I'm hoping to find out whether canine-human communication is possible."

Matthew shakes his head. "No," he says. "I mean, what are you hoping to learn about Lexy?"

I look away. I've never mentioned to Matthew that my project has anything to do with Lexy. I hadn't realized my motives were so transparent.

"I mean, that's it, isn't it, Paul?" Matthew asks when I don't say anything. "You're hoping to find out something about Lexy?"

I nod. "After she died," I begin. "There were some incongruities."

"What do you mean, 'incongruities'?"

I tell him about what I found, the steak bone and supermarket wrappings, the re-configuration of books on the shelf. "Even the fact that she was in the tree," I say. "That's an incongruity. What was she doing up there?"

"You think Lexy may have killed herself," he says.

I look away and try to concentrate on a painting hanging on the opposite wall. I don't like hearing the words spoken out loud.

"And you think Lorelei can help you find out the truth?"

I look at Matthew. I look him square in the eyes. "She's a witness," I say. "Don't you see? She's the only one who knows for sure."

He nods slowly. "You know, Paul," he says, "the loss of a spouse is a very difficult thing to deal with. Have you thought, maybe, about talking to someone? A pro-fessional? Someone who could offer you some help?"

I try to smile. "I have all the help I need," I say. "I have Lorelei."

Matthew sighs. "Okay," he says. "Okay." He pauses. "Well, you know you're always welcome back at work. It might do you good to come back. Even half-time."

"No," I say firmly. "I have my hands full."

"All right," he says. "Well, think about it, anyway."

We sit silent for a few moments. Lorelei wakes abruptly from her sleep and turns to gnaw at a sudden itch near the base of her tail.

"Have you heard about this dognapping case?" Matthew asks. "That dog, Hero?"

I nod. "Dog J," I say.

"Right." He laughs awkwardly. "I have to admit," he says, "that I was half afraid I'd come here and find out you were the one hiding that dog."

"Well, I certainly wish I'd thought of it first." Matthew gives me a searching look. "I'm kidding," I say. "I haven't turned criminal just yet."

"No, of course not." He leans forward to pick up a brownie. "What a lunatic, eh? The guy who did that to that dog."

I look around guiltily. My letter from Wendell Hollis was on the coffee table when Matthew and Eleanor arrived, but it appears that Eleanor has cleared it away with everything else.

"Insane," I say. "It's a terrible case. But you can't argue with his results."

Matthew looks at me warily.

"I mean, there you have it," I say. "There's the proof that I'm not crazy. A real live talking dog."

"If that's really what he is."

"What do you mean? People have heard him talk. A whole courtroom heard him talk."

He shrugs. "Parlor tricks," he says. "Or wishful thinking. Whole courtrooms in Salem were convinced they'd seen witchcraft performed." I must look stricken, because he softens. "Well, who knows?" he says. "Anything's possible. Maybe it's all true."

"It is," I say. "It has to be."

We sit and talk for a while longer, with Matthew filling me in on the latest department gossip. By the time Eleanor's done cleaning, the house gleams. She's washed the floors and polished the bathroom fixtures, cleaned out the refrigerator and remade my bed with fresh sheets. She's gathered up the clothes from my bedroom floor and turned them into neat piles of fluffy, clean laundry. The house smells like lemons and pine.

"Thank you," I say, kissing her cheek. "Thank you so much."

"Any time," she says. "All you have to do is ask."

"Keep in touch," Matthew says. "Take care of yourself."

I stand in the doorway and wave as they drive off. Then I turn and go back inside my shining house.

"Come on, Lorelei," I say. "Time to practice our typing."

THIRTY

I don't have to wait long to hear from Hollis's friend Remo. Five days after Hollis's letter arrives, I find a note in my mailbox. It hasn't been mailed; apparently this man I've never met, this man who's been referred to me by a psychopath, has been to my house. The note is handwritten on lined notebook paper. It reads as follows:

Dear Paul,
   I've done some checking up on you, and it doesn't appear that you're a cop or anything, so I decided to trust Wendell's recommendation and get in touch with you. We're always glad to get new members. We're having our monthly meeting on Saturday night at 7 o'clock. Come a little early, say around

6—that way, I can show you around the facility. Hope to see you then.

Yours,

Remo and The Cerberus Society

P.S. And bring your dog. We want to see what she can do.

I read the letter with some uneasiness. What is this "facility" he's talking about? Am I getting myself into something I might not want to be involved in? And what do they want with Lorelei? Will I be putting her in danger if I bring her? Underneath these fears, another concern begins to take shape, a concern that has more to do with my own vanity than Lorelei's safety: If I bring her with me, what will I be able to show them, for all my months of hard work? Lorelei poking at random keys on a key-board? Lorelei picking out the wrong flash card from the three I offer? If I tell my pa-thetic story about the time she almost said *wa*, what will they think of me? I could fake it, I suppose, rub meat on the keys I want her to push. But what would I gain from that?

There's a map enclosed with the note, with directions to the building where the meeting will be held. It looks to me as though the "facility" is an ordinary house in a neighborhood not far from where I live. I get in my car and take a drive past. It's a small brick house with a neatly trimmed lawn. It doesn't look like the kind of place that might contain a basement laboratory or a soundproofed shed where unspeakable experiments might be conducted. We never know, do we, what our neighbors might be doing behind their fences, what love affairs and bloody rituals might be taking place right next door? The world is a more interesting place than we ever think.

But back to the question at hand: Should I go to this meeting? Will they hit me over the head, spike my drink, take my dog away from me? Or will it be like any other meeting—speakers, perhaps, a group discussion, someone jotting down the minutes, coffee and refreshments to follow? The truth is, of course—and I suppose you knew this already—the truth is that I want to go. I'm curious. An underground society of canine linguists right in my very hometown? So close to my house that I could actually walk to their meetings? How can I resist? And the prospect of conversation with other people, people who won't look at me as if I've lost my mind when I speak of what I've been working on, well, it fills me with excitement. It seems to me just now that I might find I have more in common with these people than I do with any of my so-called colleagues at the university.

And so it is that on this balmy Saturday night I've showered and shaved, clipped Lorelei's leash to her collar, and set off to join the Cerberus Society.

When Lorelei and I reach Remo's house, I can see that the driveway is full and the street is packed with cars. It certainly looks like somebody's having a party. I find a parking space and let Lorelei out of the car. She trots happily along next to me until I start to lead her up the front walk; then something strange happens. She stops and refuses to go any farther. I pull and pull, but she resists.

"Come on, girl," I say. "What's the matter?"

As I struggle with the dog—she does, after all, weigh more than eighty pounds, and she's pulling back with all her strength—the front door of the house opens, and a man steps out onto the porch. He looks to be about my age, maybe a little older. He's a heavy man with long white hair and a full beard. He reminds me of a king in a pack of playing cards. When Lorelei sees him, she begins to bark.

"Hi, there," he says. "Having some trouble?"

"A little bit," I say. "She's not usually like this. I'm Paul, by the way."

"That's what I figured," he says. "I'm Remo."

Remo comes down the front steps and walks over to us. Lorelei shrinks away from him and tries to hide behind my legs. She's still barking, but it's a different kind of bark. I recognize it as the one I've categorized as Frightened Bark #1.

Remo kneels down beside Lorelei and takes hold of her head. Lorelei twists her face toward his hand and snarls, making a move as if to bite him. I'm horrified, but Remo acts quickly, grabbing her snout in one hand and snapping her mouth shut. With his other hand, he fingers a spot just behind her left ear. He parts the fur and exposes the skin beneath. I lean over to see what he's doing, and I can see that there's a

tiny red dot there. I've never noticed it before; I've never thought to look.

"Look at that," says Remo. "She's one of
ours."

I stare at him, then look back at the dot
with a profound sense of unease. "What *is*
that?" I ask.

"It's a tattoo," says Remo. He releases
Lorelei and stands up. Lorelei retreats behind me, pulling her leash across the backs
of my legs. "We do it to all the puppies we
use. This one must've gotten away. Sometimes they do."

"I don't understand," I say. "We've had
Lorelei since she was a puppy."

"Well, it looks like we had her first. The
dot doesn't lie." He gives me a toothy smile.
"This one must've gotten out early. Let me
think, now—seems to me we had a litter of
Ridgebacks maybe seven or eight years
ago, and there might've been a pup or two
who ran. That sound about right to you?
Seven or eight years?"

"Yeah," I say. My head is fairly spinning
with the import of what he's telling me.
"That sounds about right."

"Thought she was making a clean break,"
Remo says, "but look where she ended up."

He laughs deeply. "Welcome back, girl," he says to Lorelei. "Welcome back to the fold."

I start to back away. "You know, I'm not so sure this is a good idea. Lorelei seems upset. I've never seen her like this. I think I should take her home."

"Nonsense," he says. "We're old friends. Isn't that right, girl?" He extends a hand toward Lorelei, as if to pet her. She shrinks away.

"Well, I'll tell you what," he says. "She does seem a little out of sorts. How about we put her in the back kennels while you come to the meeting? Let her calm down a little. She'll be okay there. You can pick her up afterwards."

I look at Lorelei, cowering behind me. She's terrified. I shouldn't have come here. And to think that this is the secret of Lorelei's puppyhood. This is what she was running from when she came wet and bloody to Lexy's porch. Who knows what kind of horror she endured here before escaping? I should just take her home and never come back. I should call the cops on these people.

Remo sees me hesitating. "I think you might be interested in staying," he says, lowering his voice. "Tonight's a very special meeting. We've got a speaker you might like to hear. A speaker who's not exactly human, if you catch my drift."

I stare at him. "You don't mean—"

He smiles that wide smile again. "That's right," he says. "We've got Dog J."

THIRTY-ONE

I stare at Remo. "Dog J?" I say. "He's here?"

Remo smiles something close to a smirk. "You got it," he says. "So what do you say we put your dog away in the kennels and show you around?"

I look down at Lorelei, still cowering behind me. Should I just take her home and forget I've ever seen this place? I imagine the evening ahead of me, sitting quietly at home with Lorelei, knowing that only a few blocks away, a group of men are gathered to hear a dog speak. I don't think I could bear it. Lately, I have to admit it, I've begun to lose faith in my project. I've begun to wonder if I'm wasting my time. It would be a great boost to my morale to see the living proof that all my efforts have not been in vain. To see that it *is* possible, after all. What hope it would give me! I look up at Remo's house, ordinary and unprepossessing as it is. Somewhere in that house, the world's only known talking dog is waiting, waiting to tell us what he has to say. How can I not stay for that?

"I'll tell you what," I say to Remo. "I'll just run her home. It won't take me a minute."

"You sure?" he says. "The kennels are just around back. I'm sure she'd be perfectly comfy."

I look down at my frightened dog and feel a surge of protectiveness. "No," I say. "She'll be better off at home." I kneel down to comfort her. "Shh, girl," I say. I can feel her trembling. "It's going to be all right. What a good girl." Remo's looking at me strangely.

"You talk to her like that, do you?" he says. "Well, I guess we've all got our methods."

"Come on, girl," I say, leading Lorelei to the sidewalk. She bounds ahead of me, panting with relief. She pulls me all the way to the car. I open the back door, and Lorelei leaps in. "Don't worry, girl," I say to her softly as I crack the window open. "I'll take you home." She settles herself on the seat and rests her head on her paws.

I drive home quickly and deposit Lorelei in the backyard. I give her a quick pat and dump a small pile of biscuits at her feet to apologize for the evening's ordeal, then I head back to Remo's. The street is packed with cars by the time I return. I end up parking two blocks away. As I walk toward the house, I can see that Remo is sitting on his porch, waiting for me.

"You get her all settled in?" he asks as I head up the front walk.

"Yeah," I say. "She's fine."

"All right, then," he says. "Let's show you around."

He leads me to the rear of the house. "We don't get too many newcomers," he says to me as we walk. "And we have to be pretty careful about outsiders. You never know when somebody might get skittish and call the police. But like I said in my note, we checked you out a little. And you come recommended by Wendell Hollis—can't do much better than that."

I try to return his smile. "Right," I say.

We're standing in front of a large outbuilding in the yard. I can hear barking and yelping coming from inside. It's a terrible noise.

"This would be the kennel," he says.

"Don't the neighbors ever complain?" I ask.

"Well, they used to," he says. "But I made things pretty unpleasant for them, until they all either just shut up or moved." He laughs. "Yep, I made things pretty unpleasant. The houses on either side of this one are owned by Society members now, so we don't get too many complaints."

He swings open the door to the building and ushers me inside. I see that we're in a long, narrow corridor with rows of cages on either side. The cages are filled with dogs of various breeds, most of them two to a cage. There must be thirty dogs in here. Most of them are pathetically skinny, and some of them have bandages on different parts of their bodies. The cages haven't been cleaned anytime recently, and the smell is overwhelming. I'm very glad I didn't agree to leave Lorelei here.

"These are the dogs we're currently working with," he says. Dogs on either side of us fling themselves against the bars of their cages, yowling at us as we walk past.

"They don't seem very happy," I say.

"Oh, they're fine. They're just looking for their dinner."

We walk back out into the yard, and Remo closes the kennel door behind us. "The meeting's going to be upstairs in the main part of the house," he says, "but we've still got a little time. Why don't I take you down to the lab and show you around?"

I take a deep breath. "Sure," I say. "Sounds good."

There's a cellar door that opens into the yard, the slanty kind of door that opens outward to reveal stairs leading down to the basement. I remember suddenly that my grandmother's house had a cellar door like this and that I used to like to slide down it when I was very small. Remo opens the door and gestures to the stairs inside. "After you," he says.

I walk down the stairs cautiously. It's dark until Remo flicks the light switch. I'm prepared for any number of horrible things, but it looks pretty much like a regular basement. There's a large table in the middle of the room, a sink in the corner, and a row of cupboards along one of the walls. I flinch slightly when I notice a display of knives and surgical equipment laid out on the counter next to the sink.

"This is where it all happens," Remo says. "Now, once you've joined the Society and paid your dues, you'll have access to all this. I assume you're working out of your house now?"

I nod.

"Well, you'll probably find this a little easier. The room's soundproofed, and we've got a good supply of tools and ether, suture materials, just about everything you need."

I nod again. "Great," I say, in a hollow voice.

Remo continues. "Now, it didn't look to me like your bitch has been altered in any way. Am I right about that? You haven't started operating on her yet?"

"Uh, no. See, my background is in linguistics, and I thought I'd try a nonsurgical approach first."

Remo looks skeptical. "What have you been doing with her, then?"

"Well, lately I've been working with flash cards, trying to get her to associate certain words with a set of pictorial symbols I've devised," I begin. "I've had a special typewriter made up with these symbols, and I'm trying to get her to the point where she can type a sentence with her nose." I stop talking. It sounds ridiculous, even to me.

Remo's smirking. "Yeah, and how's that working out for you?" he asks.

"Well, I admit it's going a bit slower than I'd like."

Remo laughs. "Yeah, I thought so. Listen, you're not the first one to try going at it from that angle, but here at the Cerberus Society we pretty much believe that there's no progress without surgery. If you decide to join, you'll also have access to our library"—here he points to a corner of the basement that has a couple of bookshelves lined with three-ring notebooks and veterinary textbooks—"and I think after you do some reading, you'll probably come to the same conclusion for yourself."

Remo walks over to a filing cabinet that's next to the "library." He opens a drawer and pulls out some papers. He hands them to me.

"Here's our membership packet. You can look it over and let me know after the meeting whether or not you'll be joining us. Dues are three hundred dollars a year, which may sound a little steep, but it goes toward covering the cost of our medical supplies, feeding the dogs, and paying for whatever guest speakers we have." He smiles. "Of course, we didn't have to pay tonight's speaker anything. We'll give him his honorarium in kibble."

I force a smile. "Okay," I say. "I'll look these over."

Remo checks his watch. "Well, we'd better be getting upstairs," he says. He walks toward the staircase, then stops and turns around. "I forgot to ask you," he says. "Are you married?"

"No," I say. "I'm a widower."

"Well, I'm sorry to hear that, but it's probably for the best. We've found that most women don't seem to understand the work we're doing here. We have a little saying around here: 'The only bitches we allow are the ones that bark.' " He laughs deeply.

I look away. Remo sees I'm not laughing.

"Well," he says. "Meaning no disrespect to your late wife."

"No," I say. "Of course not."

Remo leads me up the cellar stairs and back out into the yard. I listen to the noise coming from the kennels, and I feel a little bit sick.

Remo and I walk around to the front of the house and up the steps. Remo opens the front door, and we walk into a little entrance hall. To the right is the living room, and I can see that there are several rows of chairs set up, facing a podium. Funny to think they've provided Dog J with a podium. There are about twenty men standing in groups, talking.

"Come on," Remo says. "I'll introduce you."

He leads me over to a group of three men. He claps one of them on the back, a big, bulky man with thinning hair, holding a clipboard.

"Lucas," he says, "I want you to meet Paul. He's thinking about joining our little society. Paul, Lucas here is our treasurer. He's the one you'll be giving your check to."

"No, give it to me," says another man, with red hair and very white skin. "I'll take your money." The men all laugh.

"That's Aaron," Remo says. "Don't pay any attention to him."

"And don't give him your money, whatever you do," adds the third man, a short, mousy guy with big eyes. More laughter. "I'm Tom," he adds.

I shake the men's hands. "Paul here's got himself a Ridgeback bitch," Remo says. "Turns out she used to be one of ours."

"A runner?" Tom asks.

"Yup," Remo says. "But they all end up back here sooner or later, don't they?" He turns to Lucas. "You were working with that litter of Ridgebacks seven or eight years ago, weren't you?"

"That's right, I was. I guess this must be my prodigal daughter. She out in the kennel?"

"Nope," Remo says. "Paul took her back home. She seemed a mite upset to be here." The men laugh. "Paul here was real concerned for her feelings." Remo and Lucas exchange a look I can't read. "Maybe he'll let you take a gander at her sometime, if you ask real nice."

"I'd enjoy that," Lucas says. "Perhaps I'll come by sometime. Let's see, you're on"— he consults his clipboard—"you're on Turner Street, is that right?"

"Yes, that's right," I say. I don't like these men knowing where I live.

Remo sees the expression on my face

and smiles. "I told you, we can't be too careful," he says.

"Of course," I say.

"So Paul," Lucas says. "Have you done any throat work on her yet?"

"No," I say. "Um, not yet."

"Paul's kind of new to all this," Remo tells them. "He's been trying a *'nonsurgical approach.'*" The other three men burst into laughter.

"Oh, you're one of *those,* are you?" Lucas says to me.

I stand there uncomfortably, not sure what to say. Remo claps me on the arm. "Don't take offense, buddy," he says. "We're just joshing you."

"We've all been there," says Tom, the mousy man. "I started out that way, too. Spent three years trying to get my beagle to say 'Mary Had a Little Lamb.' Finally occurred to me that he was designed wrong, and I wasn't going to get a word out of him unless I fixed him."

"And how did that work?" I ask uneasily.

"Well, that one didn't make it through. But I've got one I'm working on now that's able to make a *k* sound."

"We're all making good progress," Remo

tells me. "But none of us has had the kind of success Wendell had. That man is a genius." The other men murmur assent.

"That's why we're all so excited about our guest of honor tonight," Lucas says. "Speaking of which"—he glances at his watch—"I think it's about time to get this show on the road."

"Take a seat," Remo says to me. "I'm gonna go see if his canine highness is ready."

"I'll excuse myself, too," Lucas says. "I've got a few things I want to take care of before the festivities." He and Remo walk off into the next room, and Tom goes to tell the other men that the meeting's about to start. Aaron and I find seats next to each other.

"So how'd you get into this?" Aaron asks me.

I hesitate, unsure if I want to tell him the truth. But what other story would be plausible? "My wife passed away last fall," I say. "And our dog Lorelei was the only one there when it happened. I guess . . . I guess I just wanted to find out what she saw."

I feel myself blushing at the ludicrousness of it, but Aaron just nods.

"That's not too far off from my story," he

says. "I had some suspicions that my wife—my ex-wife, I should say—was cheating on me. I figured that the only one I could trust to tell me the truth was her poodle, Fluffer." He smiles ruefully. "Always hated that name."

"And did . . . Fluffer tell you?"

"She didn't have to. I came home one day and found my wife in bed with the other guy. She left and took Fluffer with her. But by that time, I'd already met up with these guys"—he waves his hand to include everyone in the room—"and it was too late. I was hooked on the idea."

I nod. This is a very strange group I've wandered into. But, in a way, I'm one of them.

The meeting begins with a brief greeting from a man named Jeff who seems to be the secretary. He reads a few announcements, then goes through the minutes of the last meeting. It feels just as ordinary and routine as any meeting I've ever been to, except for the vaguely sinister details that keep popping up: Jeff announces that a veterinary textbook has gone missing from the library and asks that it be returned as soon as possible; he reminds us that proper cleaning of surgical instruments is one of the conditions of membership. A man in the audience raises his hand and announces that he's found a place that sells cheap dog food in bulk; another member announces that one of his dogs is pregnant, if anyone's looking for puppies. I'm feeling more and more uncomfortable being here. I look at my watch. We've been sitting here almost twenty minutes.

Just then a hush falls over the room as Remo and Lucas return. They're carrying a large dog crate between them, covered with a dark cloth. They set the crate down carefully, and Remo walks up to the podium. Jeff steps away and takes a seat in the front row.

"Good evening, gentlemen," Remo says into the microphone. "And thank you, Jeff. This is a proud night for the Cerberus Society. It was about eleven years ago that I first made the acquaintance of a man named Wendell Hollis. I was nothing but an amateur then, trying the odd experiment here and there with a stray mutt I'd picked up at the pound. But meeting Wendell Hollis changed my life. Never had I met a man with such clarity of purpose, such unflinching devotion to a cause. He was a visionary in this new field, a true visionary, and everything I know I've learned from him. Unfortunately, as we all know, Wendell can't be here tonight, due to the ignorance and shortsightedness of the United States penal system. But we have something even better. We have Wendell Hollis's crowning achievement. Some people call him Hero, but I choose to call him by his true name. Gentlemen, I present to you . . . Dog J."

Applause thunders through the room. Next to me, Aaron stands up and whistles through his teeth. Remo walks over to the crate, lifts the cloth, and opens the front grate. I crane my neck to see over the crowd, but as soon as the dog walks out of the cage, I have to look away. He has almost no face left. From the shoulders back, he looks like a normal yellow Lab, full grown but still young enough to walk with a puppy's lope. But his head has been completely reconstructed. His snout has been shortened so much that his face looks almost caved in. His jaw has been squared and broadened to resemble the shape of a human jaw. Even from four rows away, I can see the scar tissue on his neck where, I know from the newspaper reports, Hollis opened him up to operate on his larynx.

Aaron leans over to me. "Beautiful work, isn't it?" he whispers.

Remo picks the big creature up in his arms and sets him down on a wide stool in front of the podium. He adjusts the microphone so it's level with Dog J's poor scarred mouth. The room falls silent, and Dog J opens his mouth to speak.

The sound that comes out is unearthly. A cross between a howl and a yelp, the noise shapes itself into a string of random vowels and consonants. I've never heard a living creature make a noise like this before. It's the saddest thing I've ever heard. But it isn't speech.

"*Ayayay,*" the dog says. "*Kafofwayo.*"

I look around the room. The men are smiling and staring raptly.

"*Woganowoo,*" enunciates Dog J. "*Jukaluk.*"

"Amazing," Aaron whispers. "*J*'s and *k*'s are very hard."

I sit there, listening to the unholy noise and waiting for someone to react. But they all seem satisfied. Next to the podium, Remo is smiling beatifically. There's a new light in his eyes, one that I see reflected in every face around me.

I wonder if it's me. "What's he saying?" I whisper to Aaron, but he waves me away.

"Just listen," he says. "It couldn't be clearer."

Suddenly, there's a pounding on the door. It's loud enough to drown out the sad yowling, and I'm grateful.

"Police," someone yells from the other side of the door. "Open up."

Panic fills the room as the people around me jump up and run for the back door. Up at the podium, Remo grabs Dog J and heaves him back into his crate. I see him say something to Lucas, and they both turn to look at me for an instant. Then the two of them pick up the unwieldy crate and carry it out the back door. I stand still for a moment in the chaos, with people pushing past me on all sides. Chairs are overturned as everyone struggles to get out.

I'm glad the police are here. I want these people arrested, and I want those dogs freed. I'm on the verge of going to open the door for them, when something occurs to me: the police will think I'm one of *them*. How will I explain my presence here, interacting with criminals? The best thing is for me to go, to get in the car and drive home as fast as I can. I reach the back door just as the police break through the front. With all the chaos in the backyard, it looks like I can still get away. I run a convoluted path through neighbors' yards until I get to the block I'm parked on. I jump in my car and drive home at top speed.

I pull into the driveway, drunk with adrenaline, and turn off the engine. I sit in the car for a moment, my heart beating wildly in the sudden quiet. I've just fled from the police. Am I in trouble? I remind myself that, apart from the actual running, all I did was attend a meeting. I try to think whether the police will find my name anywhere among Remo's belongings. I never signed up, I never paid a membership fee, so I wouldn't be listed anywhere on the club's rosters. But of course—and here I feel a pang of fear—Wendell Hollis sent Remo my name and address. Certainly the police will want to examine all correspondence from Hollis, given the Dog J connection. And Lucas had my name and address on his clipboard. Calm down, I tell myself. Surely it will be clear that I'm no more than a bit player in this

drama. I had nothing to do with the kidnapping of Dog J, and I've never taken part in
the mutilation of a dog. I've done nothing
wrong.

But right away I know it's not true. I
should never have been there. What the hell
was I thinking, going to a place like that? I
feel as if I'm going to spend the rest of my
life trying to forget the things I saw this
evening. All I can think of, the only thing
that will help, is to go get my dog and wrap
my arms around the great furry mass of her.
I step out of the car and fairly run across the
front lawn.

But once I get to the back gate, I stop
short and my skin turns cold. Because the
yard is empty.

T H I R T Y - T W O

Lexy and I had fallen into a kind of quiet peace together after that awful night when she destroyed the first death mask, the night she tried to disappear and I brought her back by holding her fast in my arms. I knew she was embarrassed by her anger that night, by the unruly way it had pre-sented itself, bounding forth like a big, muddy dog to leave its marks on the pris-tine fabric of the day. But I thought that she was being a bit too careful with me now, that she was keeping herself in check. I didn't like this change in her; I wanted her the way she was, my wild and tempest-tossed girl. It concerned me, too, that she was spending so much time among the dead. It was time to bring her back to the world of the living.

I decided to whisk her away. She'd never been to Mardi Gras—can you imagine? Lexy, my maker of masks, and somehow she'd never gone. It was perfect. I'd take her away, spur of the moment, a sweet reminder of that first week we spent together. An escape from our dreary, soup-eating, winter selves. I would pack outrageous things for her. A sequined gown. A feather boa. We needed masquerade, disguise, revelry. A drunken debauch. I would take her where she needed to go. A romantic hotel with balconies and French doors and a lurid history. I would dress her up, her bosom sparkling with glitter. I would make her buy me with beads.

The timing worked out perfectly. Easter was late that year, not till mid-April, and spring break came a little earlier than it usually did. Of course, my spontaneity is never truly spontaneous—show up in New Orleans the week of Mardi Gras and expect to find a hotel room? The idea made me faintly ill. I spent months planning it, and somehow I managed to keep it a secret.

I told her the day before we were supposed to leave. I tried to pass it off as a spur-of-the-moment idea, but she saw through me pretty quickly.

"Hey, I have an idea," I said. It was a Friday evening, the first night of my spring break. Just exactly the time of year when we'd first met. "Let's fly down to New Orleans. For Mardi Gras."

She looked up from her book. "Really? Just like that?"

"Just like that," I said, snapping my fingers in a way that immediately struck me as too contrived. But she seemed not to notice. "It'll be fun," I added.

"What'll we do with Lorelei?" she asked. "I think Jim's out of town." Our neighbor Jim sometimes looked after Lorelei when we went away.

"We'll board her."

"They might not have space for her on such short notice. You know, they get booked up weeks in advance. Remember last Thanksgiving when we had to take her with us to your sister's?"

"Well, that's a particularly busy time. Why don't I call them? You never know, they might have a space open."

She studied my face for a moment and broke into a smile. "You've already called, haven't you? You probably called a month ago."

"I don't know what you're talking about," I said, trying to keep my face nonchalant. I've never been much of a liar.

"So if I go through your desk right now, I won't find any plane tickets? Or computer printouts about the hotel we're staying at?"

"Of course not," I said. "I just came up with the idea two minutes ago."

"So you haven't gone out and bought a guidebook and reserved a rental car and printed out a list of New Orleans's best restaurants?"

It was the restaurant list that got me. It had seemed a perfectly good idea—after all, why take a chance on a bad restaurant when it's so easy to find a good one?—but the fact that she knew me so well made me laugh.

"Okay, okay," I said. "You caught me. I did all that stuff. But so what? It's the thought that counts, isn't it?"

"Yes, and I'll bet you've put *a lot* of thought into it."

"Yeah, yeah, yeah," I said. "Well, tomorrow morning I'll be on a plane bound for New Orleans. Are you coming or not?"

"I'll be there," she said, giving me a kiss.
"With bells on," I said.
"Well, I don't know about that."
"I do. I've already packed your suitcase."

The only thing I'd left for Lexy to do was to pack masks for the two of us.

"Whatever you want," I told her. "Whoever you want us to be."

"I wish you'd told me earlier," she said. "I could have made something special."

"But then it wouldn't have been so spontaneous and romantic."

She smiled. "Well, romantic anyway," she said. "That's okay. I've got a lot to choose from. I'll find something."

She wouldn't show me what she'd chosen. She packed the masks in a separate suitcase and told me I'd have to wait.

In New Orleans, we stayed at a hotel that was said to have a ghost in it: a young woman whose lover had been killed in a duel. She was known as Blue Mary for the cobalt of the gown she wore. There was a little pamphlet about her at the check-in desk. Look for her in the courtyard on warm nights, it told us, look for a woman with a gown of blue and a mass of dark ringlets piled on top of her head. She died of a broken heart, the story went, and now she walks the grounds, crying her lover's name. Some claim they have seen him, as well, the lover. He walks across the courtyard with his dueling pistol still in his hand. They're never in the same place at the same time. A pair of ghosts, eternally missing each other.

If you should meet Blue Mary, the pamphlet said, if you should come upon her on a moonless night, don't run away. Sit with her and talk a while. Tell her what you know. Try to ease her mind. If you should see Blue Mary, take her hand. Try it. You will be surprised at the substance of it. It will be cold to the touch. Tell her to stay with you, to stay put for a while. When she asks if you have seen her lover, say yes. Say that he sends his love, and he wants her to rest. Tell her she can stop looking. Give her a single rose, the pamphlet advised. Tell her it's from him. She will tell you she's so very cold. Give her your jacket, lay it gently across her shoulders. And when she disappears, as she always does, say a prayer that this time it's for good. There's nothing scary about ghosts, after all. They are sad stories, all of them. She wanders forever, awaiting his kiss. The pretty girl in blue. You can go see her grave, if you like. They believe it's this one here. Notice the angel carved on top. Run your hands over it. Go ahead.

Lexy was entranced by the story, but I didn't believe it for a minute. I suspected the hotel of fabricating the whole thing, although the desk clerk seemed quite sincere about explaining it to us. It was all too neat, it was the stuff of those tragic sixties pop songs, "Last Kiss" and "Leader of the Pack" and all that. It smacked of urban legend, the hitchhiker who vanishes before you can take her home, the old woman answering the door with a sad smile on her face: "She died ten years ago tonight." We've heard it so many times.

Anyway, I thought, it's wishful thinking, all this talk of ghosts. If the dead wandered among us, their spirits still present on this earth, what need would we have for grief? Scary as it is, it's what we hope for. How else can we go on living?

But Lexy shushed me when I began to voice my objections.

"It's a sweet story," she said. "And who are you to say it's not true? Can't you give yourself over, just once, to something that doesn't make any logical sense?"

No, I thought. I can't. Of course I can't. But this was our vacation, and I wanted Lexy to be happy, so I kept the snide remarks to a minimum.

The first night, we went to the French Quarter. The reality of it was nothing like I'd imagined: there was none of the mystery, none of the dark magic I had expected. The streets were filled with loud music, with drunken frat boys flashing their penises, with girls lifting their shirts and showing their breasts for beads. The forced revelry of it was all wrong. I was too old for this.

"Let's go back to the hotel," I said.

"Oh, come on," Lexy said. She was drinking a grain alcohol concoction she'd purchased from a walk-up window. It was in a plastic cup shaped like a hand grenade. "We just got here. It's fun. Let's make the best of it. Let's go someplace and dance."

"I don't think so," I said. "This really isn't my kind of scene."

"Well, of course it isn't. That's the point. Let's do something a little out of character. Isn't that why you brought me here?"

I wasn't sure anymore why I'd brought her there. It was late, and I wanted to go to bed. In situations like this, I was always reminded that Lexy was eight years younger than I was. Or maybe age had nothing to do with it. Would I ever have liked being in a crowd like this?

"Don't sulk," she said. "Let me buy you a drink. You want the one that comes in the monkey's head or the one that comes in the fake coconut?"

"Neither," I said, making a face. "I had wine with dinner, and I don't think I should mix."

"Well, you're not going to find wine here."

"Let's just go back," I said. We'd stopped in the middle of the street, and people were pushing past us on all sides. I took Lexy's arm and pulled her off to the side of the street. "There are parades tomorrow, and we have to get up early to get a good spot along the route."

"I don't believe you," she said. "You whisk me away on this trip, which is, like, the most romantic thing you've ever done, and once we get here, you don't want to have any fun."

"I feel out of place with all these kids. What if I run into one of my students?"

"If you did, they'd think you were a lot cooler than they'd ever imagined."

"Well, I'm going back to the hotel. Are you coming or not?"

"No," she said. "I'm going to stay and have fun."

"Fine," I said. I felt irritated, and I was starting to get a headache. "Do you remember how to get back to the hotel?"

"Yeah, I'll be fine." She turned and walked away from me. I could tell she was annoyed with me, and as I started to make my way through the crowd, I was starting to wish I'd stayed. I almost decided to stay, but when I turned around to look for her, she was already out of sight.

By the time I reached the hotel, I felt terrible. Lexy was right—I'd brought her here to have fun, and then I refused to enjoy myself. I began to worry about her out in the crowds all by herself. What if something happened to her? Or what if she simply decided not to come back at all? Would I ever find her again in this city full of people?

By the time I heard her key turn in the lock an hour later, I was ready to fall at her feet and beg her forgiveness. But when she walked in, she looked flushed and excited. She didn't look angry at all.

"Lexy," I said, jumping up from the chair I'd been sitting in. "I'm so sorry. You were right. I was a jerk. I'm sorry I ruined everything."

"That's okay," she said. "You were right. It wasn't that much fun. It was kind of an obnoxious scene. I only stayed another fifteen minutes or so after you left."

"Then how come it took you so long to get back?"

"Paul," she said, her face lit with excitement. "I saw her. I saw Blue Mary."

THIRTY-THREE

Lexy was convinced she'd seen Blue Mary. She told me that she'd come back to the hotel and had decided to walk through the open courtyard on her way back to our room. She was standing by the swimming pool, enjoying the cool night air, when she noticed a woman in a formal blue gown sitting on the edge of a deck chair with her face in her hands. She appeared to be crying. Lexy didn't think anything of her elaborate, old-fashioned dress; after all, this was Mardi Gras, with masquerade balls every night. Lexy walked over and stood beside her.

"Are you okay?" she asked.

This is the kind of person my Lexy was—she would approach a crying stranger to see if she was all right.

The woman looked up, and Lexy could see that she was very pale.

"I can't seem to find him," she said to Lexy. "I don't know where he went."

As she spoke, she took Lexy's hand in her own, and her touch was as cold as ice. It was then, Lexy said, that she understood whom she was speaking to.

"I'm sorry," Lexy said. "Maybe It's time to stop looking."

At that, Lexy told me, the woman became furious. "Stop looking for him?" she said, her voice rising to a screech. "What have you done with him?" Her face grew ugly before Lexy's eyes, and when she stood up, she seemed to tower over Lexy. "What have you done with him?" she said again.

"I haven't done anything," Lexy said.

"Well, where is he, then?" she roared.

Lexy stood straight and tall and looked her in the eye. "He's gone," she said. "You're not going to find him now."

The look on the woman's face in the instant before she turned and ran away was one of horror and terrible, terrible pain. Lexy immediately regretted what she had said, and she reached out to take her arm. But the woman was already gone.

"What do you think?" Lexy said to me now as we sat on our hotel bed. "It was her, it had to be."

"I don't know," I said, skeptical bastard that I always was. If Lexy could see me now, putting my faith in a talking dog! "It could have been some hotel guest coming back from a costume party, and you go and tell her her husband is gone."

"If you could have felt how cold her hands were," Lexy said.

"So she had cold hands. Some people always have cold hands. They have trouble regulating their body temperature." God, would you listen to me?

"She disappeared, Paul. She vanished into thin air. Right in front of me."

"Maybe you looked away for a minute and she ran away."

"I didn't look away."

"Well, I don't know, Lexy. But I don't believe you saw a ghost."

"Well, I know you don't believe me," she said, lying back on the bed. "But I know what I saw."

Later that night, I awoke to find Lexy sobbing. "I'm so afraid," she said. "I'm so afraid you're going to die." I held her to me until my chest was damp.

The next morning, while Lexy was still asleep, I woke early, dressed, and slipped out to go get beignets and coffee. When I returned with my bag of sweets, I found Lexy sitting on the couch in her nightgown, looking at the Blue Mary pamphlet. She looked so lovely sitting there in the morning light that my breath caught in my chest.

"Good morning," I said. "I brought breakfast."

"Good," she said, without looking up.

"What are you reading?" I asked, although I could see perfectly well from where I was standing.

"I'm reading about Blue Mary," she said. She looked up at me. "Whether you believe it or not, I'm sure that's who I saw last night."

I nodded. I didn't want to argue. "Well, come and have some beignets," I said. "They're still warm. And then we'll go find ourselves a spot along the parade route."

"I don't think so," she said. "I'd like to go to the cemetery. I'd like to find Mary's grave."

"But what about the parade? That's the reason we came."

"Paul, there are, like, five more parades between now and Tuesday. We can go to those."

I sighed. "Lexy, I'm worried about you," I said. "You seem to be so concerned with death lately, with the death masks and everything. I brought you here to take you away from that."

She looked up at me and smiled. "There's nothing to worry about," she said. "The death masks are important to me—it's a new direction for my work, and I'm excited about it. But I'm not going to let it turn me into a morbid person, I promise. This Blue Mary thing is something different, though. I've just never had an experience like this. I want to investigate it a little further. We could have fun with it, if you weren't such a skeptic."

"Okay," I said. "I'll try to be more open-minded." I hesitated a moment. "What about last night?" I asked. "When you were crying."

"Yeah," she said, looking down. "I don't know what that was. Sometimes I just get so scared that I'll lose you."

"You don't have to worry about me," I said. "I'm not going anywhere." I walked over to the couch where she was sitting and kissed the top of her head. "Now come and have some breakfast while it's still warm."

So we went to find Blue Mary's grave. The cemetery was one of those strange New Orleans boneyards, with all the graves aboveground. It was quite picturesque, actually, with the old marble stones and the Spanish moss hanging from the trees. I was surprised to find I wasn't sorry we'd come.

We followed the directions on the hotel pamphlet and finally located the grave. It was a tall block of granite with the head and wings of a cherub carved on top. I read the words aloud.

" 'Here lies the body of an Unknown Girl, found on the streets of New Orleans on the 27th day of December, 1872. Since no Kin or Well-Wishing Friend stepped forward to claim the Fair Young Lady in the Blue Dress, this Memorial was erected with Funds raised by the Citizens of New Orleans on the 24th day of August, 1873. May she rest in Peace, in God's Bosom at last.' "

Lexy bent to run her hands over the

faded lettering. "I wish I'd brought some paper to do a rubbing," she said.

"What for?"

"Just as a keepsake."

I felt around in my pockets and came up with the three-page itinerary I'd made for the trip. I glanced for a moment at the entry on the first page for what we were supposed to be doing just then—the parade, followed by lunch at a carefully selected restaurant and an afternoon of browsing in mask shops—before I ripped the page off.

"Do you have a pencil?" I asked.

Lexy smiled at me. "I think I do," she said. She rummaged through her bag. And that was how we spent our second afternoon in New Orleans, husband and wife kneeling in the moist grass, rubbing the words from a stranger's grave. It took all the pages of my itinerary to get them all down.

After that strange day, though, our trip seemed to get back on track, and things started going more or less the way I'd planned. There were more parades than we could manage to see, and it didn't really matter that we'd missed one. The whole city was infused with an air of revelry and masquerade, and it was infectious. We saw wonderful things: acrobats who seemed to walk on air, and a big white dog whose fur had been dyed to match his master's tie-dyed shirt. Throughout it all, Lexy was buoyant. Something about the trip, whether it was my good planning (as I'd have liked to believe) or her encounter with Blue Mary, seemed to have lifted her spirits, and it was more than I could have hoped for.

On our last night there, the night of Mardi Gras itself, as we were getting ready to go out, Lexy opened the suitcase that contained our masks. She handed me a mask with a lion's face, surrounded by a wild mane.

I was pleased. "Why a lion?" I asked.

"Oh, no reason. I just thought it'd look good on you."

I must have looked disappointed, because she laughed. "Okay, let's see," she said. "I brought you the lion mask because you're so strong and fierce and wild." She came up beside me and made a growling sound in my ear. "No one better get in your way."

"Well, you don't have to make stuff up."

She smiled. "There aren't always reasons

for everything. It's just dress-up. I didn't have a lot of time to think about it, you know. But I guess you *are* kind of a big pussycat, if that helps."

"Yeah, thanks, that helps a lot. What are you wearing?"

"I thought we'd go as a matching pair," she said, and she pulled out a lovely lioness mask, topped with a garland of papier-mâché flowers that seemed to be twined through the fur.

"Perfect," I said. I turned my mask over in my hands. "I've never seen these before. When did you make them? I know you didn't have time before we left."

"I was just playing around with designs. I thought I might save them for our anniversary," she said. "But this seemed like a good opportunity to unveil them."

"Well, I love them," I said. "We'll be the best-dressed couple of the night."

We went down to the lobby, with our masks still in our hands. We were standing in line at the front desk—our hotel subscribed to the old-fashioned policy of leaving your key with the desk clerk when you went out for the evening—when a woman came up and tapped Lexy on the arm. She was a young woman, very pretty, with dark hair. She was wearing a red ball gown.

"Hi," she said. "Remember me?"

Lexy turned and stared at her. She didn't answer.

"From the other night?" the woman said. "Out by the pool? I was hoping I'd run into you, so I could apologize." She turned to me and explained. "I was coming back from a party, and I'd had a lot to drink, and I'd had a big fight with my husband, and I was sitting there crying, and your friend here was so nice to me, and I really acted horribly. I think I yelled at you, didn't I?" she said, smiling at Lexy. "And then I just ran away."

I looked at Lexy. She had turned very pale. "I thought you were someone else," she said finally. "Your hands were so cold."

The woman looked at Lexy curiously. "Were they?" she said. "Well, anyway, I just wanted to tell you I was sorry." She looked down at the mask Lexy held in her hand. "What a great mask!" she said. "Put it on, and let me see!"

Lexy put the mask over her face. She didn't say a word.

"Oh, that's just beautiful!" the woman said. "Wherever did you get it?"

I stepped in for Lexy. "My wife makes them," I said. "I have one, too." I put it on.

The woman exclaimed over our masks, and then she stood by us, making small talk until it was our turn in line. When she'd finally walked away after apologizing to Lexy one last time, I took Lexy's hand. "Are you okay?" I asked.

"Fine," she said, and I couldn't tell by her voice whether she meant it or not. "I guess you were right."

"I'm sorry," I said. "I wish I wasn't."

We walked out into the noisy street. It was a warm night, and I began to feel hot under the mask almost immediately. Lexy didn't speak as we negotiated our passage through the crowds. What was she thinking as we pushed our way through those packed streets, the sweat running down my face beneath my mask? I don't know. I couldn't see her face.

We stayed out late, walking through the festivities without really joining in. Lexy didn't take her mask off once. When we finally returned to the quiet of our hotel room, I lifted the mask from her face.

"Are you all right?" I asked. I took her in my arms, and she rested her head against my chest.

She shrugged.

"You know," I said, "just because that woman wasn't Blue Mary doesn't mean she doesn't exist. We could go out and look for her right now."

She shook her head and put a finger to my lips. Then she took my hand and led me to the bed. Slowly, she began undressing me.

"Oh," I said. "I see."

When I was naked, she pushed me down gently until I was sitting on the bed. She leaned down and kissed me long and soft. Then she held up one finger, indicating that I should wait a minute. She went into the bathroom.

I settled myself underneath the sheets. It was dim in the room, but when Lexy came in a moment later, I could see that she was wearing a white nightgown and that she had her mask on.

"Ooh," I said. "That's unusual. Should I wear one, too?"

She didn't answer me. She got into bed next to me and pulled the sheet off me. I closed my eyes as she rolled herself on top of me and began to move against me. I could feel the stiff edge of her mask against my face as she lifted herself up and guided me inside her.

"Hey, slow down a little," I said. "What's your hurry?" I opened my eyes, and in the moonlight from the window, I saw that Lexy wasn't wearing the lioness mask. She was wearing Jennifer's mask. The mask of the smiling girl.

I started to pull away. "No, Lexy," I said. "Take that off."

She held me down on the bed and shook her head no.

I could have resisted more. If I could go back to that night, I would. If I could take that moment back, I would lift the mask from her face and kiss her own soft lips. But I didn't. I let her go on. She made love to me wearing the mask of a smiling girl, and I lay there and let her do it. When I came, I felt as if I had betrayed us both.

That was March. Lexy died in October. We were already running out of time.

THIRTY-FOUR

The yard is empty. I look around wildly, but Lorelei is nowhere in sight. I know I latched the gate on my way out; I remember the feel of the metal hook in my hand as I fastened it through its loop, and I remember Lorelei jumping up to nose my hand as I pulled on the door to make sure it held fast. But now the gate is standing wide open. The dog is gone, and I know she did not get out of here on her own.

I sit down on the grass, feeling dizzy. Lorelei is gone, Lorelei is gone—I turn the phrase over in my head, looking for a way for it not to be true. It's my own fault, I know it is. I put Lorelei in danger. I dragged her back to the site of her puppyhood trauma, and I brought her to the attention of men who meant her harm. Which one of the men in that room took my dog? And then I remember Lucas standing next to me, leaning toward me slightly when he heard that Lorelei was a Ridgeback, peering at me with eyes made tiny by the thickness of his face. *I guess this must be my prodigal daughter,* he'd said. He must have been the one who took her; he must think he still has some claim to her. Some unfinished business with the one who got away. Maybe Remo was in on it, too. But when did they have the chance? It couldn't have been after the police arrived; there was no time. It must have been during that first part of the meeting, before they brought Dog J in. I remember Lucas excusing himself, saying he had a few things he wanted to take care of. I remember him reading my address off his clipboard and looking me up and down.

I feel a chill run through me as I try to imagine what they're doing to her now. I've got to get her back—but I don't even know their last names. I'll go to the police, there's no other way. I'll tell them what I know. And maybe they'll help me find her.

I get up and go inside the house to look in the phone book—to find out where the nearest police station is. My mind is reeling.

Beneath my worry for Lorelei, another thought tugs at me, one I don't even want to turn my mind to. Dog J. Dog J can't talk. All these months with Lorelei, the story of Dog J has been a beacon for me: See, it can be done after all. Whenever I started to feel that I was on a fool's mission, that my work would never amount to anything, I would open up my desk drawer and take out the stack of newspaper clippings about Dog J. And they gave me hope. Now I don't know what to think. Everyone in that room heard the same garbled noise I heard, and everyone but me interpreted that noise as speech. What did they think he was saying, that poor mutilated dog? And what about the jurors, the ones who convicted Wendell Hollis after hearing Dog J's testimony? What about the newspaper reporters who printed Dog J's words? Was it all a case of the emperor's new clothes, of hearing what you want to hear and believing what you want to believe? No. It can't be. Because no one wanted to believe more than I did.

As I look through the phone book, I turn on the local news channel. There it is, top story. "The police are calling this the worst case of animal cruelty they've ever seen," the anchorwoman says. There's footage of animal control people leading dog after dog out of the kennels in Remo's yard. Some of the dogs seem barely able to walk. I look to see if Lorelei is among them, but she's not there. "Earlier tonight," the anchorwoman continues, "acting on an anonymous tip, police raided the home of Remo Platt. They were looking for Hero, the famous talking dog who disappeared last week from his owner's New York City apartment. They didn't find Hero, but what they did find was enough to turn any animal lover's stomach." The news team cuts to a reporter standing outside Remo's house, who explains that the police interrupted a meeting of a "bizarre animal mutilation cult," most of whose members fled when the police arrived. "Upon searching the premises," he says, "police found a makeshift laboratory where Platt and his associates had apparently been conducting experiments on dogs. Literature found at the scene"—here the reporter holds up a membership packet identical to the one Remo gave me earlier this evening—"suggests that the group had been surgically altering dogs in the hopes of giving them the power of speech. The group members seem to have drawn their inspiration from Hero's former owner, Wendell Hollis, the so-called Dog Butcher of Brooklyn."

There's some inane banter between the field reporter and the anchorwoman, then photos appear on the screen of the three men the police managed to arrest. One of them is Aaron, the red haired man with the unfaithful wife; the other two I recognize vaguely from the meeting.

"Platt is still at large," the anchorwoman says. "If you have any information, please notify the police."

So Remo managed to get away with Dog J. And Lucas managed to get away with Lorelei. I turn off the TV and pace around the living room for another couple of minutes. I put on my jacket and get ready to leave for the police station, but before I get a chance, the doorbell rings. It's a police officer.

"Paul Iverson?" he asks when I open the door. I nod. "Come with me," he says. "We'd like to ask you a few questions."

It's nearly daybreak by the time I return home. I'm exhausted; it's been a grueling night. It turns out that the police have been keeping an eye on me. After Dog J's disappearance, they did some research into Wendell Hollis's recent correspondence, and of course my name came up. In fact, they followed me to the meeting tonight. It took some time for me to convince them that I'm not exactly a key player in the Cerberus Society. And the words "I was just on my way to the police station when you arrived" didn't seem to carry much weight. In the end, of course, I didn't have any information that could help them. I had no idea where Remo might have gone; I knew nothing about the details of the kidnapping or about Remo's plans for Dog J. And though they took down a description of Lorelei and told me they'd let me know if she turned up, it was clear it wasn't going to be a priority for them. She's not the dog the public wants them to find.

At least they didn't arrest me. It certainly seemed like a possibility at first, although I was able to establish fairly quickly that I hadn't had anything to do with the kidnapping. But rarely in my life have I been so humiliated. The detective I spoke to, a great bully of a man named Caffrey, was very menacing until he'd decided I wasn't a threat. Then he treated me like an imbecile. When I told him the story of Lexy's death and my subsequent work with Lorelei—it seemed important that I explain the circumstances that had led me to attend the meeting—he actually laughed.

"So should I put the word out that we've got another talking doggy on our hands?" he asked, smirking.

"No," I said quietly. "She hasn't learned yet."

"I see," he said. "She hasn't learned *yet*. Well, we'll certainly let you know if she comes in here asking for help."

Just then, Detective Anthony Stack, the man who had presided over the scene of Lexy's death, walked in.

"Dr. Iverson," he said. I could have hugged him for calling me doctor. "I heard you were here, and I thought I'd come say hello."

"Detective Stack," I said. "It's so nice to see you. I was hoping I might be of some help with the Cerberus Society case, but it doesn't look like I have any useful information."

"I was a little bit surprised when I saw

your name come up. I couldn't believe you were mixed up with those guys."

"Well, I'm not really," I said. "I was just telling Detective Caffrey, here . . ."

"The professor here is trying to teach his dog to talk," Caffrey said. "He's going to turn her into a police dog. She's going to solve the mystery of his wife's death."

"Dr. Iverson," said Detective Stack, "you know your wife's death was ruled accidental."

"Yes, well," I said. "I just wanted to . . . There were some incongruities," I finished lamely.

Detective Stack gave me a searching look. He nodded doubtfully.

"But as I was telling Detective Caffrey," I went on, "my dog's disappeared. One of the men from the meeting took her." I could hear how I must have sounded.

"And apparently," Caffrey said, "the dog's the only one who can figure out those 'incongruities.' "

Stack shot Caffrey a warning look. "Well, we'll see what we can do about your dog," he said to me. His voice was gentle. "Now, why don't you go home. Do you need someone to take you back?"

For an instant, I saw myself as he must have seen me—shabby, frail, broken—and I felt ashamed. "No," I said. "Thank you." I walked out of the police station into the starless night.

Now I'm back in my empty house, and the sun is starting to come up. Late as it is, I don't feel much like sleeping. So I do what I always do lately when I have a few moments' time on my hands. I pick up the phone and dial the number I've learned by heart.

"Thank you for calling our Psychic Helpline," the woman on the other end says. "This is Lady Arabelle."

THIRTY-FIVE

"This is Lady Arabelle," she says again when I don't answer. "Extension 43981. I'm going to do a tarot card reading for you, so why don't you start by giving me your name, your birthday, and your address."

"Is this really Lady Arabelle?" I ask, though I know her voice by heart.

"Yes, it is," she says. "And who am I speaking to?"

"Paul," I say.

"Well, Paul, honey, why don't you tell Lady Arabelle your birthday, so we can get started."

"September twentieth," I say. "But I'm not calling for a reading."

"Oh, no?" she says. Her voice is smooth as warm caramel.

"No," I say. I try to figure out where to begin. "I've been trying to reach you for weeks. You see, my wife died last October, and then a couple of months ago, I was watching TV, and I heard you talking to her on one of your commercials. She's the one who said, 'I'm lost, I don't know what to do.' Do you know the one I'm talking about?"

"Well, of course I know the commercial, but I'm afraid I can't tell you anything about any one particular call. It's confidential, for one thing, and to be honest with you, I can't say I remember the details of every call I take."

"No, of course not. But if you could just think about it for a minute, if you could just try to remember. It's very important to me."

She starts to say something, but I interrupt her and go on in a rush. "As for confidentiality," I say, "I'm sure you have your rules, but do they still apply when the person you spoke to is dead?"

Lady Arabelle sighs. "You know," she says, "it may not even have been your wife's voice that you heard. It might have been another woman entirely. Isn't it possible that in your grief you might have been mistaken?"

"I know my wife's voice," I say. I'm surprised at the coldness of my tone. I take a breath and compose myself. "Anyway," I say, "I found it on my phone bill. October twenty-third. Eleven twenty-three P.M. Eastern time. You spoke to her for forty-six minutes. Surely you can remember *something*. You can at least try." She doesn't say anything, so I continue. "Look, you've got me on the phone for five dollars a minute, and I'm not planning on hanging up until I get an answer out of you. How often does an opportunity like that come along?"

She doesn't laugh, but when she speaks, I can hear she's softened. "Why don't you tell me about your wife?" she says.

And so I do. I tell her everything I can think of. I tell her about how I met Lexy; I tell her about how Lexy died. I tell her about the lonely months I've spent since then, unraveling clues that may not be clues at all. My work with Lorelei, the open gate, the empty yard. I have no idea how long I've talked, but when I finally stop, my throat is dry.

There's a long silence after I finish talking. "Lady Arabelle," I say. "Are you there?"

"I'm here, baby," she says.

"So . . . did that help?" I say. "Did it help

you remember anything about Lexy's call?" My voice cracks. I don't think I'll be able to bear it if she says no.

"I think I can help you," she says. I let out a breath that sounds like a sob. "I don't remember the call, I have to be honest with you. I get a couple hundred calls a month, and most of them sound pretty much the same after a while. But I do keep notes."

Notes! Oh, God, she has notes from Lexy's phone call! I don't trust my voice to answer her.

"I'm writing a book," she says. "About my experiences as Lady Arabelle. Starting last fall, I've kept notes on every call I've taken. If you give me the date and time again, I can look and see what I have, and I'll call you back."

"Thank you," I say. "Thank you. I can't tell you . . ."

"I know, baby," she says.

I give her the information and my phone number, and we hang up. I'm shaking all over. I feel jubilant, and I feel afraid.

It's full morning now, and the sun is coming through the windows. I've got to calm down. I've got to find something to occupy my mind while I wait for Lady Arabelle to call me back. I sit down to compose a Lost Dog ad, but as soon I write the words "Missing: Eight-year-old Rhodesian Ridgeback," tears come to my eyes and I have to put down the pen. Instead, I go into my office and turn on my laptop. I still haven't finished listing the books on the shelf. I stretch out on the floor in front of the bookcase and begin to list the books on the bottom two shelves.

To Have and to Hold (Ours. It's a book about writing your own wedding vows. We bought it before we got married.)

The Toad Not Taken: The Linguistic Value of Puns (Mine.)

Out of the Rat Race and into the Chips (Mine. It was written by the grandfather of a girl I dated in college. It describes how the author started his own mail-order business and was able to make lots of money and still play golf every afternoon.)

Your Fortune in Mail-Order Selling (Mine. Same girlfriend, same grandfather.)

Exercises for a Healthy Heart (Mine. It's a novel that I found misshelved in the fitness section of a bookstore.)

A Handbook of Dreams (Hers. A book on dream interpretation.)

Flesh Wounds (Hers. A wryly funny collection of short stories.)

Papier-Mâché Arts and Crafts (Hers.)

Put a Lid on It: Managing Your Anger (Hers.)

Learn to Play Piano in Fourteen Days (Mine.)

The City of One (Mine. A futuristic sci-fi thriller.)

A History of the English Language (Mine.)

Stone Shoes and Other Fables (Hers.)

That's all of them, and I still know nothing. I'm beginning to feel sleepy. I was up all night, after all. I put my head down on the carpet. It feels blessedly soft against my cheek. I close my eyes and sleep.

I dream that I come upon Lexy sitting in the kitchen, chopping an onion. In the dream, I can feel my eyes stinging from the sharp smell.

She looks up at me and smiles. "I was going to peel it," she says. "But you can only peel so many layers before you have to cut it."

"Lexy," I say, "you're alive." But what I

feel isn't surprise or joy or wonder. I'm furious at her. I've never been so angry.

"I meant to call," she says.

"You meant to call?" I say sharply. "Well, that does me a lot of good."

Lexy laughs. "Sorry," she says.

"You can't just come back here," I say. "Do you have any idea what I've been through? What the fuck were you thinking?" I'm shouting at her now.

"Do you want me to go?" she says, standing up from the table.

"No," I say. "Just go back to cutting your fucking onion."

The dream gets strange after that—there's something else, something about how Lexy needs her body back, the body I buried. I don't know how we're going to get it back for her. "This is your fault," I yell at Lexy. I'm screaming, I'm out of control. "If you hadn't let it go in the first place, we wouldn't have to get it back."

I wake up with the anger still hot in my stomach. The phone is ringing. I look at it for a moment, disoriented, before picking it up.

It's Lady Arabelle. "I found my notes,"

she says. "There's something you're not going to want to hear."

I take a deep breath. "I've got to know," I
say.

"All right, honey. Listen to me, now." She
waits a moment. I can hear her rustling
through pages of notes, although I know
she already knows what she's going to say.
Break down *Lady Arabelle* and what do you
find? *Read* and *bleed. Lay bare.*

"Your wife," Lady Arabelle says. "She
was pregnant."

I'm silent for a long time. When I finally
speak, my voice sounds very far away.

"Yes," I say. "I know."

THIRTY-SIX

I didn't know before she died. She never told me herself. It showed up in the autopsy, of course; Detective Stack called to give me the news. She was two months along. But I knew even before that. I had found a scrap of paper, a corner of cardboard from a box that had contained a home pregnancy test. I didn't find the test itself; she was careful to get rid of that. But in the bathroom trash—I'll admit now that in those first days, I tore apart the house looking for hints as to what had happened, I went through every piece of lint on the carpet and every soggy, coffee-stained envelope in the garbage—and in the bathroom trash, underneath the tissues and cotton swabs and tangles of minted floss, I found a scrap of pink cardboard that she must have missed. It was one of the . . . anomalies I found during those terrible days. One of the clues that started me down this path. The piece of cardboard had three letters on it: CLE. I didn't recognize the lettering or the color of the cardboard as anything we had had in the house recently, so I went to the drugstore with my little pink scrap in my hand, and I walked the aisles until I found the box it matched up with. The letters were from the word "clear," and the box contained a home pregnancy test. And I knew.

It didn't happen in New Orleans, certainly; that's much too early. But when? We were using birth control all along, and I don't remember any specific incident when we thought it might have failed. I suppose I'd always had some romantic notion that when you conceived a child, there would be some cataclysm, some indication that something momentous had occurred. But there was nothing like that. I've looked at the calendar, using the autopsy report as my guide, and I've pinpointed the week when it must have happened. I can recall certain things about that week, some of them quite happy, but there was nothing special, nothing earthshaking. It was just another week in my life.

What does it change, though, to know that she was pregnant? What good does it do me? It hasn't made things any clearer. It has only widened the circle of images at play in my mind. I've thought, for example, well, if she was pregnant, then she might have been dizzy. She climbed a tree for reasons I cannot fathom, but that may have made perfect sense in the moment, and she got dizzy and fell. Or hormones. Pregnant women have mood swings. A wave of despair just as she attained the highest branch. A wave of despair caused by a hormonal shift, having nothing to do with how she felt about me or her life or our child. There are so many ways it could have happened. She had not yet begun to show. Or had she? Had there been a new roundness to her that I was slow to notice? I've racked my brain but I can't remember how she looked the last time I saw her naked. I can't even remember when it was.

How we come to take these things for granted when we see them every day! There was a time when the sight of her bare body would make me lose my breath. When

I couldn't even look upon her without a wave of arousal passing through me like fire. How long had it been since I came up behind her and cupped her breasts in my palms? How long since the sight of her stepping out of the shower had begun to seem commonplace? My body singing at the sight of her. It's not that we were making love less frequently than before—well, of course, it was a little less frequent than it had been in those early, heady days. Who can maintain such constant passion for more than the first year or so? But sex was no longer the underlying current of everything we did. Did she notice that? Did she feel I no longer loved her as well as I could? Did she feel rejected? Had my lust for her fallen too far into the background, become too much the wallpaper of our lives and not enough the centerpiece? Oh, God, oh, God, did she think I no longer found her beautiful? Did she worry about the changes a baby would write on her body? No. She wasn't that petty, that insecure. What, then? What did I do and what did I neglect to do? How did I fail her? How many different ways? In what way am I to blame—I know I must be, the problem is figuring out the details of my failure. The problem is explaining it in a way I can understand. Perhaps even Lexy couldn't have done that.

Lady Arabelle's notes aren't able to tell me much more. The rest of our conversation focuses on the tarot card reading she did for Lexy.

"I do a ten-card tarot reading," she says, "in a Celtic cross spread. Do you know anything about tarot cards?"

"No," I say.

"Well, in a reading, I lay out ten cards, and each one has a specific role in the reading. Taken all together, the cards give me a picture of a particular moment in a person's life, you see? And I can look at the spread and get an idea of what paths this person might take from here. I'm not telling the future, you understand. The future isn't fixed in place. It all depends on what actions you choose to take from this moment we're looking at right now. And the cards can help determine the best course of action. You got that, honey?"

"Okay," I say. "Yes."

"All right. Now with your wife, the first card I laid out was the Magician."

"The magician?" I say. I'm looking around for a piece of paper to write this down.

"That's right. The Magician card was in the Significator position, which is the position that represents the overall place your wife was in her life the night she called."

"That sounds important," I say.

"Well, sure," she says. "They're all important. They all work together. For the Magician to appear in this space, it means that your wife was in a position to control what was going to happen to her. The Magician represents unexplored potential, you see, he represents opportunities and possibilities. And your wife had the power to follow those opportunities. She was in control of her world."

"Okay," I say. "That sounds good."

"Now the second card, that's the Crossing card. This is the card that indicates the basic problem the seeker—that would be your wife—is facing. In this reading, that card was the Lovers."

"All right," I say, writing it down.

"The Lovers card indicates a choice, a very important choice that has to be made. The decision you make is going to affect the course of your life. There are conflicting forces at work, and you have to look carefully at the implications of your decision. Okay, now, the third card is the Crowning card. That represents the overall situation hanging over the person's head at this particular moment. For your wife, this card was the Page of Cups, which indicates that she had received some news. Usually it's news of a birth, or a new start. I took that to be the baby."

"Yes," I say. "I'm sure that's right."

"The fourth card is the Base of the Matter. That shows you what's really at the root of the current situation. For her, it was the Ace of Wands, but it was reversed."

"What does that mean?"

"It means the card came up upside down, so it has a slightly different meaning than it would otherwise. Usually, the Ace of Wands means a new beginning—again, sometimes a birth or sometimes just a new business undertaking or something like that—but when it's reversed, it means that this new beginning wasn't well thought out. The circumstances aren't right, and the seeker might not succeed in the undertaking. Or it could mean that she could succeed, but she doesn't have the confidence to find out."

"How did she take it when you told her that?"

"I'm afraid that's not in my notes, sweetheart. But I don't think she took it badly. I'm sure I would have played up the positive aspect, that if she believed in herself, she'd do okay. I'm sure I would have told her that."

"Okay," I say. This is all starting to run together in my mind. It all sounds so weighty, but I don't know what to make of any of it. I write it down dutifully. The fifth card, she tells me, represents past influences, and in Lexy's reading it was the Six of Cups; apparently, it has something to do with looking back on happy memories, but beyond that, the significance is lost on me. I shake my head to clear it and resolve to listen more carefully.

"The next card," Lady Arabelle says, "the sixth, is the opposite; it represents forthcoming influences. Here it was the Seven of Wands. This is a card that tells the seeker it's time for her to take action. She may be unsure about what to do next, but she has to do something. Any action is better than nothing."

"Any action is better than nothing," I say.

"Right. The seventh card is called Where One Finds Oneself. It's kind of like the Significator, but it takes it a little further. It represents the inner state of the seeker and gives an idea of what she's likely to do next. For your wife, the card here was the Fool."

"Are you calling Lexy a fool?" I say, sort of trying for a joke. I'm feeling punchy.

"No, not at all. But the Fool represents someone who . . . well, if you could see the card, it's a picture of a man walking off a cliff. And in the picture, it varies from deck to deck, but there's usually an animal trying to stop him, sometimes a dog or something like that."

"A dog?" I say, sitting up.

"Or sometimes a bird. The point is, those around the fool can see he's making a mistake, and most likely the fool knows it himself. But he's refusing to see it, and if he keeps going the way he's going, he's going to walk right off that cliff."

"So it's a card of death?"

"No, it's not usually that literal. It just means the person has a choice to make, and if he makes the wrong choice, the consequences could be great."

"Okay," I say.

The eighth card, she tells me, is the card that represents the way other people saw Lexy. It was the Ace of Cups, which Lady Arabelle says is a very good card. It represents happiness, love, fertility. A happy marriage and family life.

"But that's how other people saw Lexy?" I ask. "Not how she saw herself?"

"Well, that's the position of the card. But that doesn't mean anything, sweetie. I didn't see anything to suggest she wasn't happy with your marriage. I didn't see anything like that at all."

I nod, unable to speak. I have a sudden lump in my throat.

"The ninth card—hang in there, baby, we're almost at the end—is the Hopes and Fears card. The idea is that hope and fear are two sides of the same coin. The Five of Swords came up here. That's a very negative card, implying great loss and tragedy. Complete ruin. I guess that's what your wife was afraid of."

"Well, isn't everyone?" I say.

"Sure, sweetie," Lady Arabelle says. "That's what we're all afraid of. Now, the last card, the tenth card, that represents the

Final Outcome. But that's a little misleading, because, like I said, and I would have told this to her, too, there's nothing written in stone. 'Final Outcome' just means the likely outgrowth of the current circumstances."

"Okay. And what card was that?"

"Well, I don't want you to make too much of this, baby, but it was the Hanged Man."

"Good Lord," I say.

"The Hanged Man doesn't mean death, though, sweetie. It just means self-sacrifice. It's a card of renunciation. It means you may have to give something up for the sake of something more important."

"I see," I say. "And that's it?"

"That's it," she says. She pauses. "I want to emphasize," she says, "that this was not a bad reading. There was nothing in here that made me worry about this woman's future."

"Okay," I say. "And that's all you have in your notes?"

"Well, let me see. I have that she was thirty-five years old, married and pregnant, and that she hadn't told her husband about her pregnancy. That much she told me up front. I have her birthday, and I have a list of the cards I read for her. I also wrote that she had stopped crying by the time she hung up. She thanked me, and she said I'd helped her. I've got a plus sign next to the call, which means I thought it went well. And that's all I've got."

"Thank you," I say. "Thank you very much."

"You're welcome, baby," she says. "Keep yourself well. Try to let go of this. I'm sure that's what she would have wanted."

"Yes," I say. "Thank you."

I hang up feeling lost. For so long I've been pinning my hopes on this call, and now it's over, and I know no more than I did before. I have my pages of careful notes to file away with all the other pages of notes I've taken—notes on Lorelei's behavior, notes on canine physiology, lists of books shelved side by side in an order that seems to mean nothing at all. I suddenly miss Lorelei very much. What I want most, more than all of death's secrets revealed, more even perhaps than my wife back in my arms, is to crawl into bed and to feel the comfort of Lorelei's great, furry heft beside me. To rest my hand on her warm, breathing flank as I drift off to sleep. I get up and go into the bedroom, stopping to close the curtains against the bright day. I lie down on my bed and slip into a troubled, bereft sleep full of falling women and the barking of dogs always out of sight.

THIRTY-SEVEN

After our trip to New Orleans, Lexy and I returned home in a somber state. Lexy kept silent, refusing to talk about Blue Mary or the night she came to me wearing the mask. She had thrown away the rubbings from Blue Mary's grave, and when I rescued them from the trash and smoothed them out, she told me she didn't want them anymore. Even so, I packed them away carefully in my suitcase in case she changed her mind.

Lexy went back to her death masks, but her interest in them seemed to have waned. I don't know if it had anything to do with Blue Mary or if she had merely exhausted her enthusiasm for the medium. She continued doing them when asked, but she stopped advertising, and eventually the requests dropped off. But she didn't seem to want to return to the kind of masks she'd made before, either. She came up with new ideas she didn't follow through on, drawing up elaborate plans for series of masks she never started. She had an idea for a line of children's Halloween masks, good ones— grotesque hags and demons that would have been a million times better than the cheap plastic and rubber ones I remember from my childhood—but she decided that the prices she'd have to charge were more than most parents would be willing to pay. For a few days, she was excited about a series called Laundry-shaped Souls, based on a phrase half remembered from a dream she'd had. She wasn't able to tell me what the phrase meant exactly, but the dream had been so evocative, the words so mysterious when she woke with them on her lips, that she felt she had to do something to bring them to life. But after a few days, as so often happens with dreams, the urgency of her memory faded, and she found that she'd lost the ability to put herself in the frame of mind she'd been in when she'd first awakened. Another idea, inspired by some of the dogs in disguise we'd seen at

Mardi Gras, was to make human-faced masks for animals to wear, sort of a counterpart to the animal-faced masks for humans that had always been among her most popular items. She did make one of these, using Lorelei's face as a model, and the effect was quite eerie—a Victorian-looking child's face, with rosy cheeks and blond ringlets and Lorelei's snout protruding underneath—but again, she soon lost interest. Lorelei, for her part, walked around the house for days with plaster stuck to her fur until we could get her an appointment at the groomer's.

I was worried about Lexy. Some days I'd come home to find her lying on the couch with Lorelei curled up beside her. "I didn't do a damn thing all day," she'd say. She was having trouble sleeping, too. One night, I woke up to find her gone from the bed. I went to look for her and found her down in her workshop, pacing the floor.

"What are you doing?" I asked.

"Just thinking," she said. "Just trying to think what to do next."

I wanted to do something to help her out, so I talked to a friend of mine in the theater department, Patricia Wellman, who was going to be directing a summer-stock production of *Macbeth*. She had some rather ambitious ideas for the staging of the play— she'd cast women in all the men's roles, for example, and men in all the women's, and she'd set the whole thing in a karaoke bar in Hackensack—and when I suggested to her that she consider having masks made for all the characters, she was very excited.

Lexy wasn't thrilled by the assignment at first. It wasn't exactly groundbreaking work for her, and Patricia's ideas were a bit vague and subject to change at a moment's notice—one week, she wanted all the characters to wear blank white faces with no features at all, and the next week she changed it to yellow have-a-nice-day smiley faces— but it seemed to do Lexy some good to have steady work, deadlines, a task at hand. She enjoyed going to the rehearsals and watching the show take shape, and the two of us had fun laughing together about some of Patricia's more outlandish ideas.

On opening night, Lexy and I went to see the play, which turned out to be a bit better than I'd expected. Lexy's masks were a focal point of the production. She'd managed to talk Patricia out of the smiley faces, and

they'd settled instead on masks that revealed the inner torment of each character,
which lent a striking and harrowing effect to
an otherwise rather silly production. Afterward, Patricia invited us to join the cast for
the opening night party, which was held—
where else?—at a karaoke bar. I remember
we had a very good time that night. We
drank shots of tequila, and after several
drinks, Lexy was able to persuade me to
get up with her and perform a duet of "I Got
You, Babe." I have a snapshot in my mind
of Lexy standing there, flushed and laughing, with a microphone in her hand, singing
the words of a love song to me. When I
sang "Put your little hand in mine," she
reached out to me, and her grasp was
warm and soft. Afterward, we kissed in the
taxicab on the way home, making out like
teenagers while the cabdriver studiously ig-
nored us. It was a moment of pure happiness, not just for me, but for us both. She
was happy that night, do you see? *She was
happy.*

That was somewhere around the middle
of August. That was, according to the best
estimates of the medical examiner, the
week our child was conceived.

THIRTY - EIGHT

I think about the baby all the time. It's been a week since Lorelei disappeared, and I don't have much else to do. I've papered the neighborhood with her picture, I've placed ads in the local papers, and I call the police every day, but there's still nothing. So I sit at home, waiting for news of my dog, and I think about what I've lost. It's July now; the baby would be two months old, almost old enough to hold up its head by itself, old enough perhaps to smile. I try to imagine that other life, that other winter, the one where I get to watch Lexy's body grow heavy with new life. The one where her water breaks in the middle of the night, and we time her contractions on a stopwatch. The one where we drive home on a bright spring day and I hold Lexy's elbow as she carries our child into the house for the first time. I imagine a girl baby first, a tiny girl with dimpled fingers and a scalp covered in soft fuzz. Then a boy, a sweet little boy with a mouth like a rose. And I find, at last, that I am angry.

I'm angry at a dead woman. It's not a welcome feeling. And when I try to catch hold of the thread of my anger, to follow it through to its other end, I hit knot after tangled knot. I'm angry, I suppose, that she climbed to the top of a tree, knowing that she held our child within her. I'm angry that she never told me she was pregnant, that she never gave me the gift of that knowledge and all the potential it held. And I'm angry, of course—but you don't know anything, I tell myself, you don't know anything at all—I'm angry that if she took her own life, she did it knowing that she was taking a second life with it.

I feel like yelling, I feel like pounding the walls with my fists, I feel like ripping apart everything in the house. My blood feels hot in my veins, and I want to jump out of my body. I pace back and forth through my empty rooms, sampling the flavor of this untested emotion. It feeds on itself and gains weight in my body until I think I must do something to let it out. It's only after I've walked past the basement door fifty times or more that I decide to open it and walk down the stairs to Lexy's workshop. It's not the first time I've been down here since her death, of course, but it's the first time I've looked around this room with my eyes un-clouded by the exquisite tenderness of fresh grief. I want to wreak havoc down here, I want to tear the masks from the god-damned walls, but I hold myself back. What I *really* want is to understand. I want to see Lexy as she really was. There has to be something down here that can help me un-derstand.

In the corner, there's a small desk where she kept her files, her receipts of masks sold, her sketches for future designs. I throw myself on the desk and start pulling papers out of the drawers. I tear through drawer after drawer, looking for something, anything, that will tell me something new. And it's in this reckless frenzy, this disre-spectful pawing through the things that mattered to Lexy, that I come upon her book of dreams.

I recognize it immediately, of course—

how many times have I seen it in her hands?—and I can't believe it's never occurred to me to look for it before. It's a beautiful book, made by Lexy herself, with a blue velvet cover and soft pages of grainy, handmade paper. It's not the original book, of course, the one she started in childhood. That first book, a tattered red notebook with the cover torn nearly off and the spiral binding poking out at dangerous angles, was the one she was still using when I met her. But for our first Christmas together, I bought her a paper-making kit, and she spent weeks carefully transcribing each dream from the old book into the new one she'd created.

I hold the book in my hands, stunned at the discovery. For a frightened moment, I think that I shouldn't open it at all, that I should hide it away again, burn it, bury it the way the parents of Lexy's dead girl, Jennifer, had buried their daughter's diary without ever seeing what secrets it held. But in an instant, I know I will read it. How can I possibly not?

I take the book over to the sofa and sit down. The dreams are listed in chronological order. Lexy was eleven when she first started writing them down, and she began by listing every dream she could ever remember having. The very first one, dated tentatively with a question mark as being from the year she was four, is one of the ones I remember her telling me during our drive to Disney World: "I was in a castle, but there was only one room. A king came in and I hid behind his throne, but he saw me and yelled at me, and I was scared." The next one, dated two years later, is also a nightmare: "There were spiders everywhere. I wasn't even in the dream, just the spiders." And when she was nine: "My dog Sunshine died and I was sad." At age ten, she writes, "I got married to Jonathan Weiss, this boy I liked at school. When I woke up, I thought he would really be there, and I went walking all over the house looking for him." As she gets older, as she and her dreams age and mature a bit, the descriptions become more detailed, as in this one, written when she was twelve: "I was in my friend Lisa's house, but it was also the same as the McDonald's at the Wal-Lex shopping center. I tried to find Lisa to tell her that this wasn't really her house, but her mother kept taking me behind the counter and making me cook hot dogs. I was yelling at her that they don't even *have* hot dogs at McDonald's, but she wouldn't listen." So many of them are like this: ordinary, mean-dering, shaped by the kind of internal logic found only in dreams. And that's it—they're only dreams. What can I hope to learn?

I turn the pages, skimming through the magical and mundane dreams of little girls. One of them, dated when she was sixteen, makes me catch my breath: "I was on top of a high building, and I was walking close to the edge, and I fell off. I thought I was going to fall all the way to the ground, but halfway down, I found I could fly." The height, the fall—it makes me dizzy for a mo-ment. But so many people have dreams of falling, dreams of flight—I've had them my-self, dreams where I wake with my heart pounding, convinced I've just fallen to the bed from a great height—that I have to con-clude it doesn't mean a thing.

I skip ahead past college dreams of missed exams and sex with strangers, past a recurring nightmare in her twenties about driving a car down a flight of stone steps. I skip to the part after she and I have met. And there I am, a new fixture in her dreams, sometimes a key figure, sometimes just a bit player: "Paul and I decide to buy a new house, but it's so big I get lost. He keeps calling to me, and I try to follow his voice, but I can never find him." Or "I'm on a train somewhere in Europe, and I'm not sure where I'm supposed to get off, but I'm not too concerned about it. I'm eating delicious pastries. Paul's there, too." I enjoy reading the ones that I'm in, even when the role I play in them is small. It's gratifying to know that you've appeared in someone else's dreams. It's proof that you exist, in a way, proof that you have substance and value outside the walls of your own mind.

So many of the dreams are ones that Lexy told me herself—here are the laundry-shaped souls, here is "I remember my wife in white"—that I begin to feel ashamed. There's nothing she kept from me, at least nothing that's going to be found in this book. Of the ones I don't recognize, some of them are very cryptic, as though she herself didn't remember any more than the sketchiest details. "Snake eating money," one of them reads. "So many people gave it to him." And another one says only: "I put one in metal, one in glass, and one in wood."

In the entries from the first winter after we were married, dreams of pregnancy and birth begin to appear. "I gave birth to a little girl who was afraid of me," says one of them. And another: "I had a baby, but it wasn't really mine." In one dream, Lorelei has puppies, then swallows them one by one. In another, Lexy finds herself hugely pregnant and sitting in a courtroom. "I'm sorry," the judge says to her, "but we have to put a stop to this." She looks down to find her belly flat once again.

Looking at the dates of these dreams, I can see that they occurred around the time I was trying to convince Lexy that we should have a baby. It seemed to me then that she was dismissing the idea rather easily, without giving it the consideration it deserved, but I can see now that the decision weighed heavily on her, coloring even her sleep. Well, what of it, I think, a glimmer of my earlier anger rising within me. It was a reasonable expectation, that we might have a family together. I'm not going to feel guilty for wanting the things that everyone wants.

I'm expecting that the dreams will take a

rather macabre turn around the time that she began making death masks, but this is not the case. In fact, I find only one dream about death during that entire period, although it seems to be a fairly significant one: "I've died," she writes, "and I'm at my funeral. Paul is in the front row, and he's crying. I want to comfort him, so I go up to him and put my hand on his shoulder, but he can't feel me. Then he looks right at me, even though I know somehow that he can't really see me. 'I'm crying,' he says, 'because it's such a relief.' That's when I wake up."

But I have to emphasize that not all the dreams are like this. For every dream that seems to sing out with symbolism and revelation, there are ten others that are nothing more than ordinary. The week before the funeral dream, for example, she writes, "I'm in the supermarket, and I'm buying a lot of pineapples." And the very night after she dreamed that I felt relief at her death, she had a dream that "Paul and Lorelei and I are taking a long car ride. Lorelei has her head out the window, and Paul and I are laughing."

After our trip to New Orleans, there's a

period of a month or so with no dreams at all. I don't know what to make of this; did Lexy really not dream at all during this period, or was she just not writing them down? The first dream listed after this fallow time sheds little light: "I'm swimming in a pool, but it turns out it's actually the ocean. When I open my eyes underwater, I can see that there are colorful fish swimming all around me."

I feel some trepidation as I near the end, as the dates move inexorably toward the day of Lexy's death. I don't know when exactly she learned that she was pregnant, when she first suspected it, and when she took the test, but I feel sure it will be reflected in her dreams. But again I'm wrong. This isn't a diary, after all; it's a record of random synaptic movements that defy my attempts to imbue them with meaning. There are no dreams of babies in her last days. There is one dream a week before her death—"My body is covered with scars from head to toe"—that might perhaps reflect a preoccupation with bodily changes. But then again, it might not. Four days before her death, she dreamed she went to the dry cleaner's; a night later, she dreamed that she was cooking a wonderful meal. The last dream of her life, or at least the last one she wrote down, is this one, dated the day before her death: "I dreamed they cut me open and found I had two hearts. The second one was small, and it was a different color. It was hidden underneath the main heart, so they didn't see it at first. I was very surprised when they told me about it, but the doctor said it was completely normal. He said that most people have two hearts, we just never know it."

I'm intrigued by this one, and not only because it's the last. It's true, isn't it, that each of us has two hearts? The secret heart, curled behind like a fist, living gnarled and shrunken beneath the plain, open one we use every day. I remember a night about a year or so ago, when I was lying awake next to Lexy, unable to sleep. For some reason, I began thinking about a woman I had known in college, a woman I had dated for only six or seven weeks. It was not a serious relationship, at least it wasn't to her, but I had fallen in love with her, and it shamed me to realize that, all these years later, I still felt pain that she had not loved me back. How can it be, I wondered, that we can be lying in bed next to a person we love wholly and helplessly, a person we love more than our own breath, and still ache to think of the one who caused us pain all those years ago? It's the betrayal of this second heart of ours, its flesh tied off like a fingertip twined tightly round with a single hair, blue-tinged from lack of blood. The shameful squeeze of it. Lying there that night, with Lexy beside me, I was surprised to find myself where I was. I was surprised to find I had lived a whole life in the meantime. And sitting here now, with all of Lexy's dreams in my lap, I realize there are things about her I will never know. It's not the content of our dreams that gives our second heart its dark color; it's the thoughts that go through our heads in those wakeful moments when sleep won't come. And those are the things we never tell anyone at all.

THIRTY-NINE

I continued to call Detective Stack every day, hoping for news of Lorelei, but so far I haven't had any luck. But today, he's the one who calls me.

"Dr. Iverson," he says. "I wanted to let you know that we arrested Remo Platt and Lucas Harrow last night. We got a tip as to their whereabouts, and we now have them in custody."

"Oh, thank God," I say. "What about Lorelei? Did you find her?"

"Well, I'm not sure," he says. "There were several dogs recovered from the location where they'd been staying, but I don't know if your dog was among them. The arresting officers handed them over to Animal Control. They're at the pound now, if you want to go take a look."

"Thank you so much, Detective," I say. "I'm so grateful."

"No problem," he says. "I hope you find your dog."

"Were the dogs . . . were they okay?" I ask.

He pauses. "Some of them were not in good shape," he says. "I'm not going to lie to you. And we found some evidence at the scene of some dogs that had been . . . that were deceased."

"I see," I say. "Well, thank you."

I drive to the pound, imagining all the possibilities: Lorelei's not there after all, or she's there, but she's badly injured. Or she's there, but she doesn't want to have anything to do with me. This last is a stretch, I know, but who could blame her? Even dogs can feel betrayal. She knows that she trusted me and I brought her back to the place where they hurt her once. She knows that a man she was afraid of came to get her, and I wasn't there to help.

I try to prepare myself for the fact that she might be dead, but I can't bear to think about it. When I imagine those men hurting her, perhaps killing her, I start shaking so much that I have to pull the car over to compose myself.

Finally, I reach the pound. I park my car and go inside. There's a young woman sitting at the front desk. She looks like a kind person. She's wearing a name tag that says Grace.

"Hello," she says when I approach the desk. She smiles at me. "Can I help you?"

"I hope so," I say. "I heard from the police that they brought some dogs in last night. I think my dog might be one of them."

"Oh," she says, her face falling a little. "You mean the dogs from the animal abuse case?"

"Yes."

"That's such a terrible story. I'm glad they've arrested those guys. If you could see what they've done to some of these . . ." She trails off. "I'm sorry. What kind of dog is your dog?"

"A Rhodesian Ridgeback. A female. Her name is Lorelei."

"That's pretty. We do have a female Ridgeback. I don't know if it's the right one—there weren't any tags or collars on any of the dogs. But she's a real sweetheart. I was sitting with her most of the morning. We've become pals."

"Is she okay?" I ask.

Grace looks down. "Well, she's . . . she's okay, don't worry, she's going to be fine. But they did some surgery on her. We had our vet examine her this morning, and it appears that . . ." She looks up into my eyes. "They removed her larynx."

"Oh, God," I say. "Oh, God."

"I'm sorry," she says. "But it's not so bad. She's recovering fine. The vet said the surgery was done really well, if that's any comfort. She's going to be fine. She just won't be able to bark or anything."

My eyes are filling with tears. "She won't be able to talk," I say. And suddenly I laugh at how ridiculous it sounds.

Grace smiles uncertainly, but when she speaks, her voice is gentle. "No," she says. "She won't be able to talk."

I nod and bow my head, willing the tears to stop running down my cheeks.

"Oh," Grace says. "Oh. Don't cry." She stands up, plucking a few tissues from a box in front of her, and walks around to stand beside me on the other side of the desk. She puts her hand on my arm and squeezes it lightly. "It's okay," she says, handing me a tissue. "It's okay."

She gives me a moment to pull myself together. I wipe my face and blow my nose, ashamed to be behaving this way in front of a stranger.

"Shall we go take a look," she says, "and see if this is your dog, after all?"

"Yes," I say. "Thank you."

She leads me through a locked door into a corridor full of cages. It reminds me, sadly, of the kennels at Remo's house. Dogs jump up on the bars of their cages, yelping and barking as we walk past. I can see that some of them are hurt, their wounds dressed with clean white bandages.

"She's in the second-to-last cage on the right," Grace says.

I quicken my steps, looking ahead, trying to see into the right cage. And then I'm in front of the cage, and there she is, my sweet Lorelei, my sweet puppy dog. She's lying down in the back of the cage, but when she sees me, she jumps up and leaps into the air, spinning her body around in a circle. She propels herself toward me with great force, landing with her front paws propped high on the bars. She looks me right in the face. I can see that her throat is freshly bandaged. She makes a sound, sort of an empty whistling whine, like the sound of air rushing through a hollow reed. I put my fingers through the bars, and she licks them furiously.

"Lorelei," I say. "What a good girl! What a good girl! I'm so sorry, girl." I laugh as she sticks her tongue through the bars, trying to reach my face.

Grace is smiling. "I'm guessing this is the right dog," she says.

I smile back, feeling happier than I have in some time. "Yes," I say. "This is the right dog."

I take Lorelei home with me, back to our little house. I give her her dinner and check her bandages, according to the vet's instructions. Afterward, she settles down in her favorite corner and falls into a deep sleep, her paws twitching and jerking as she dreams. I wonder if her dreams, such as they are—I suppose I'll never know, after all—have been changed by what she's been through. As she lies here safe in our living room is she dreaming of men with knives, men who lock her in cages and make her throat burn like acid? Why would they do this to her, these men whose goal was to *enable* dogs to speak? And then, suddenly, it hits me, and I feel so sick I have to sit down. It's because of me. I remember now that Remo and Lucas looked at me when the police broke through the door. They knew I was responsible for leading them there, unwitting fool that I was. It was all my fault. And they couldn't silence me, so they silenced her. Whether they meant it as a message to me—did they know they'd get caught?—or whether they simply wanted to take their revenge on her, I don't know. But it's my fault, just as everything seems to be my fault, and I don't know how I'll ever make it up to her.

Lorelei begins to make noises in her sleep, gaspy, wheezing sounds that might have been yelps at another time in her life. I kneel beside her and stroke her flank until she jerks awake and stares at me with wide, unrecognizing eyes.

"Shh, girl," I say. "It's okay." She sighs

and puts her head down again, settling into a quieter sleep.

A few days later, Lorelei and I head back to the animal shelter for a follow-up visit with the vet who examined her throat. On our way out, Grace at the desk calls us over.

"I was hoping to see you guys," she says, coming around the counter and stooping to say hello to Lorelei. "The police sent over some collars they found at—well, you know, at the crime scene. One of them might be Lorelei's. Do you want to take a look?"

"Sure," I say. "I'd like to get that back. She's had it practically since she was a puppy."

Grace retrieves a cardboard box from underneath the desk and sets it before me.

"You can just look through them," she says.

I begin to sort through the collars. There are thirty or forty of them, nylon collars, leather collars, collars sparkling with rhinestones. One of them has the name Oliver spelled out in silver dog biscuits. It seems very sad to me. All of these dogs had owners who loved them, and not all of them were as lucky as Lorelei and I were. Finally, I spot Lorelei's thick leather collar. It's buckled into a circle, as if it were still on her neck. I pull it out of the box.

I unbuckle the collar and turn it over. I can see that there are words written in felt-tip pen across the underside, and a sudden jolt runs through my body when I see them. It's Lexy's handwriting. It takes me a minute to make sense of it. What it says. What it says is this: *You are my finest knight.*

I feel my breath nearly stop, and I feel the world nearly stop, and I sink down to the floor and hide my face in Lorelei's bare neck. I whisper into her fur and thank her for telling me what she's known all along.

I look up at Grace. "My late wife . . . ," I say. "I never knew . . . I just never knew."

I stay on the floor with Lorelei for a few moments more. I hold on to her, solid and warm as a rock in the sun, until I'm ready to stand up and fasten her collar around her neck and take her home again.

When we get into the house, I go directly to my study. I understand now, I think I do, what I'm supposed to be looking for. And there it is, and I can't believe I never saw it before.

Mary **Had** a Little Lamb: Language Acqui-
   sition in Early Childhood
I Was George Washington
Love in the **Known** World
But That's Not a Duck!
That's Not Where I Left It **Yesterday**
What You Need to Know to Be a Game
   Show Contestant
I Wish I May, I Wish I Might
Know Your Rhodesian Ridgeback
Didn't You Used to Be Someone? Stars
   of Yesterday and Where They Are **To-
   day**
I'd Rather Be Parsing: The Linguistics of
   Bumper Stickers, Buttons, and T-shirt
   Slogans
Have You Never Been Mellow? The
   World's Worst Music
How to Buy a Used Car Without Getting
   Taken for a Ride
You're **Out!** A History of Baseball
And **Your** Little Dog Too: Hollywood Dogs
   from Rin Tin Tin to Beethoven
Cooking for **Two**
Gray Girls

*Don't Close Your **Eyes***
*First Aid for Dogs **and** Cats*
***Put** Me in the Zoo*
*Where to Stay **in** Northern California*
*A Feast for the **Eyes***
*Thrill Rides **of** North America*
***Clay** Masks from Around the World*
*I'm Taking My Hatchback to Hackensack **and** Other Travel Games*
*I **Had** a Dream: The Civil Rights Movement and Real Life*
*796 Ways to Say "**I** Love You"*
*Things I Wish I'd **Known***
*Strange **but** True: Aliens in Our Midst*
*Forget About **Yesterday** and Make the Most of Today*
***You'd** Better Believe It! The World's Most Famous Hoaxes and Practical Jokes*
*How to **Be** a Success While Doing What You Love*
*And **No** Pets Step on DNA*
***More** 10-Minute Recipes*
***My** Ántonia*
*A Room of One's **Own***
*Places **I'd** Never Dreamed Of*
*To **Have** and to Hold*
*The Toad Not **Taken:** The Linguistic Value of Puns*

Out of the Rat Race and into the Chips
Your Fortune in Mail-Order Selling
Exercises for a Healthy Heart
A Handbook of Dreams
Flesh Wounds
Papier-Mâché Arts and Crafts
Put a Lid on It: Managing Your Anger
Learn to Play Piano in Fourteen Days
The City of One
A History of the English Language
Stone Shoes and Other Fables

It's from "Tam Lin." It's what the elf queen says to Tam Lin before she releases him to the world of mortals. When she knows he is lost to her. When Lexy told me the story, I thought that these were bitter words, full of malice and spite, and perhaps for the elf queen that's all they were. But reading these words now, they seem to me very sad. I see that they can also be words of kindness, words of protection. An incantation, a wish to avoid causing pain. How often since Lexy's death have I wished for eyes that could not cry, a heart that could not grieve?

But I see now that her wish for me came true by half. I've been looking through eyes of clay all this time. And now my useless heart, my fallible heart, my heart of flesh, seems to break in two, and inside it I find the truth I suppose it has held all along. And I know at last that my Lexy killed herself.

FORTY

What was Lexy like in those last two months, the months in between the time we conceived a child and the time she climbed into that tree? She was fine, that's how it seemed to me. She was fine. The depression and lethargy that had followed our trip to New Orleans seemed to have disappeared, and she was beginning to take interest in new projects. A local café with a Venetian Carnival theme had begun to display some of her masks on its walls, and she made a few sales as a result. We spent a weekend at the beach in early September, and we walked along the ocean hand in hand. My face turned bright red with sunburn, and we ate a pound of saltwater taffy in the car on the way home. A colleague of mine got married, and we went to the wedding. My birthday came and went and was celebrated in all the usual ways. I spent a weekend repainting our bathroom. Lexy became interested in Chinese cooking and made special trips to buy ingredients at an Asian supermarket. It was normal, do you see? I didn't pay as much attention as I should have, because it all seemed so normal. I didn't know the end was so near.

But somewhere in there, something happened to change everything, and I didn't even notice. Somewhere in there, Lexy discovered she was pregnant. I remember there was one evening, maybe in mid- or late September, when she complained of feeling nauseated. And one Sunday, maybe a week later, she took a nap, which was not something she did very often. Were these the symptoms that led her to take the pregnancy test? Her periods, I think, were not very regular under the best of circumstances, but perhaps she noticed it had been a particularly long time since the last one. The question is when. How long did she live with this knowledge? How long did I live with her in that changed state without sensing that anything was different?

The only clue I have is that little corner of

pink cardboard I found in the trash. Maybe I can work backward from there. Our trash is collected once a week, of course, but that little bathroom trash can has never filled up fast enough to warrant being emptied every week. I'm not sure how often we used to empty it; that task, I confess, usually fell to Lexy. I can tell you this: Since she's been gone, I don't think I've emptied that little container more than once a month. But before that, when it was the receptacle for all of Lexy's female detritus of disposable makeup sponges and cleanser-soaked cotton balls, I think it's safe to say it would have filled up at least twice as fast. And when I went through it after her death, it was only half full. So we're looking at one week at the outside; it's only in the last week of her life that she knew she was pregnant. Knowing what I now know, knowing that the week ends with Lexy climbing that tree with the intention of ending her life, I have to try to reconstruct that week.

Lexy died on a Wednesday. I'll start with the Thursday before. She was up before me, I remember. Is that the morning when she got up early and took the test? It seems to me now that maybe she was a little more animated than usual that morning, that maybe when she said good morning to me, she smiled a little longer than she normally would have. But I'm not sure. We had breakfast together and read the paper, then I showered and dressed for work.

"What are you going to do today?" I asked her before I left.

"I've got a few Halloween orders to finish up," she said. "And this afternoon I'm going grocery shopping."

"Sounds good," I said, and kissed her. "Well, have a good day."

Do you see how ordinary it all was, how boring, the routine dailiness of that week? Try as I might, I can't coax any more meaning out of it than I saw at the time. I went to work, I met with one of my dissertation students to discuss his progress. I worked on a grant application that, as it turned out, I would never send in. I went home, and Lexy made pasta for dinner. We watched a movie, sitting close together on the couch. It was all so normal. We read in bed, each of us lost in our own book, and I fell asleep before she did. Another day of our marriage, and I was content with it. I believe, even now I believe that Lexy was, too.

Friday night, there was a thunderstorm. We'd been playing a word game together, a pen-and-paper game we both enjoyed, when the lights went out. We found candles pretty easily—for some reason, we'd received about a million decorative candleholders as wedding gifts, so we had candles everywhere—but matches proved a bit harder to find. We stumbled around clumsily, bumping into tables and calling out to each other in the dark. We'd been listening to music before the power went out, and our voices sounded strangely loud in the sudden silence. Lorelei was frantic—she was terrified of thunder and lightning—and I could hear her anxious panting as I wandered around the house. Finally, I found some matches on the windowsill above the kitchen sink, and we lit some candles. In the soft light, I could see Lorelei wedged into a small space between the couch and the wall. She was shaking violently and drooling with terror.

"Oh, poor girl," Lexy said. She went and sat down on the floor next to the dog and began petting her and speaking to her softly. I settled myself on the floor next to

Lexy, and together we tried to soothe the shuddering dog.

"I've always wondered," Lexy said, "if her fear of thunderstorms has anything to do with the storm she got lost in the day I found her."

"Maybe," I said. "But I think most dogs are afraid of the noise."

"Did I ever tell you," she said, "why I named her Lorelei?"

"No. I thought you just liked the name."

"Well, I did. But I'd also been reading a lot of mythology right around that time, trying to come up with new ideas for masks. I was sick to death of doing Medusas and Bacchuses—would that be Bacchi?"

"Yes, I suppose it would be Bacchi with an *i*. Bacchae with an *ae* refers to his female worshipers, as in the title of the Euripides play. . . ." I was being deliberately pompous. Sometimes I liked to play up my academic-gasbag persona so that Lexy could poke holes in it.

"Right," Lexy said, interrupting. "But getting back to *my* story . . ." We both laughed.

"Right," I said. "Sorry."

"So one of the myths I had come across

was the story of Lorelei. It's German. Do you know it?"

"No."

"It's about this beautiful woman who drowned herself because her lover was unfaithful, and then she became a mermaid and sat on a rock in the Rhine River and lured sailors to their deaths with her beautiful siren song."

"So you read that and thought, what a perfect name for a puppy?"

"No, of course not. But when I first saw Lorelei shivering in the rain, half drowned, I thought she looked like kind of a tragic figure. And she always has that worried expression on her face, even when she's happy. It just seemed to fit her."

I imagined a woman with Lorelei's dog-face sitting on a rock and howling an unearthly song.

"So did you ever make a Lorelei mask?" I asked. "The mythological Lorelei, I mean."

"I did, but it didn't come out that well. I was imagining her with this really harrowing, haunting look on her face, but it was hard to make it work with the eyeholes cut out. I was just never that happy with it."

"Do you still have it?"

"No, I sold it to this German couple. They actually wanted something more American, like a Bill Clinton mask or something, for a souvenir, but once I heard their accents, I started doing a real hard sell on the Lorelei mask. They were familiar with the myth, which no one else had been, and I gave them a good deal on it."

There was a loud clap of thunder, and Lorelei shuddered convulsively beneath my hand.

"Shh, girl," I said. "It's all right."

But she would not be comforted. When Lexy and I went to bed, we let her climb up and lie between us, and all through the night, my sleep was troubled by her trembling and her whining. It wasn't until the rain stopped and the morning sun showed the world washed and new that Lorelei's body relaxed, and the danger past, she closed her eyes to sleep.

My last weekend with Lexy was a quiet one, full of easy lulls when she could have told me the secret she carried. It was fall, yard sale season, and we spent Saturday afternoon driving through neighborhoods we'd never been to and trying to decipher the handwriting on signs where the writer had run out of space and had had to cram all the details into the bottom corner. It was something we liked to do together, a happy reminder of the way we'd met. I bought a sweater vest Lexy didn't like and a clock for my study; Lexy bought an electric coffee grinder and an ice-cube tray that made ice cubes in the shape of a heart. She said she liked the kitschiness of it. It's the hopeful-ness of these items that gets me now. She was still imagining a future where we would drink fresh-ground coffee together in the mornings. Where we would slip tiny ice hearts into our drinks to see how they'd float.

At our last stop of the day, Lexy paused in front of a table of children's toys. She picked up a plastic Halloween mask, the kind that's held in place with a rubber band. It was a Frankenstein mask, cheaply made and garishly colored.

"I think yours are nicer," I said to Lexy, talking quietly so that the woman sitting in the lawn chair a few feet away wouldn't hear.

"Yeah, but these are fun. They're like

everyone's memory of their childhood Halloweens. I think I'm going to get it."

She paid the woman a quarter, and we walked across the lawn to the car.

"I think," Lexy said, and it makes my chest ache to think of it, "maybe I'll start collecting these."

Sunday, we slept late and Lexy made pancakes, working from a cookbook.

"I never knew these were so easy," she said. "My mom never made anything from scratch, and I used to be so jealous when I slept over at friends' houses and they had the kind of moms who made pancakes in the morning. But it turns out it's really easy."

"See?" I said. "You could be a mom."

She looked at me for a long moment, and I think she might have told me then. But she didn't. She turned away to ladle more batter into the pan, and what she said was, "Yeah, I guess I could."

I filed that away in my brain as a small triumph. I thought I'd bring it out another time, if the topic of having children came up again. I ate my pancakes happily, pleased with this small concession. Maybe there's hope, I thought.

We went for a walk in the afternoon, and then to a movie. We had dinner at our favorite pizza place. Sunday was a lovely day. And Monday was fine.

But Tuesday. Tuesday is when we had our last fight.

FORTY-ONE

We're getting nearer. We're nearing the end, of course you know that, you've known from the beginning, from the very first sentence I spoke. I'm tensing up as we get closer, I can feel myself wanting to slow down and to speed up at the same time.

I had a slow day at work on Tuesday—I was supposed to be finishing up a symposium paper, but I kept getting distracted. I found myself, at one point, thinking about the myth of Lorelei. The image that kept popping into my mind was the one I had envisioned the night of the storm—a combination of the two Loreleis, the dog and the siren, a woman with flowing hair and a deadly song, her human face replaced with a Rhodesian Ridgeback's earnest, furrowed features. It was a captivating image, at least in my mind, and it started me thinking that maybe this could be Lexy's next big project. She'd seemed a bit aimless since finishing the *Macbeth* masks over the summer, and I thought this might be the answer. It drew on some elements she'd worked with in the past, and it allowed for endless combinations; she had all of mythology to work with, and all the dogs of the world. Didn't the Egyptians have a dog-faced god? Why not carry that over to other mythologies? I imagined Medusa with the snarling face of a Doberman, her snaky hair sprouting from the glossy black fur of her forehead. I imagined Botticelli's Venus rising from a clamshell with the sweet face of a sheltie. I made some clumsy sketches. I drew a pug-faced Cupid, a dalmatianfaced Athena bursting forth from the Labrador forehead of her father, Zeus. I drew Hermes with his winged hat resting gently on the ears of a Jack Russell terrier. I was quite taken with the idea. My drawings were mediocre, but surely Lexy would be able to do a better job.

I looked at the clock. It was four o'clock, and it was clear I wasn't going to get any more real work done that day. I left my office and headed for the library. I found an illustrated book on world mythology and one on dog breeds. Using the photocopy machine and some scissors and tape borrowed from the reference desk, I created a few prototypes. Here was Poseidon with the face of a Portuguese water dog. Here was Hades with a bull-dog's bloated grimace. I laughed out loud at what I had made, causing several nearby students—it was close to midterms, and the library was packed—to cast annoyed looks in my direction. The images I'd created were crude and out of proportion, but there was something about them that made sense to me. At least they would give Lexy some idea of what I had in mind. I made one final picture, with a Ridgeback's face on top of a siren's body—I wasn't able to find a picture of the German Lorelei, so I used one of the Greek sirens—and I headed home to show my creations to Lexy.

When I got home, Lexy was chopping vegetables for dinner. I kissed her on the top of her head and sat down across from her at the kitchen table. She smiled at me.

"Hi," she said. "How was your day?"

"Good," I said. "Excellent. I had a great idea."

"Tell me about it," she said. She pushed aside the onion slices she'd been working on and started in on a red pepper.

"Well, it's an idea for you, actually. I've got your next project for you."

She put down her knife and looked at me warily. "Okay," she said. "But you know I don't really tend to take other people's ideas for my work. It kind of has to come from me, you know? I have to be inspired by something on my own. It's like, remember when you published your first linguistics textbook, and all of a sudden your uncle started telling you all his ideas for mystery novels? It's not like you were about to give up all your own work to work on someone else's ideas."

"Well, no, of course not. His ideas were terrible. But I think what I've got is pretty good. Just let me show it to you."

She sighed. "Fine, but just be aware that I may not want to take your advice."

I pulled my drawings and photocopy art out of my jacket pocket and smoothed the pages on the table. Lexy looked at them skeptically. She didn't smile.

"See," I said, "it's figures from mythology done with dog faces. Isn't that kind of interesting?"

She shrugged. "I guess so," she said.

"Well, these aren't done very well, of course, but I think that if *you* did them . . ." She didn't say anything. She was staring at the table. She wouldn't meet my eyes.

"See," I went on, "I got the idea from your story about the myth of Lorelei and the way that when Lorelei, the dog, showed up, she kind of looked like the character from the myth. And I just started envisioning this mythical mermaid with Lorelei's face." I shuffled through the pages until I found the one with the Ridgeback. "Look, it's this one here."

She picked up the paper and looked at it, then let it fall to the table.

"It's just not that simple, Paul," she said. There was a sudden sharpness to her voice. "Look, some of these can't even be done as masks. This Venus on the clamshell thing—if you just did her head, no one would understand what it was supposed to be."

"Well, you just give it a title that explains it—that's what artists do, isn't it? You call it

'Sheltie Venus' or something. 'Sheltie Venus Number 1.' "

"Oh, so now I'm supposed to do more than one of them? A whole series of sheltie Venuses? And this is going to be my claim to fame?"

"Lexy, I spent half the day working on this. You could at least . . ."

"Well, I didn't ask you to."

"I don't know why you're getting so up-set," I said, my own voice rising. "I was just trying to help. You've been sitting around for weeks, trying to come up with some-thing new to work on. Why won't you at least consider this?"

"Because it's a bullshit idea."

"I don't see what makes it worse than some of the things you've come up with. 'Laundry-shaped Souls'? What the hell is that?"

She stood up from the table and glared at me with such rage that I had to look away. "I can't believe you just said that," she said, her voice shaking. She was clenching and unclenching her fists. She made a noise of strangled anger and frustration, and in a single motion swept everything off the table, the papers, the vegetables, the cutting board. The knife hit the floor with such force that it bounced up at her, and she had to step back to avoid being hit by it.

I was not charitable. "Great," I said coldly. "Here we go again."

She raised her fist and banged it hard on the table once, twice, then stopped and rubbed her hand as if she'd hurt it.

"Go to hell," she said, and left the room, her movements stiff and jerky. I heard the basement door slam.

I picked my papers off the floor and smoothed them out, but I left the mess of the vegetables. The wooden cutting board, I saw, had broken in half.

I paced the kitchen floor, growing more and more angry. Why did everything have to be so damn hard? There are people, I thought, whose lives are easier than this. There are people who don't have to worry that their tiniest acts of kindness will be met with fury by the ones they love. It was in that moment that I thought, for the first time, about leaving Lexy. For a moment, only for a moment, I saw my life without her and I saw it to be better. Easier. Lighter. In that moment, that second heart of mine seemed to soar free. And it was in that same moment that I heard a cry from downstairs.

I went down to Lexy's workshop to find her sitting on the couch, crying. She had a book on her lap, a big coffee-table book of African masks, with a piece of paper on top of it. She was holding her hands in front of her, looking at them. They were covered with a red liquid that I thought at first was blood. There was a pool of the same liquid seeping into the paper.

"What happened?" I asked.

"I was just so mad," she said. "I just didn't know what to do with it."

"What did you do?" I asked.

"Well, I thought maybe it would help if I tried to write it down, but as soon as I started writing, I lost control and started pounding the pen into the paper as hard as I could, and I was stabbing the paper with it, and the pen just broke."

"That's ink?" I said.

She nodded. She dropped her head and began to sob harder.

"What's wrong with me?" she said. "I broke a pen. What kind of person does that?"

I just stood there and watched her cry. I

tried to summon the strength to go to her, to comfort her, but then I saw the wreckage of the pen in her hands, and I realized what pen it was she had broken. It was a gold pen I had received from my parents when I graduated college. I used it to grade papers and exams; I kept it filled with red ink for that purpose. It was a pen that meant a great deal to me, and even though I've spent every day since then wishing I had acted differently, in that one moment I just couldn't bring myself to be kind.

"I'm going upstairs," I said. "Do you think you can avoid damaging any more of my things?"

I left her sitting there, crying, her hands covered with ink like blood.

I didn't see her for the rest of the night. She stayed in the basement until after I'd gone to bed. And even though my anger had waned by the time I went to sleep, even though I cleaned the vegetables from the floor and left a note saying I was sorry, the harm was already done. That night, while I slept, Lexy picked up the phone and called Lady Arabelle and told her the secret she had not seen fit to tell me. "I'm lost," she said. "I don't know what to do." And

Wednesday morning, when she woke up, when she got dressed, when she apologized to me over breakfast, when she kissed me once on the mouth before I left for work, she did so knowing it was the last day of her life.

Or perhaps not. I think I may be wrong on that last point. Knowing my Lexy, with her faith in impulse, her "suicide is just a moment," I think she may not have known for sure until she reached the top of that tree and looked down at what lay below. And that, I can see now, is the great lie of her life and the great lie of her death. Because for most of us, suicide is a moment we'll never choose. It's only people like Lexy, who know they might choose it eventually, who believe they have a choice to make. And so Lexy, walking through her day, laying puzzles for me to solve, let herself believe there was a chance she might climb down from that tree unharmed. And so she granted herself absolution.

What's it like, Lexy? You wake up and you feel—what? Heaviness, an ache inside, a weight, yes. A soft crumpling of flesh. A feeling like all the surfaces inside you have been rubbed raw. A voice in your head—no, not voices, not like hearing voices, nothing that crazy, just your own inner voice, the one that says "Turn left at the corner" or "Don't forget to stop at the post office," only now it's saying "I hate myself." It's saying "I want to die." It starts in the morning, as soon as you wake up. You see the sun through the curtains, it's a beautiful day maybe, it doesn't matter. You turn over to see if you can sleep some more, but it's already too late for that. The day is upon you. You want to hide, to curl up in a ball, but that's not really what you want either. After all. It doesn't stop your mind, does it, it doesn't stop the ache. It's not an escape. The whole day in front of you. How will you bear it? You want to escape, but there's no place you can go where it won't be with you. Inside you like a nausea. Even sleep, really—you wake up with a jaw sore from clenching your teeth in the night and a feeling inside you like you've spent the whole night dreading this moment of waking up. The shining sun is of no use to you. Crying helps sometimes, the way that the wrenching act of vomiting can lead to a few moments' respite from nausea. And the way it racks your gut is exactly the same.

You don't want to get out of bed, but you don't want to turn into that cliché, you know danger lies that way. So you get up, and you try to find pleasure in the little things, the first cup of coffee in a mug you like, the mint-burst in your mouth when you brush your teeth, but you can tell you're trying too hard. You have breakfast with your husband, your sweet unknowing husband, who can't see anything but the promise of a bright new day. And you say your apologies—you're sorry, you're always sorry, it's a feeling as familiar as the taste of water on your tongue—and you kiss him on the lips as he walks out the door, and he's gone.

You go through your morning, but your interactions feel false, all the little things you take for granted at other times, the need to smile at the neighbors on the street, the need to speak pleasantly to the awkward boy with the terrible face ringing up your groceries. The smile feels wrong on your face. You look at other people, and you know they have their problems, too, but it seems to come easier to them, all of it. They don't have that hollow sound in their voices when they talk.

You force yourself to go through the immediate stuff, the stuff that must be done, write the check for the gas bill, put the frozen things away in the freezer, but the more amorphous tasks, the things that are not so crucial right this minute but will ultimately shape your life into something worth remembering, those are harder to face. You'd rather lose yourself in something stupid that wastes your time but occupies your mind for a few moments—TV, a crossword puzzle, a magazine about celebrities. You've spent whole days doing things like that. And then you get scared because another day of your life is gone, and what have you done with it? What will they find, you wonder, when they find me dead? Years can pass this way. Years. The pleasures of the body, food and sex, walking under the autumn leaves, these can give you some small comfort, but even then your mind is running in the background, worrying, hurting, hating, despairing. Those snakes on your scalp don't protect you from a thing. Maybe they never did. What can you do to make yourself happy? In all the wide world, there seems to be nothing. So how, how can you even imagine bringing a child into this life of yours? You don't trust yourself for a second. You don't trust yourself with anything. What will you do when you get like this? You will damage the child, it seems inevitable. How can you take that chance? Your child, Paul's child, would deserve better than that.

You, giving in to temptation to lie in bed in the middle of the afternoon. Leaving the nonperishable groceries in their bags on the floor for two days. You notice a book under the couch, and it's days before you bother to pick it up. Letting dust collect. How can you put a child in the middle of that? You wouldn't do it right, and the stakes are too high to chance it. The funny thing is, it's what you've always wanted. More than anything.

You felt hope in that moment, didn't you, that moment when you found out you carried life inside you? You felt hope. You thought, yes. Maybe I can do this after all. But then we had a fight and anger ripped through your body. You remembered who you were. And had you known but yesterday what you know today . . .

But you know yourself. It can't be done. You may need to give something up, that's what the psychic told you, you may need to

give something up for the sake of something more important. And any action is
better than nothing. The relinquishing, it's
the hardest thing you've ever done. But
perhaps the bravest. The most grown-up.
You're doing the right thing.

Your only worry is about Paul, about the
pain you'll cause him. But you know he'll
get through it. You leave him a note, written
in book titles, a message in a collar, a puzzle for him to work out. Something to make
him forget his grief. And Lorelei—you leave
him Lorelei. That's all that's left to do. You
do it, and you're done.

So you go outside and you climb a tree.
It's harder to do than you remember from
childhood, and by the time you reach the
top, your hands are sore from gripping the
rough, unyielding bark. You settle yourself
on a branch, and you see what the view is
from here. You wait to see if it makes things
any clearer, this perspective, this view from
on high. And it does. You don't think about
it, you don't waver. You stand, balancing
yourself on the branch. It's a heady feeling,
standing there like that. You feel like you've
broken some law of physics. You feel like
you're walking on air. You stretch out your

arms and you close your eyes. You lean backward, tipping your head back to feel the sun on your face. And you let go of everything, and it's such a relief. And you fall.

This is where we'll stop, with Lexy still in midair. A freeze-frame, a cinematic measure that keeps her from ever hitting the ground. Look at her, floating in the autumn sun, her hair blown upward by the force of the wind. Her arms are stretched wide, and her blouse billows out softly as it catches the air beneath it. She's not looking down at the ground rushing toward her; she's looking up at the sky. But her head is turned slightly away from us, and that's what I keep coming back to. No matter how many times I look, I cannot see her face.

FORTY-TWO

I find myself at a loss now. I find myself unsure what I'm to do next. There are no more
puzzles to figure out, no more clues to follow. My research is at an end; even if I
didn't have Lorelei's wheezy rasping to remind me daily that my work will never succeed, I have the memory of Dog J to remind
me that some things should never be attempted in the name of science or love.
And yet I can't seem to let it go. I sit here in
my house, the house of Paul, with all my
clues around me, and none of them seem
to help. No matter how I lay them out, none
of them seem to be able to tell me how to
go on living.

I keep thinking about the steak Lexy
cooked for Lorelei. I can see the picture of
it—Lexy standing at the stove, Lorelei hov-

ering nearby, drawn by the scent of the cooking meat. Lexy laying the steak down on the floor. The trail of meat juice and grease, waiting for Lorelei to lap it up. And Lexy's body, maybe just minutes later, lying on the ground. What is the thread that ties it together? The blood spilled in the dirt and the blood spilled on the kitchen floor. What does it mean?

It's partly to get away from these wearying thoughts that I decide to climb the tree. I just want to see how the world looks from up there. I just want to see what Lexy saw.

I close Lorelei in the kitchen and go out to the yard. It's a hot day, but I've put on long pants and a shirt with long sleeves. It's been quite a while since I've climbed a tree, and a middle-aged man with skinned knees and elbows makes a pathetic figure.

It takes me a few tries before I get the right grip to start shinnying upward. As I hoist myself onto one of the lower branches, wondering if it's strong enough to hold my weight, I hear a curious scratching sound from the kitchen door. It's Lorelei, trying to get out. We have a dog door that leads into the yard, but Lorelei never uses it. It was installed by a previous owner, who must have had a smaller dog, and it's too tight for Lorelei; she has to squeeze to get through it. But now as I watch, I see the door flip open and Lorelei's nose pokes through. Whining her soft, whistling whine, she wedges herself into the small space. I'm afraid she'll get stuck.

"Lorelei," I call out to her. "Stay inside. It's okay, girl."

But she wriggles and twists until she's gotten her midsection through the hole, and then she comes barreling through, wide-eyed and alarmed, leaping and making the noise that now passes for barking. She bounds toward the tree. Staring up at me with wide, urgent eyes, she leaps and dances around the base of the trunk, barking her near-soundless bark.

An image pops into my mind, the image of the dog in the tarot cards Lady Arabelle described to me, the dog barking at the Fool about to walk off the cliff, and it hits me all at once. Lorelei tried to stop Lexy. It hits me like a blow, like a fall. It knocks the wind out of me. That's why she cooked the steak for Lorelei. To distract her, to keep her quiet. Lexy went outside to climb that tree, her mind filled with thoughts of sacrifice,

thoughts of the end. But Lorelei wasn't going to let her go that easily. And how could
Lexy complete her task, how could she do
what she planned to do, in the face of such
fierce, feral love? She couldn't. There was
no way. So she went inside and she gave
her dog one last treat. She took the steak
from the pan and put it on the floor at
Lorelei's feet, without even the playful teas-
ing dialogue that dog owners love so much,
the usual preliminary tantalus of "Who'd like
a yummy treat?" And Lorelei, her tail wag-
ging, Lorelei accepted it gratefully.

Look at it from Lorelei's perspective. A
steak laid at her feet. A gift, a reward for her
vigilance. She'd done good, and here was
the proof. I imagine her gratitude, her relief.
And Lexy, pausing to watch this display of
animal hunger and fulfillment, this voracious
enjoyment of the appetites that give life its
shape, did she stop and question what she
was about to do? Did it give her pause? Did
it make her reconsider, even for a moment?
Or was she too focused on her goal—the
time she had to fulfill it limited to the time it
takes a hungry dog to gobble a piece of
meat—to stop and think about it? Lorelei
lost herself for a moment, only a moment, in

the smell of the meat that filled the kitchen, the task of tearing apart the flesh with her teeth, and by the time she looked up, by the time she had finished licking the floor clean of the meaty juices, Lexy was gone. She was gone. Lorelei, betrayed by her belly and her fine sense of smell. Betrayed by the way her nose twitched at the aroma of the cooking meat and the way the saliva filled her mouth. It only takes a moment of inattention, the moment when a mother turns to answer the phone as her child nears the open window, the moment when the traveler, forgetting that the traffic goes the other way here, looks right instead of left. It only takes an instant, and all is lost. Lexy, dead on the ground. Lorelei, inconsolable, bereft. And all for a piece of meat.

Below me, Lorelei is jumping and gasping, spinning her body in frantic circles.

"It's okay, girl," I call to her. "I'm coming down."

I measure the distance to the ground—I'm still pretty low—and I jump, landing on my feet with a small stagger. Lorelei leaps up onto me, nearly knocking me over. She licks my hands, my arms, whatever she can reach. I bend down to her and give her a hug.

"It's okay, girl," I say. "I'm here. I'm not going anywhere."

Later on, I put Lorelei in the car and drive to the supermarket. She loves to go for rides, and these days I like to give her whatever small pleasures I can. I crack a window for her and leave her to snarl ferociously at all who dare pass by her car, while I run inside to the meat counter. I buy the two best steaks they have, one for me and one for my dog. At home, while I'm warming the grill, I pick up the phone and I call Matthew Rice.

"Matthew," I say. "I want to come back to work."

And so it is that a year has passed since Lexy's death. Lorelei and I lead a quiet life. We go for long walks, the fallen leaves crunching beneath the weight of our six feet. I teach my classes and chat with my colleagues, who seem a little less wary of me with each day that goes by. I'm beginning to enjoy the pleasures of the living again, eating and reading and throwing a ball for my dog to retrieve. And when Grace from the animal shelter called me up last week and asked if I'd like to get together for a cup of coffee sometime, I only hesitated for a moment before I said yes.

Not too long ago, I had a dream that Lorelei and I walked into a bar, just like all the jokes had said we would.

"No dogs allowed," the bartender said, just like I always knew he would.

"But you don't understand," I said, following a script I knew by heart. "This is a very special dog. This dog can talk."

"Okay," said the bartender. "Let's hear it."

I lifted Lorelei onto a bar stool. She opened her mouth, and the bartender and I waited to hear what she would say. But she didn't speak. Instead, she leaned over to me and licked my face. Then, distracted by an itch, she turned away and started chewing on her paw.

"See?" I said to the bartender.

"You're right," he said, without a trace of sarcasm. "That's quite a dog."

When I woke up, I found that I was smiling.

I remember my wife in white. I remember her walking toward me on our wedding day, a bouquet of red flowers in her hand, and I remember her turning away from me in anger, her body stiff as a stone. I remember the sound of her breath as she slept. I remember the way her body felt in my arms. I remember, always I remember, that she brought solace to my life as well as grief. That for every dark moment we shared between us, there was a moment of such brightness I almost could not bear to look at it head-on. I try to remember the woman she was and not the woman I have built out of spare parts to comfort me in my mourning. And I find, more and more, as the days go by and the balm of my forgiveness washes over the cracked and parched surface of my heart, I find that remembering her as she was is a gift I can give us both.

ACKNOWLEDGMENTS

Thank you, first of all, to my parents, Doreen C. Parkhurst, M.D., and William Parkhurst, my stepmother, Molly Katz, and my grandmother Claire T. Carney, for passing along their wisdom and for being my first and most supportive readers.

Thank you to Kim Alleyne, Cybelle Clevenger, Lee Damsky, Paula Whyman, and Katrin Wilde for their friendship, advice, insightful reading, and humor.

Thank you to my agent, Douglas Stewart, for all his incredible work, and to everyone at Curtis Brown, especially Ed Wintle and Dave Barbor.

Thank you to my wonderful editor, Asya Muchnick, and to everyone at Little, Brown, especially Alison Vandenberg, Heather

Rizzo, Michael Pietsch, Laura Quinn, and Sophie Cottrell.

Thank you to all the great teachers I've had, especially Kermit Moyer, Richard Mc-Cann, Matthew Klam, Ann duCille, and Roberta Rubenstein.

Thank you to Barbara Fuegner for talking to me about dogs and to Annie Hallatt for talking to me about masks.

Thank you to my son, Henry, whose impending birth provided me with the deadline I needed to finish this book and whose happy face reminds me daily of what really matters. And thank you, above all, to my husband, Evan, who has supported me in every way and who has provided the invaluable service of making me happy.

Finally, though they will not read this, I would like to thank all of the dogs who have let me share their lives, especially Chelsea, who was such a good puppy dog it's hard for the layman to understand.

ABOUT THE AUTHOR

Carolyn Parkhurst holds a B.A. from Wesleyan University and an M.F.A. in creative writing from American University. She has published fiction in the *North American Review*, the *Minnesota Review*, *Hawai'i Review*, and the *Crescent Review*. She lives in Washington, D.C., with her husband and their son.